STAY

BOOK 2 – THE SEQUEL TO *FLEE*

"STAY"
Written by EK Jonathan
Cover design by EK Jonathan
©2018. All rights reserved.
www.fleenovel.blogspot.com
www.ekjonathan.blogspot.com
Edition 1.1

David Pod

This is a work of fiction and as such is nothing more than a product of the author's imagination. Although the events portrayed in this novel are based on things foretold in the Bible, they should not be viewed as predictions. Any similarities between characters portrayed within this novel and real life persons are completely unintentional. Keeping in mind the principle at Romans 15:1, readers are reminded to be respectful of the consciences of others who may be uncomfortable reading this kind of fiction.

This book is in no way sponsored by the Watchtower Bible and Tract Society.

Dedicated to my love

Give orders to those who are rich in the present system of things not to be high-minded, and to rest their hope, not on uncertain riches, but on God, who furnishes us all things richly for our enjoyment

-1 Timothy 6:17,
New World Translation of the Holy Scriptures (1984 Edition)

Previously in *FLEE:*

Aboard Rig 7 in New Orleans, PETER and RACHEL BURTON reunite with the rest of Monte Vista Congregation, including their neighbor and evacuee tag-along, RON FELDMAN. They are relieved to finally make contact with Rachel's younger sister, CLAIRE ABERDEEN.

Fearing that a sickness CLAIRE contracted from a terrorist attack in Seattle may be fatal and contagious, JOYCE TUCKER secretly leaves the camp in Burrard Harbor, Vancouver, to find iodide pills, unbeknownst to her husband, ALVIN, and contrary to the organization's instructions. Days prior, another sister from their congregation, STACY OWEN, leaves the camp as well, for reasons undisclosed.

Back in San Jose, DARREN and RITA HUGHES refuse to evacuate with the rest of their congregation, choosing instead to continue to fight a legal battle with a large drug company.

Meanwhile, THIAGO is hired by ANGELICA PARRY's jealous ex-husband, CHAD HARKETT, to kidnap both her and their son EVAN, and to carry out a hit on PETER BURTON and TED WATKINS. Thiago assumes the identity JAMES CASTILLO and boards a ferry in New Orleans headed for the rigs…

CHAPTER 1

Chad Harkett gazed down at the valley through the glass walls. The setting sun bled through the smog and bathed everything in crimson light. He swirled a glass of white wine in his hand and tilted back his head to sniff the air of Martin's apartment.

"You'd better not be burning my mahi mahi," he said without a glance over his shoulder. In the kitchen behind him, Martin stirred something in a saucepan and snickered.

"Yeah, yeah," he said. Chad popped the joints in his neck, stretched, and strode across the living room to one of the bar stools directly across from the burners where Martin stood.

"The man lives in a four million dollar house and still won't pay for a personal chef. Classic," Chad said, shaking his head.

Martin shrugged it off. "I like cooking. They say it's therapeutic, you know." He gave his business partner a look.

"You trying to imply something?"

"Should I be?"

"And here I thought you were having me over for dinner because you liked my company. Do I get to kick back on a leather couch and stare at inkblots next?"

Martin only chuckled. "Sure, why not?"

Chad shook his head and gazed back out the window. "Been a long time since I've been up here. The hill out back looks different. You been landscaping?"

Martin said nothing as he scooped the seared fish from the grill and set it over two plates of brown rice and steaming vegetables. He handed one to Chad and refilled his glass. "Eat first. I'll tell you all about the hill later," Martin said. "What I want to know first is: where'd you disappear to two weeks ago?"

Chad glanced at him, frowned, then shrugged.

"Look, Chad, we're not some college dorm buddies selling keygen software and jailbreaking iPhones anymore. There's big money floating around us."

"Thanks, dad," Chad said.

"I'm serious, man. You disappear for even a few days and news gets out about it, our shares take a hit. Investors start getting anxious. Lawyers start calling. It was nothing but damage control that whole week."

"What, I can't take a vacation?" Chad wouldn't look in Martin's eyes as he emptied his glass.

"Not you, no. Not without letting someone know. I mean, would it have killed you to shoot me a text or an email? I even called your housekeeper. She had no idea what was going on. No one did. So what was it? You have a breakdown? Some kind of mental episode?"

"What is this?" Chad sneered, pushing away his plate.

"So what, then? DUI? You get picked up by the cops? Couldn't pass the breathalyzer?"

"*Excuse* me?"

"Oh, come on, Chad. Your drinking is no secret. No one cares, so long as it doesn't interfere with work."

"Geez."

"I won't let it. And neither will the board. Don't forget they're fifty-one percent. You and I may be the founders of the company but they're the ones holding the leash. They have to take action, they will."

"That some kind of threat?" Chad asked. Martin took a deep breath, leaned back, and sipped his wine.

"No. No, Chad. It's not a threat. I'm just saying times have changed. You–*we*–answer to people. We can't just play it off the cuff like the old days." Martin unfolded his napkin and started on his fish in a way that told Chad the conversation was over. Chad snorted but said nothing. The two finished their dinner and Martin loaded the dishwasher.

"Now. You asked about the hill," Martin said, a curt smile playing on his lips. Chad returned a casual stare, but Martin knew he'd gotten his attention. "Follow me."

The valley below the house sat in a soft evening mist. It was nearly dark now, the air cold and crisp and tinged with pine and burning cedar. The two men exited the main house and followed a stone pathway as it threaded down the hill and abruptly came to an end at a concrete doorway that jutted at a sharp angle from the earth. The door itself was of heavy, rough steel. A plate glass window the size of a paperback book was embedded at eye level.

Martin glanced over his shoulder to catch Chad's reaction. It was one of puzzlement, if not amusement. "This what I think it is?" Chad asked.

"Wait'll you see the inside." Martin slid back a metal panel beside the door and keyed in an eight-digit code. Chad heard the groan of loud, heavy machinery within the door as the lock disengaged. "After you," Martin said, opening the door.

Motion-activated LED bulbs plinked on one by one as the men entered. The air was dry and warmer than outside by a few degrees. Chad ducked his head as he passed under a crossbeam and felt the walkway beneath his feet slope downwards. It was utterly silent; the sounds of distant highway traffic, airplanes, even night crickets, all vanished completely in this dark space beneath the ground. Chad jumped as he heard the door clamp shut behind them. He could feel the air vacuumed from the empty space as it closed, the work of a carefully hidden network of ventilators and pressurizers.

"When? And why?" Chad asked, turning back to look at Martin, who strolled past him to a power box and pumped a series of levers. More lights glowed to life above them, illuminating the space. Chad could now see that the place was basically shaped like a long cylinder lying on its side. At its end, he could make out a few doorways leading to other rooms.

The place was furnished simply but comfortably. There were couches near the entrance opposite a large flatscreen. On the other end, a couple of bunk beds and a kitchenette. Each wall was lined with sturdy metal shelves stocked with board games, video game consoles, books, lab apparatus, and blankets. A pair of heavy-duty wire grated lockers stood beside the kitchenette. Martin walked over, opened a refrigerator, and extracted a couple of beers. He threw one across the room to Chad and invited him to sit.

"Ten months," Martin said, peeling back the beer tab and taking a hearty swig. "Most of the bunker is pre-fabbed. You specify the dimensions, they put it together. Excavators show up, dig the hole, a big crane sticks it in the ground. They even hook up the generators, the septic tanks—"

"You've got a septic tank down here?"

"Sure," Martin said. He threw a thumb over his shoulder to indicate one of the walls.

"All right. And the *why?*" Chad asked.

"What, you don't watch the news?" Martin asked.

"Not religiously. You referring to something specific?"

"Shouldn't have to. You do know that we live on an earthquake fault, right? And that there was a series of highly coordinated terror attacks…"

"So you subscribe to those doomsday theories, then?" Chad said, scoffing.

"No, not necessarily. But if something does happen, I don't wanna get caught with my pants down. It's insurance."

"Right."

"I never did tell you about my trip to South Korea back in 2013, did I?" Martin said, his voice taking on an eerie quality in the near absolute silence of the underground chamber. Chad shook his head.

"I had lunch with a guy out there—a Brit—he was working for a microchip manufacturer in Incheon. He said they were independently contracting software developers to help them put together a zero day."

"The computer virus? What was it, corporate espionage?"

Martin shook his head. "Nah. More like anti-corporate espionage. See, this microchip company kept getting their designs ripped off by Chinese companies. They'd filed all sorts of copyright lawsuits, but... You know China."

Chad gave a dramatic roll of his eyes.

"Anyways, they got sick of waiting on the courts, so they hired hackers to build a worm."

"Self-replicating, no doubt," Chad said, feeling a tingling at the base of his spine. Computer viruses were the bane of modern corporate America's biggest players' existences, and zero day viruses were especially scary. They were able to embed themselves quietly into a computer system and sit idly for months or years without being detected before suddenly coming to life and wreaking all sorts of havoc.

"Yeah," Martin said, grimacing. "Anyway, they designed one to specifically target the factory machinery of the Chinese companies stealing their designs."

"And?"

Martin shrugged. "Don't know. It hadn't been implemented yet, so far as that guy knew. But you remember all those Shenzhen factory fires a few years ago?"

Chad nodded warily.

"Could be a coincidence, but then again..." Martin shook his head and finished his beer. "The thing is, we know the US has developed similar stuff and used it against other countries. South Korea's just implementing it at the corporate level. But if South Korea's got it, then it's just a matter of time before North Korea gets their hands on it–or the Chinese. You take a destructive virus like that, one that can manipulate *real-world devices*... That's a scary world, man."

***

Just seven miles to the east of New Orleans proper lays Lake Borgne. It curls below the southern coast of Mississippi and Louisiana before opening its jaws and swallowing the marshlands like an enormous sea serpent. Its name, however, is a misnomer; after years of coastal erosion and rising water levels, it is no longer a lake but a lagoon, connecting at its north-easternmost point to Chandeleur Sound before it bleeds into the

Gulf of Mexico.

In its milder moods, the sea here is calm, even pleasant. But the region is known for its unpredictable nature, and sudden storms frequent the seas. Jagged, gunmetal clouds can sweep low over the lagoon at a moment's notice and churn the water until it spits and sputters in whitecaps and agitated swells. It was this black, tempestuous sea that Thiago found himself chugging across in the two-hundred-passenger ferry. He turned to watch the coast slip back into a mist, the lamps and lights there blurring, dulling, and finally winking out as the distance between them grew.

Thiago tightened his grip on the rail as an icy curtain of rain slid over him. He didn't feel its sting; his calculating mind focused only on the job ahead and the deception it would require. The fact that his targets were out at sea rather than in some land camp as their website had suggested complicated things. He would need to commandeer and pilot a boat–somehow undetected–back to the safety of shore. Thiago knew enough about boats to pilot them, but he suspected that procuring one would prove difficult, and he could hardly risk the task of recruiting the help of others. It was a challenging task, but one that he found his mind quite enjoyed prying at, trying to solve.

"Can I get your name again, brother?" asked a voice at his side. Thiago turned to look as a thin man leaned forward and tilted his head. His inky black raincoat shed droplets through the steel grating walkway. Thiago reached out a hand to steady himself as a sudden swell surged below the ferry, rocking their craft to one side. The man before him bent a leg and shifted his weight effortlessly to compensate. It was clear he'd been on the sea for some time.

"James. James Castillo," Thiago said. The man glanced down at a binder and flipped through several laminated pages.

"You said you were with which congregation again?" the man asked, frowning.

"3-4-0-1-9."

"Yes, but the name?" asked the man. Thiago narrowed his eyes. The man glanced up and caught his expression, held it for a moment, then looked back down at the binder.

"Ah, here it is. West Palo Alto. 3-4-0-1-9."

Thiago sighed imperceptibly. "Thank you."

"It looks like we don't have much space left on the rig where the other brothers and sisters from your congregation are housed, so you'll be living for now on one of the VLCCs." The brother paused to turn and point through the night out at the sea. In the far distance, two red lights blinked through the mist. "I'll let the brothers on board fill you in on the rooming situation. But rule number one: we always wear life vests and locators when on deck," the man said, tapping the back of his pen against a sign that had been fastened to the wall.

A woman stepped forward from behind the brother and opened a plastic crate. She removed a rigid orange flotation vest and handed it to Thiago.

"Whistle," the man with the clipboard said, indicating a small red tube protruding from one of the shoulders. Then he pointed at a square block of plastic on the other shoulder. "Locator is here. You press the button and it'll start flashing. Bright enough to see for miles out here. Well, when it's not raining, anyways. Battery will last you six hours. But let's hope it won't come to that, huh?" The man's lips formed a tight smile. Thiago nodded grimly as he slipped the vest over his raincoat.

"When will we get to the ship?" he asked, snugging up the straps. He hated the way it felt.

"Thirty minutes, give or take. It's slow going in this weather. Hope you took your Dramamine."

In fact, Thiago had taken nothing for seasickness. A day earlier he hadn't even known this job would require him stepping foot on a boat. After a mere thirty minutes aboard the vessel, he was beginning to feel the sea's effect. His stomach rose and fell and turned, the bile ebbing up closer and closer to the back of his throat. Thiago focused harder.

It was only now beginning to sink in just how many people were out here. It was clear that his earlier estimates had been grossly inaccurate. Despite the soupy weather conditions, Thiago could make out eight rigs hovering high above the waves in the distance. The original structures had clearly been altered; the upper decks were stacked high with shipping containers. On two of the rigs, cranes arced slowly in the night, moving supplies and casting roving white beams of light across the decks. How many people were actually out here? *Ten thousand? Twenty?*

Thiago braced himself as another swell caught the underside of their craft and tossed saltwater over the prow. He wiped the water from his face, tightened the muscles in his gut, and tried to shake off the motion sickness.

Thiago made his way around the deck to a large room walled in from the outside. Several dozen passengers sat huddled around plastic benches. A large pile of backpacks, suitcases, and camping gear was strapped to the deck with nylon webbing. A small girl knelt beside a pink backpack, her fingers squirming through the straps to remove something before her father scooped her up in his arms and returned to their bench.

The girl looked up at Thiago and smiled for a moment before closing her eyes and resting her head on her father's shoulder. Thiago let his eyes comb over the crowd, trying to absorb as many details as possible. His ears caught only snippets of conversations. Few were talking and most of the voices were smothered by the sound of rain spattering against the windows and the outside decks.

"Traveling alone?" asked the man with the little girl in his arms.

"Sure," Thiago said, looking away.

"Name's Frank. Frank Henley. This is Alyssa."

"Nice to meet you. I'm James."

"So are you a brother or a student?" Frank asked. Thiago didn't understand the question, but could hear from the man's tone that it ought to be a simple one to answer so he didn't take long considering his options.

"A brother."

"Oh, ok. You from California?"

Thiago frowned before he could curb the reflex. "I am. How'd you know?"

Frank blinked. "Well, I think most of us are from Cali.

Everyone I've asked so far has been from the Bay Area. I guess most of those congregations came here. We're from Hayward. You?"

"Palo Alto."

"Palo Alto, ok," Frank said, looking up at the ceiling as if trying to recall something. "So, made it out just under the wire, huh?"

"Yeah. Whew," Thiago said, hoping the man would elaborate. "You guys too, huh?"

"Yep. Our congregation left about a week ago–they're already on one of the rigs. Number 13, I think. But we got tied up. Made it here just in time. Tomorrow's it."

"Right," Thiago said, making a mental note. "I was told by one of the men that the rigs are all filled up. Any idea how many people are on each rig?"

Frank shrugged. His little girl fidgeted in his arms and he stroked the back of her head with his hand. "I heard someone say five thousand of the friends are on the biggest rig, but who knows."

"Five thousand people on a rig?"

"I know, right? But that's what people are saying."

"And how many rigs are out here?" Thiago asked.

"Well, at least thirteen. Oh, wait." Frank thought of something suddenly and dug a hand into his outer coat pocket. He pulled out a folded sheet of paper and handed it over. "Didn't get one of these?"

Thiago shook his head and studied the document.

"It's a map of the place. Grey area's the lake. The harbor is the star, where we departed from. Those triangles are the rigs."

Thiago counted them quickly. Twenty-two. And that wasn't including the supertankers, which didn't appear on the map. He did the math and shook his head in disbelief.

"Okay, friends, we have some news from the rigs," bellowed a deep voice from the center of the sitting room. Thiago's head turned along with the others to see a large man in a bright yellow raincoat and a matching inflatable vest.

"Unfortunately, we've confirmed that the rigs you all were

14

assigned to are filled to capacity." The man paused as a wave of hushed, anxious voices flooded the space. "However, the nearest VLCC still has available space, so we're taking you there."

Someone raised a hand; the man gave it a nod. "What if our family is aboard a rig? Are there any exceptions for us?"

"I'm sorry, sister, our instructions are clear. We can't overfill the rigs. There's simply no space for more people."

"But it's my husband, you see. I had to return back to California for his medication, and–"

"I'm very sorry," the man said, showing the woman his palms. "But rules are rules. Maybe they'll shift people around in the future but I can't promise anything." The woman gave her lap a dejected look and began crying softly.

"How long till we get to the VL…?"

"VLCC. Stands for *very large crude carrier*. Supertankers. We'll be abreast of her in another fifteen minutes."

"How will we board in these seas?"

The man in the raincoat stared for a moment at his inquirer, cleared his throat, and politely stifled a chuckle.

"These seas aren't all that bad, my brother. It's a little breezy but the swells are manageable. Our friends aboard the VLCCs have trained for months. You'll all be fine."

The man stepped over to the luggage webbing and disabled the spring-loaded latches with the toe of his thick-soled boot. Then, without another word, he clambered up a metal staircase set into the wall and disappeared.

***

Alvin Tucker was exhausted. In the past two weeks he'd learned how the apartment pods' electrical and sewage systems worked, how they'd been pieced together, how they'd be disassembled when the time came. With his other responsibilities, it was unlikely that Alvin would have to handle much of the physical labor; still, he'd need a thorough understanding of the minutiae of details to ensure the safety of everyone involved, including those who'd be living in the pods.

Similar training programs were being conducted throughout the camp, where teams of brothers were taught how to tie off the ships, how to operate the loading and offloading cranes, how the laundry and food distribution worked, and a hundred other tasks.

Alvin enjoyed the work, enjoyed the brothers, enjoyed the atmosphere, but he felt… old. *Too old.* Never mind that his body wasn't what it used to be–he was well accustomed to the aches and pains of middle age. But his *mind*, that was going too, he could feel it. He couldn't remember things like the younger overseers. He often had to be told things twice, sometimes even more than that. It was exhausting and humiliating.

Alvin sighed as he turned the handle on their apartment door and let himself in. He was surprised to find the place empty. He glanced at his watch; it was already past ten. Where was Joyce? Alvin grabbed a change of clothes and headed downstairs for a shower, certain Joyce would be there when he got back. She wasn't. He frowned, dug his phone out of the jacket hanging from a peg on the wall, and called.

No answer. No texts from her, either.

Alvin combed his hair, stifled a yawn, and threw on his jacket. He plodded down the catwalk and the steel girder stairs and trudged over to Claire's apartment, a five minute walk. But as he approached, he came to a halt. The windows of Claire's pod were dark, the lights off.

Where was she?

Alvin called his wife's cell again. Nothing.

Alvin felt an unsettling sensation in his stomach begin to tease his nerves. It crept up from his belly until it sat in his chest like an uncomfortable weight pinning him to the ground.

No. No. Please. Alvin thought. He felt his hands go clammy as they clenched at the lining of his pockets. He began the long walk to the parking area. *Surely not my Joyce.*

Alvin bit his lip, his intestines crumpling into a hard knot deep in his belly where the worry blossomed into dread. His strides were slow but purposeful as he passed row after row, lot after lot of cars. A light, icy drizzle rained down on him from the cold night until his face was slick and wet. He ignored it.

He entered the lot where they'd parked their Subaru, located the column of cars. He squeezed his eyes shut, not wanting to see the empty space, not wanting to face his awful reality. Surely Joyce was somewhere else, somewhere within the camp. *Just a misunderstanding. That's it*, Alvin's mind begged.

When he got to the space, finding nothing but an empty spot on the asphalt where their car had been, he collapsed. He opened his mouth and heaved, but nothing exited his body. His throat was dry and racked with pain; his body shook. His palms and knees sank into the wet macadam beneath him.

"Brother! Brother! Are you ok?" came a young man's voice from over his shoulder. A beam of light flashed in his eyes and was quickly drawn away. Two men were helping him up now, lifting him to his feet.

"She's gone," Alvin groaned, the words barely forming between his lips.

"What'd he say?" asked one brother of the other.

"I don't know. Let's get him in the booth," said the other as they coordinated their steps and navigated the large man towards one of the night watchmen's booths. Alvin's feet half-stepped, half-dragged behind him as he moved. Cold rainwater streamed off his face and into the collar of his jacket.

The watchmen set Alvin down on a folding cot. One brought him a bowl of noodle soup and placed it in his hands.

"You feeling ok, brother? We can call up the nurses' office, see if someone can come out to take a look at you," the shorter of the watchmen suggested. He removed the hood of his raincoat and Alvin heard the water *plink, plink, plink* against the metal floor.

"Did either of you… see a woman…" Alvin struggled, gazing back and forth between to two faces.

"A woman?"

"Yes, a woman…Leave this parking lot… Tonight… A maroon Subaru." The words came with great difficulty; the room spun. The two men took a half step back and shared a look as Alvin's heart sunk a little deeper into his stomach.

17

"Yeah. We did. Maybe two hours ago. Right, Joe?"

"Yeah, I'd say two hours."

"You didn't… *stop* her?" Alvin asked incredulously. The two young men shook their heads. "But why not? Those letters… They specifically said the friends must *stay*. Doesn't that mean anything to you two?"

The watchmen exchanged a glance. "I'm sorry. But we're not supposed to keep anyone from leaving."

Alvin took a deep breath, looked out at the drizzling sky, and wept.

CHAPTER 2

Leaving Burrard Harbor had not been difficult. Sure, there had been some delays as Joyce Tucker struggled to track down their Subaru in the black winter night with only a vague memory and a flashlight. And yes, she'd gotten her fair share of strange looks from the night watchmen as she'd entered her car, pulled from the space, and drove off the lot. But no one had stopped her. No one had asked for her ID. Coming had been difficult; leaving was easy.

Joyce breathed a little easier as she slipped onto the freeway and headed south for Seattle. She hadn't been behind the wheel in two weeks and was surprised by how strange it felt. At half past nine there were few cars on the roads; Joyce imagined she might even get home before she'd planned.

She slipped her phone from her pocket, plugged in the charger, and glanced down at her texts. She'd messaged Sami Raphesh, the doctor at West Hill Medical, who'd confirmed that they still had plenty of iodide pills on hand, and that it would be no problem to procure them for her. The price would be high–$120 a bottle, thanks to the recent rise in demand–but it was fine. Joyce would put it on her credit card and that would be that. You couldn't put a price tag on life.

It was just past eleven o'clock when Joyce Tucker pulled into the visitor's parking deck, found a spot, and slid in through the hospital doors. A handful of orderlies and janitors recognized her and nodded, but no words were exchanged. She navigated the halls to the ward where Doctor Raphesh's office was located and took the elevator up. But when the elevator doors opened, she froze.

The entire area was cordoned off by white plastic sheets. Narrow window slits revealed men and women roving about in Hazmat suits. Many held medical apparatus Joyce had never seen before. Two of the men held guns. A woman emerged from a doorway at the far end of the hall holding what looked like a yellow car battery. A cable running from the device was attached to a chrome wand, which she waved carefully over the walls and floors. A knot formed in Joyce's throat; she realized she was holding her breath. The woman holding the Geiger counter turned, spotted Joyce, and pointed.

"Civilian! We've got a civilian on the premises!" she shouted.

Joyce stumbled backwards a few steps, hands fumbling for the elevator buttons on the panel behind her. The DOWN button lit up, but the elevator climbed at an impossibly slow pace. Joyce glanced back at the woman, who stood in the middle of the hall, her face lit up dreadfully inside the plastic mask of her suit, her eyes wide with intent. She held a small walkie-talkie to her mouth and said something Joyce couldn't make out.

Another moment passed, and the elevator still hadn't arrived. Joyce pounded the button again with her fist as two soldiers emerged from a stairwell behind her. They grabbed her arms and lifted her off into the shadows.

***

Chad rose from behind his desk and walked to the corner of the office, where he poured himself a glass of bourbon. He sucked the liquid between his teeth and squinted out at the dark sky. He'd been at the office all day on conference calls. There were a million balls in the air at once, as usual. He bent his neck, felt the joints strain and pop. Truth be told, he missed the old days, the simple times before investors and a board of directors and project managers constantly nagging him to make decisions he'd already delegated. The old days, when it was just him and Martin pulling all-nighters in their dorm at Stanford, writing cracks for PC games or installing modchips in their classmates'

Playstations. All that petty pirating stuff that had scrounged up enough change to keep them fed on Papa John's and Cherry Coke. Simpler times, less stress.

It was a different world now. A *changed* world. The money was nice, of course; in many ways it meant freedom. In other ways, though, success had become an anchor. Now there were people to answer to. Now there was liability. Martin had it right the night before: the old days were gone. It was enough to make a guy sentimental.

And yet… and yet *what*? What was bugging him about the night before? Well, plenty of things, really. That doomsday bunker, for starters. That was the oddest part of it. Ok, so Martin had his misgivings about the future; Chad had known that for some time. But to actually go out and build an apocalypse shelter seemed paranoid, even for him. And why hadn't he mentioned it before? After all, Chad had the contact details of some of the best contractors in Silicon Valley. Surely they could've done a much better job, given the place a little more *style* at least.

That gun cabinet, though. That had been impressive. But why had Martin been so coy about it? Chad had practically twisted Martin's arm just to get a look inside that grey metal cage at the back of the room. He wasn't disappointed. What he'd seen in there was enough to equip a small militia. Semiautomatic handguns, hunting rifles, grenades, gas masks, even an M-16, and stacked cases chock full of ammunition. Martin had been tight-lipped, but Chad knew his friend well enough to know that this went beyond just ordinary precautionary measures. Martin was scared.

But why? What had spooked him so bad that he'd dropped an unknown sum (half a million? one mil?) on a fully stocked underground shelter? Chad didn't buy the Korea story. Not for one second. Martin couldn't even look him in the eye when he'd told that little tall tale. What, so he just went to Asia and happened to meet some coder who spilled his guts about corporate espionage? No way. Not in a million years. Chad knew zero day worms. Anyone worth his salt in the computing and software industry did. They were the stuff of legends; a single zero day could go for hundreds of thousands on the dark web.

No, there was more to the story than Martin had let on. Chad could feel it, could see it when he'd looked into Martin's eyes in the cold, reflected light of those glowing LED tubes. In his jacket pocket, Chad felt the prepaid cell buzzing. The cell to which only one person had the number.

"Thiago, my man," Chad said, falling back into his leather chair, putting his feet on the desk, and holding the glass of bourbon to the side of his face. "Good to know you haven't run off with my money."

"Funny. I have some news."

"Yeah?"

"I've tracked down your wife and son."

"I'm listening."

"They're aboard an oil rig off the coast of Louisiana."

"Are you kidding me?"

Silence.

"You've seen them? How do you know?"

"I was able to access a database here. They've got their own computer network set up, anyone can log in. It wasn't hard to find them. Turns out almost everyone out here is housed on the oil rigs. Either there or on supertankers."

"What are they doing there?"

"No idea. None of this makes sense."

"And the two men?"

"I think they're together. I saw the names you gave me in the same group as your wife–they call them *congregations*–but I haven't confirmed they're the same as the guys in the pictures you gave me. There's no way for you to get me their last names?"

"No. And you? Where are you?"

"On one of the tankers. Not sure how close. Visibility is bad in this storm."

"Yeah, I've been watching the news. Looks ugly."

"Yeah, and I still need to find a way onto their rig. Not an easy task."

"Did you expect it to be?"

"I'm only one man, Chad."

"I'm sure you'll think of something. I didn't drop one hundred and fifty grand in your lap to pick up my dry cleaning."

"I'm not complaining. I just want you to know what I'm up against. Don't expect overnight results. It'll take me at least a couple of days to get a handle on the situation and figure out a way to get over there. Might have to wait for the storm to pass. Unless you're willing to charter me a chopper."

"You've got my cash. You figure it out."

There was a tense silence on the other end that Chad didn't much care for. What was this guy's deal, anyway? Was he a professional or not?

"Fine. I'll get it done."

"You'd better," Chad said coolly. He ended the call without another word, feeling irritated at Thiago for derailing his train of thought and telling him something he didn't really need to know. Whatever the man was up against in Louisiana was not Chad's problem. Still, his tone had changed somewhat since their last interaction, back when he was loitering at that sushi bar in Dallas. Chad had paid several sets of eyes to keep tabs on Thiago ever since he'd tracked down the man's apartment complex. It had added several thousand to the cost of this whole endeavor, but it was insurance, and Chad never skimped on insurance.

Insurance.

Martin had mentioned something about that the night before, hadn't he? The bunker was *insurance*. Chad closed his eyes, ignored a looming headache, and pressed the back of his skull into his recliner. What *exactly* had Martin said?

Chad leaned forward, brought up a browser on his screen, and entered:

'SHENZHEN FACTORY FIRES.'

***

The man before her squinted in the harsh overhead lighting and scratched the graying bristles of a two-day beard. The color of his lips matched the skin folds beneath his eyes: purple, dark enough to belong to a cadaver downstairs, Joyce thought. The creases in his forehead were deep and black and hardly changed their shape as the man pulled a Zippo and a crumpled pack of cigarettes from his fatigues and began to smoke.

Joyce pursed her lips, trying not to breathe as a nicotine-laden cloud filled the utility closet they'd turned into an interrogation room. She couldn't decipher the insignias and badges on the man's lapel, but she was smart enough to know that he probably had enough rank to be above the No Smoking law for the hospital, even if it was a federal one.

"All right. Talk," the man finally said. His lips parted at one corner of his mouth and expunged a thin funnel of grey-blue smoke. His voice sounded more tired than threatening, and Joyce wondered when he'd last slept.

"My name is Joyce Tucker. I'm here to pick up some pills. That's all."

"So you admit you were here to steal meds? That was easy." The soldier's expression remained unchanged.

"Steal? No, of course not!"

"How else were you supposed to pick them up then?"

"I was going to purchase them."

"You sneak into a hospital in the middle of the night to purchase some pills. Believable."

"I didn't *sneak* in. I parked in my usual parking space and went in through one of the employee entrances."

"So you work here, is that it?" asked the man.

"I… I'm not exactly sure how to answer that."

"The truth would be a good place to start."

"It's not that simple… See, I was a nurse here. You can ask anyone here. I've worked in this hospital for years. But I left recently… For personal reasons. I'm not sure if I'm still employed here or not. You'd have to ask the head nurse."

The man's eyes narrowed even further and he snubbed out his cigarette on the cement floor with the heel of his boot.

"Head nurse is dead."

Joyce's mouth fell open. "Dead?"

"They think she contracted whatever it is that's going around. Took her out within days."

24

Joyce covered her mouth.

"Look, I'm going to level with you. By walking in here tonight without any kind of credentials–no army ID, no CDC badges, no nothing–I could have you thrown straight into a military prison."

"Military prison," Joyce repeated, her voice wavering as she shook her head. Her body trembled in terror and she felt dizzy. "I… I don't understand. I was simply coming to get some pills. I was in contact with a doctor here. You must know who he is–he's one of the head neurologists here at West Hill, his name is–"

The man shot a hand into the air, halting the stream of words.

"I don't care if you had a written invitation from Pope Francis. This whole area is on lockdown. Do you have any idea what's happening in here?" The man lowered his head, and the way the light and shadows shifted, his face somehow appeared sharper, more threatening, the blade of a knife.

"I've heard the CDC was called in. I know about the sickness. That's why I'm here–for the medicine. I have a girl with me who–" Joyce stopped, catching herself in mid-sentence. *No.* It would be a mistake to tell this man about Claire, she realized. A dangerous, costly mistake.

"Go on. A girl? Who *what?*"

"It's nothing," Joyce said, looking down at the floor between them.

"No, please. Go on. Tell me about this girl. Is she sick? Is she with you?"

Joyce's mind raced, grasping for an explanation. Her head spun with the smoke and the lights and the smell of cigarette smoke and her own fear. The man leaned forward and looked up into her downturned face. "Military prison," he whispered.

A loud crash came from behind Joyce's folding chair and she jumped. Fresh air flooded into the room and she turned to find a dark face staring at her from behind a plastic hood.

"There you are!" Sami Raphesh said, grabbing Joyce by the arm and forcibly pulling her from her seat.

25

"Hey, you can't take her!" barked the soldier. Doctor Raphesh lifted a badge at the man. It flashed by too quickly for Joyce to see the details. "I need her on the fourteenth floor, stat. I'm getting her suited up." The soldier mouthed something inaudible as he stood, frowned, and froze. Sami yanked Joyce from the room and the two scampered up a side stairwell.

They made it up three floors before Joyce stopped to catch her breath on a landing. Her nerves were still buzzing from the interrogation. Her head spun and she felt her lunch coming up.

"Please… Sami… Just give me a minute." Sami clawed at his back for a large zipper pull and removed his baggy mask. His head was soaked in sweat, wet hair plastered to the sides of his face.

"We don't *have* a minute, Joyce."

"*What is going on here?* What was that all about? Why is the army involved?"

"I told you, *everyone* is involved. They showed up several days ago, said they were just here for an inspection of the patients, the next thing we know they start suiting up their soldiers and patrolling the hallways with guns."

"What?! Why?"

"I don't know. No one is telling us anything."

"He said… Something about a military prison. I'm so scared, Sami." Sami only shook his head and grimaced. "Well? Was he serious?"

"I don't know and I don't want to find out. We need to get you out of here. Now please, keep up," Sami said, turning to head farther up the stairs. Joyce pressed her fingers into a cramp at her side and struggled to follow him. He was taking two steps at a time and the gap between them grew.

"You said… You needed me… For something," Joyce said between gasps.

"I lied. I had to say *something* to get you out of there. Right now we need to put as much distance between you and this place as possible. I should've never told you to meet me here."

"What will happen to you, though?" Joyce asked. She could hear the doctor's steps slow on the stairwell above her, one floor up.

"Nothing yet, I guess. They need me right now. We're studying the patients. They wouldn't risk our work for anything."

"What's the latest? How are they?" Joyce asked, struggling to keep up.

"More of the same. The symptoms keep changing. As soon as we think it's one thing, it looks like something else. It has a mind of its own and people are dying."

"I heard about Anita."

"It's not just her."

"What about you? Are you showing symptoms?"

"Not yet, at least nothing visible. It all seems so random. You're ok, too?"

"So far, so good. What about the iodide pills? You said they were the only hope."

"They seem to work with some of the patients, but we have no idea why. This thing–whatever it is–isn't purely radioactive. It's like some kind of… biochemical cocktail."

"I'm not going to be able to get those pills tonight, am I?" Joyce said after they'd put another two flights of stairs behind them. Sami paused to pull something from a pocket inside his suit. He handed the white plastic bottle to Joyce.

"Thank you, Sami. You have no idea–"

"Keep moving," said the doctor, as he turned and continued his brisk pace up the stairs. At the ninth floor they slipped into a dark hallway and over a suspended walkway that led to another building. Sami stopped and turned to face Joyce, his eyes hard and wet.

"This ward should be safe. We're not keeping any of the blast patients here. Still, I'd take the stairwell just in case they're watching the elevator cameras."

"You think they're looking for us?" Joyce said, that awful fear rising again in her bones. Sami closed his eyes and shook his head.

"I have no idea. I know *nothing* about what's going on here, Joyce. It's just a precaution."

"I just don't understand. There weren't any military

27

vehicles outside that I could see, no one on the ground floors–"

"They're trying to keep this very quiet. That's probably why you spooked them so bad. Now get out of here. Take those stairs and go. If they catch you again, there's nothing I'll be able to do."

Joyce nodded, gave a brisk thanks, and turned to run down the hallway and into the stairwell. She only turned back once, to see Sami standing there, a resigned look on his face, as he sweated in the confines of his plastic suit. A sick feeling in her chest told her that she'd never see him again.

***

Sami had been right: the halls were mercifully quiet and empty as Joyce made her way down the stairwell of the south ward. She peeked occasionally through the stairwell access door windows, but they revealed nothing of alarm. Orderlies and janitors on a few of the floors went about their usual tasks while the rest were completely empty. Joyce began to breathe normally, her heart slowing, as she slowly descended the last of the stairs.

At the ground level Joyce slipped into a supply hallway and out through a side exit. Conscious of the surveillance cameras suspended from the ceiling, she scratched her forehead, kept her face down, and prayed feverishly.

It was clear now that this had all been a grave mistake. Leaving the camp had felt right only hours ago, but now Joyce wished now that she'd thought things over a bit more, had given the idea a night of rest, and perhaps attempted a final conversation with Alvin.

Alvin.

Joyce could just imagine the turmoil she'd put him through with all this. It was well past midnight and by now he was probably out searching for her, calling frantically... Joyce froze.

She stood there in the middle of the alley, realizing suddenly that she'd left her phone behind, in her purse, back in the closet where she'd been interrogated. Her eyes swung in a slow, hopeless arc up to the windows of the west ward and she covered her mouth with a trembling hand. It had all happened so fast, Sami bursting in like that and grabbing her and marching her off down the corridors. She hadn't had time to think or react or...

Her *purse*. Her *wallet*. Her *phone*. Her *keys*. Her *keys!*

Joyce felt a cold wind wash over her, felt her feet guide her in circles as she tried to untie the knots in her head. What was she going to do? How would she leave? How would she get back to Vancouver?

Stupid! Joyce thought. *So stupid! Why did you ever leave! Why didn't you listen!*

Joyce shook her head, fingernails digging into her head and scraping along her scalp as she forced herself to think. *No. I can't go back. I can't risk those men again*, she thought. *Sami told me to get as far away from this place as possible. So that's what I'll do. I'll find a phone. I'll call the hospital in the morning and have Sami meet me somewhere with my purse. Yes, of course. That's it. I just need time. Just another few hours. Please Jehovah. Just give me that. I'm sorry I was so stupid but just give me that.*

Her pulse racing once again, Joyce hurried down the alley until it opened onto the street and turned right. She moved quickly, getting as far away from the hospital as possible. It was her only choice.

Joyce had never felt so utterly alone in all her life. There were no friends to go to, no Kingdom Hall to track down local brothers and sisters. No phone to call for help. She tried several hotel lobbies, asking politely to use their phones to make a call, but was promptly turned away each time. She considered the police station but thought better of it, just in case.

She wandered around on the cold, empty streets, avoiding shadows as best she could, mind racing, cursing her decisions and half expecting to freeze to death before the sun rose the next morning. Then again, perhaps that was just what she deserved. Perhaps this was what it felt like to lose Jehovah's protection and suffer the consequences. Joyce plodded along, shivering against the cold and feeling the sobs rise from her chest and erupt.

I was only trying to save her, Jehovah, Joyce pleaded, the words leaking from her lips like blood from a fresh wound. *Please don't punish me for it. I was only trying to save her. I couldn't lose another daughter. I just couldn't. It's too much for me.*

That's what she saw when she looked in Claire's eyes, wasn't it? Another sick daughter.

Jasmin. Their light, their little shining star. So bright, full of life. And oh, those eyes. Those beautiful caramel eyes. How they lit up and twinkled when they asked questions like *Why can't the animals talk?* and *Why can't we lay eggs?* and *How come we can feel the wind and the music but can't see it?* Wind and music. That's exactly what Jasmin had been. A warm wind that rushed into their lives and brought with it music and every joy and laugh and reason to smile, and then, just as suddenly, was gone.

The cancer had torn through her little body like an axe through tissue paper. No sense to it, no mercy. Just a constant, monstrous gnawing at her bones and her tiny, innocent organs. Joyce had watched as all the colors and dreams and life bled from her daughter, her precious little Jasmin.

Nine months. Just nine hellish months for those caramel gemstone eyes to dim and fade and eventually close and never open again. Joyce had been hysterical, had totally broken down. Her screams and thrashing had been so unhinged, so dangerous in their desperation, that the hospital security guards were called to haul her away. In another two months she'd stopped speaking and had lost forty pounds. It took therapy and countless calls and visits from the elders and friends to bring her back.

But she could feel herself slipping back there. All it would take was another Jasmin. Another failure to save her child. Joyce found a bench on the side of the street and sat, burying her face in her hands and weeping uncontrollably. Her thoughts, like her tears, were an endless stream of pain.

From down the street, an engine revved. Joyce heard it pick up speed as it approached but failed to acknowledge it. As it roared past, a bottle flew from its window and shattered just inches from her feet.

"Take it to Plymouth, you stinkin' bum!" a voice squawked, followed by raucous teenage whoops and cheers as the car sped away. Joyce glanced up in disbelief as the taillights streaked down the street and rounded a corner. For a moment, she was too shocked to continue crying.

Plymouth, she thought. Why did that stick in her head? Where had she heard that name before?

Plymouth. Plymouth Shelter. Of course.

***

Plymouth Women's Shelter was housed in an old building that had been converted from a warehouse a decade earlier by a non-profit. Its chipped brick facade and rusted front gate would've given it an almost charming aesthetic had it been an intentional design choice and not simply a result of neglect and lack of sufficient funding. Withered vines crept up through the cracks in the walkway, having died and shriveled away in the January cold like the trees out front.

Joyce pushed through the front door open, an old, heavy wooden thing that groaned on ancient hinges. The smell was the first thing she noticed. It was a sad, heavy, dusty scent that soaked into every corner of the large space. The building's interior was only half lit at this hour. Most of its residents were strewn about on rows of cots and old mattresses. A few wandered the aisles, heads down, arms limp at their sides, mumbling things no one could understand. A small room set into a wall to her left held a sign for a check-in counter.

"Hi there, are there any beds available?" Joyce asked. A large woman in a bulging pink sweater gave a slow, indolent look from behind the pages of a well-worn romance novel. She stood from her rolling office chair, donned a pair of glasses, and waddled over to a clipboard hanging from a nail in the wall.

"Sorry, we're at capacity. You can try again tomorrow."

Joyce frowned as the wind howled outside. "I'm sorry, but it's just so cold out there. I've never stayed at a place like this

31

before, but I'm out of options. I lost my purse tonight, and…" Joyce stuttered and brought a hand to her face. The weight of the world settled on her shoulders.

The woman grunted and leaned over the counter to gaze at the cots. "I'm sorry, rules are rules. You're welcome to wait around, see if one of the beds opens up, but otherwise…" the woman tipped her head in the direction of a clock on the wall and shrugged.

"What about a phone? Have you got one I can use? I'll only be a minute."

The woman shook her head. "No, but the nearest payphone is only a block east of here."

Joyce dropped her head and sighed. Without even a scrap of loose change on her, a payphone was useless. "All right. Thanks anyway."

The woman shrugged and returned to her novel, leaving Joyce to wander through the aisles of cots and bunks. The hundred or so beds were all occupied by bodies that appeared to have simply collapsed in place. A few of the unconscious women appeared drunk. One was cursing in her sleep. Joyce checked and double-checked the beds, and when she'd confirmed that none were available, she took a seat on a folding chair beside a closed roll top door and struggled to get comfortable. She was cold, scared, and hungry. She zipped up her jacket as high as it would go, buried her hands in the pockets, and tried to drift off.

CHAPTER 3

Martin Landretti peeled the sheets off his bed and glared at his bedside clock. Seriously? Who was ringing his doorbell at nine o'clock on a Sunday morning? If it was the *Witnesses* again... he thought, clenching his teeth as he slipped into a pair of jeans and a t-shirt.

"I'm *coming*! For god's sake!" Martin shouted, scowling as he came down the stairwell and spotted the blurry figure on the other side of the frosted glass. *How'd they even get past the gates?* A security guard. That's what he needed. He'd been holding off for years but this was getting ridiculous. What was the use of owning an exclusive private property if the front door was public access?

Martin ripped open the front door and froze. Standing there on his doorstep was none other than Chad Harkett. He grinned and lifted a case of IPA in one hand before brushing past Martin into the foyer.

"What is this, Chad?" Martin groaned, closing the front door as Chad helped himself into the kitchen and began searching for a bottle opener. "Chad. Seriously? It's nine in the morning."

"What are Sundays for, if not booze and buddies?" Chad said, still grinning. The bottle in his hand hissed as he pried the cap off and tossed it in the sink. He held it out to Martin; Martin shook his head.

"Some of us like to sleep in on Sundays," Martin said dryly. He walked to the fridge and made himself a bowl of cereal.

"I couldn't sleep last night," Chad said. Half of his first bottle was already empty and Martin caught him eyeing the second. "Kept thinking about our dinner on Friday night."

"This better be going somewhere good."

"Hear me out, Marty."

Martin's eyes narrowed. He hated when people called him Marty, and Chad of all people knew this well. "Make it quick. I want to get back to bed."

"So the other night, all that talk about zero days, and I got to thinking: I wonder if my buddy Martin has ever written a zero day exploit."

Martin stopped chewing. A droplet of milk hung from the corner of his mouth; he swiped at it with the back of his hand. "Why would I do something like that?"

"Same reason you've always hacked."

"Money? Please. Look around."

Chad shook his head. "Not money. You did it for the thrill, for the challenge. You did it to show you could. It's always about cred with you guys. Who hacked into what, when."

"That's a past life man. You know I wouldn't put the company in jeopardy like that."

Chad shrugged. "We only grew up so much, you and me. We still have our vices. We just know how to hide them."

Martin stood, rinsed his bowl out in the sink. "Pretty bold move, Chad, bursting in here and accusing me of something like this."

"Here's what I think," Chad said, ignoring him. "I think you went to South Korea, like you said, and I think you maybe did talk with someone else about developing some virus, but I don't think it was a conversation in passing like you say. I think you were coordinating something with someone there."

Martin turned away, put the cereal box back on top of the fridge. "This is ridiculous."

"I think you two–or maybe there were more of you, I'm sure it takes a whole team of hackers to get the resources together for a zero day–met overseas about your little plan, and then, I think you sold it. Maybe to the Koreans, like you said, maybe to the Chinese."

Martin rolled his eyes and threw his hands up in the air.

"You're crazy, Chad. This conversation is over. I'm going to bed." He turned to walk out of the kitchen.

"So who was it, Martin? Don't tell me you sold it to the Chinese, man!" Chad yelled after him.

"I've never even been to China!" Martin yelled back as he climbed the stairs.

In the kitchen, Chad smirked to himself. He reached in his back pocket and removed the small blue booklet he'd found in Martin's desk drawer at the office the night before. He walked over to the sink and retrieved a napkin, then pulled a pen from his pocket and jotted something down on it. He flipped through the pages of the passport until he came to one he'd been looking for.

Resident Permit for Foreigner in the Peoples Republic of China: Martin Rodney Landretti.

Chad stuck the napkin between the pages, set the passport on the counter, and left.

***

Joyce groaned as she lifted her head and gradually came around. A streak of sharp pain flashed from the base of her spine up through her neck. She'd slept crooked in the folding chair, arms tightly folded, and now her body was punishing her for it. Her eyelids pried open, as dry and gritty as sandpaper. She had a funny taste in her mouth, too, as if the rot from the walls and the reek of sweat had crawled into her throat during the night. She coughed dryly and gazed around for something to drink.

Her knees popped as she stood and for a moment she fought them for balance. She was lightheaded, hungry, and possibly feverish. She brought the back of her hand to her forehead and confirmed it with a sigh. *What next?* she thought.

A commotion rose from the other end of the shelter where a line of ragged-looking women grew beside a long, narrow opening in the wall. Two of the women argued, their bird's nest hair shaking with agitated head movements. Joyce cautiously took a spot behind them in line. There were about a hundred things she needed to be doing at this moment, but right now, with the grumbling in her stomach and the pain in her neck, she could hardly think straight.

The soup wasn't much–a thin, watery broth with a few diced potatoes and chunks of salted flour dumplings served in a small paper bowl with a stale bread roll–but Joyce gobbled it down all the same. As her stomach filled, her head began to clear. She considered her options and came to the decision that returning to the hospital to track down Doctor Raphesh was her best option. She could enter the building she'd exited the day before and have someone from the lobby place a call to him. It was risky, given the military presence and general sense of lockdown the place had the night before, but it was her only hope. Without her keys, wallet, and credit cards, she was literally stranded, no better off than the homeless surrounding her. If all went well, she could be on the road in another hour and a half, and back in Vancouver by…

Joyce glanced down at her wrist, only to find a pale band of skin on her wrist where her watch had been the night before. She glanced over her shoulder at the chair she'd slept in the night before but wasn't feeling hopeful. Watches didn't just slip off in the middle of the night by themselves. Joyce looked around uneasily, half expecting to find a pair of eyes staring back at her.

It was nearly ten o'clock when Joyce finished her meager breakfast and headed back out into the cold, drizzly morning. When she reached the hospital, she found that traffic was beginning to back up around the buildings as an assortment of news crews were setting up their equipment. A woman in a bright pink blazer covered partially by a thick down coat was powdering her face as a cameraman held an umbrella over her with one hand and his camera with the other. A long line of news vans were lined up on the sidewalk beside them: people setting up lights, people crouching by the curb to find a suitable establishing shot, people positioning tripods and covering things with tarps and ponchos.

Joyce eyed them warily as she made her way around to the south ward entrance, where several news anchors stood with fingers in their ears, staring into the camera lenses. Joyce stood for a moment and listened.

"...while the military has yet to officially announce anything, this morning's eyewitness accounts corroborate what we've already heard from hospital staff–that West Hill Medical Center is under some sort of *military lockdown*. Whether or not this has anything to do with the patients from the Seattle-Tacoma airport bombing remains to be seen; still, many local residents are concerned with the steady influx of military vehicles and armed personnel."

The camera panned away from the anchor to get a shot at a lot of vehicles on the other side of the building. Joyce spotted a handful of army transport vehicles along with a white van emblazoned with the striped blue CDC logo. Joyce turned back towards the entrance and made for the door, but one of the news people stopped her.

"No use, lady. Doors are all locked."

"Locked? How can the hospital doors be locked?"

"Why do you think we're out here filming a segment in the rain?" he scoffed. Joyce frowned, stepping forward to gaze into the dark corridors. It was eerie. The lights had been turned off and she could see no movement inside.

"Are all the entrances like this?" she asked the cameraman.

"Just about. There are two more on the north side, but we can't get anywhere near them. They've got police cars and CDC vehicles blocking the roads. This was our only place to get a clear shot."

Now what? She wandered around the buildings for another ten minutes only to confirm what the man had told her. Every door she could find was sealed up. She also discovered that the north entrance was surrounded by police, and after the fiasco the night before, she was inclined to keep her distance. As bad as her current plight was, being locked behind bars would be much, much worse.

Joyce sighed and racked her brains for options. She'd been stupid for leaving, that much was clear. She could only imagine what Alvin was going through. He was probably frantic right now, and he'd no doubt go to Claire, and then she'd be worried, and the whole thing was just a mess–a mess *she'd* created. Joyce walked away from the medical center in a daze, hands shoved deep into her pockets.

After another block of wandering and struggling to think, she spotted a McDonald's and headed for it. She had no money–not even the spare change for a cup of coffee–but at least it was a warm and dry place to sit and think. And *pray*.

But before Joyce could get to its doors, the skid of tires against the asphalt caught her attention as a red pickup truck lurched to a halt beside the curb where she stood. The driver tapped the horn twice and Joyce glanced into the windows.

It was Stacy Owen.

***

"Well, don't just stand there. Get in," Stacy said. Joyce stared in disbelief for another moment before yanking open the door and climbing in.

"But how?" she asked, flabbergasted.

"I happened to be watching the news on my phone. Live coverage of the hospital lockdown. Saw you in the background trying to get into the door. Or at least, I thought it was you. So I decided I might as well spin by to take a look."

"You were close by?"

"McDonald's. Good ol' saturated fats and corn syrup. Gosh, how I missed it."

"So you came looking for me?" Joyce asked.

"Oh, don't look so surprised. I was in the area. I thought it was kind of hilarious, actually."

"Hilarious?"

"Well, yeah. I mean, all this after that long lecture you gave about me not leaving the camp…" Stacy's words trailed off as she shook her head, snickering. Joyce didn't mind the chiding. More than anything else, she felt tremendous relief at seeing a familiar face, even if it wasn't the friendliest one she could've hoped for.

"I'm glad to see you, Stacy."

"I'll bet. Hash browns?" she asked, dangling a greasy pouch in the air.

"Absolutely," Joyce said hungrily.

"All right, so let's hear the story," Stacy said.

"It was an emergency. That's why I left."

"No doubt. I'm sure someone's life depended on it." Always sarcasm with Stacy.

"As a matter of fact, it did," Joyce said, helping herself to an unopened carton of orange juice and swallowing it in two mouthfuls. She told the story of Claire, whom Stacy had somehow heard nothing about. She explained the calls she'd been exchanging with Doctor Raphesh, his advice to get the girl iodide pills, and Joyce's eventual plan to sneak out of the camp at night, and all that ensued in the wake of that misguided decision.

"Whew. I can only imagine Alvin's face right about now," Stacy said wryly.

"I'm trying not to think about it. I feel terrible."

"So you've got nothing, then? No cash, no keys, no wallet?"

Joyce nodded. "No phone, either."

"Sounds rough."

"You have no idea. I spent the night in a homeless shelter." Stacy whistled through her teeth.

"What about you? What ever happened with the house?"

"It burned down."

"Well yes, I remember that part. But why did you come back?"

Stacy bit her lip and gripped the wheel a bit tighter in her fists. Joyce decided to change the subject.

"So… I'm assuming we're headed back up to Vancouver, right?"

"That's the plan, but…" Stacy shook her head and frowned.

"But what?"

"Here, look for yourself," she said, flinging the phone by its corner across the seat. "National headlines. Not good."

Joyce grabbed the phone and opened the News app. Buried

amongst the stories of bumbling CDC interviews and the continuing aftermath of the airport bombings was an item that caught her eye: *Canada Enforces Stringent Border Crossing Protocol.*

Joyce groaned. "When? When could this have happened? I just came from there last night!"

Stacy shrugged. "Just saw it on the news a few minutes ago. It's not getting a lot of coverage with everything else going on."

Joyce brought a hand to the side of her head, where a dull headache was beginning to throb. A knot of horror, tension, and self-directed anger had wound itself tightly in her chest. She wanted to cry, to scream, to pound the dashboard in rage. But her voice conveyed none of this. She was too afraid. "This is… This is awful. What are we going to do?"

"Not much we *can* do but go check it out for ourselves, see if they'll let us in. Or sneak in."

"*Sneak* in? You're not serious, Stacy."

"You have any other options?"

"I was almost thrown into prison once in the last twenty-four hours and I'd like to avoid it happening again if at all possible."

"And if it isn't possible?"

"We're not breaking the law, Stacy."

"Suit yourself," Stacy said smugly as she shrugged and flipped the dial on the dashboard to a country music station.

CHAPTER 4

"Well," Peter said finally, looking at each of the men in turn, "I guess it *all* makes sense, now."

A chuckle rippled over the brothers. Gone was the tension and fear that had been so characteristic of their first meeting nearly a year before. They sat straight and upright on their benches, their eyes marked with confidence and determination. On each of their phones' screens was a text message from the branch:

Please immediately inform the friends: A special announcement broadcast to all camps will be made at exactly 6:00 PM (US EST) tomorrow regarding the second phase of our evacuation.

"I knew it!" Ted said, snapping his fingers. Peter chuckled at his eagerness.

"Knew what?" Marcus asked, grinning.

"I knew this was part of something *bigger*, that this was just…" Ted's hands churned the air. "Like, a *stopover*. That we were headed someplace else. The propellers! Remember, Pete?"

"Propellers?" Peter repeated.

Ted glanced around the table. "When we were going through our first training tour on the lower decks, the overseer mentioned these propellers. He said they were *specially fitted* for these rigs, like the propellers used on cruise ships. They wanted us *mobile*. I said that–you remember me saying that, right Pete? We're headed somewhere else!"

"Well, that much is clear, but *where*?" asked Jack to no one in particular. He wore his characteristic frown, but the corners of his mouth curled upwards in anticipation. The excitement was palpable.

"Well, looks like we'll have to wait till tomorrow to find out with everyone else," said Peter. The cafeteria table was silent for a moment as the group of five let the news sink in.

"Well, I suppose we ought to let everyone know, then," Ajay said finally. They nodded, and Marcus suggested they offer a prayer, after which they returned to be with the others and share the news. The ensuing buzz of excitement was not exclusive to their group; in fact, over the next few hours, similar throngs of Witnesses fleeing together on barges, supertankers, oil platforms, cruise liners, and–in a few special cases, passenger jets–could hardly stop speculating as to what the announcement would be.

That afternoon, as Rachel and Peter relaxed in their apartment, the ideas were flying.

"I'm telling you," Rachel said, "we're headed to Megiddo."

"Megiddo? As in the ancient battlefield in Galilee?" Peter laughed.

Rachel nodded emphatically. "You don't think so? That seems to be where this is headed, isn't it?"

Peter shook his head adamantly. "No way. We've always said it won't be there. It doesn't need to be. Megiddo was just a symbol. And I highly doubt the organization would send us there. It's too dangerous. Constant fighting between Jews and Arabs. There's just no way."

"O, ho, ho, mister geography buff. Sounds like someone's been brushing up on their Middle East trivia."

"Ok, I'll admit that Megiddo crossed my mind," Peter said. "But I still stand behind my earlier statement. The organization wouldn't put us in harm's way."

"So you think we're going someplace else?"

"I do."

"So? Where?" Rachel said, eyes wide with curiosity.

"Someone's in a good mood," Peter said, leaning in to plant a kiss on his wife's forehead, but she swatted him away playfully.

"Don't tease me, Peter. Really, I want to hear what you think. Where do you think we're going?"

"I honestly have no idea. We'll know tomorrow, babe. You can't wait a day?"

"Oh, come on. I heard you guys talking earlier. I know you were speculating just like everyone else."

"Oh? You admit to eavesdropping on a private elders' meeting?"

"Please. You guys were in the middle of a cafeteria with ice cream cones in your hands. I'd hardly call that official. So tell me, what does everyone *think*?"

Peter sat, took a deep breath, and wove his fingers together behind his head. "All right. Let's think it through. Apparently, we're all headed someplace else, and getting aboard this rig was just the first phase of a larger evacuation."

"Right..." Rachel said, making a cranking gesture with a finger.

"And, it would seem that this would suggest we're all going to meet up somewhere."

"Yep... however many *millions* of us."

"Right. So, we'd need a place to live. A *big* place. With water, and resources. It'd need to be in a country which agreed to have us there, which seems unlikely, given our current popularity, so..." Peter's voice trailed off as his eyes widened and locked with his wife's.

"What? What!" Rachel said, walking across the room and standing over him anxiously.

"I know where we're going!" Peter exclaimed.

"Well? Where?!"

"It's so obvious! The *moon!*" Peter said, watching his wife's expression melt into one of confusion, then annoyance.

"You're the worst," Rachel said, shaking her head and crossing her arms. "Just. The worst."

Peter held her gaze for a moment longer before throwing his head back and bursting into laughter.

"Please. It wasn't that funny," Rachel said as her husband's

43

laugher continued. Large tears spilled down his face as he rocked back and forth, clutching his sides. She watched him and the corners of her mouth curled and she tried to shake off the humor of it all and failed. Soon she was giggling as well. She hadn't laughed in… how long? She could hardly remember. Had it been months? *Years?* But now it was all coming out, all the stress and worry and anxiety and it felt like magic. A release.

Peter felt it too. Rachel could see the pure glee written on his face, his eyes red and glistening as the tears kept coming. She approached her husband and gently placed her hands on his face and brought his lips to hers and kissed them. It was warm and reassuring, a feeling they hadn't shared in a long, long time.

***

"I appreciate you being willing to take this on," the overseer said as he and Peter strolled side by side down one of Rig 7's corridors. "I know how busy you are with everything. And I heard about your sister."

"Sister-in-law, actually," Peter said. The two men squeezed to the edge of the corridor as a cart of cleaning supplies rolled by. Brief hellos were exchanged before the two men continued their brisk walk. The decks and hallways had seemed to Peter like an impossible maze when he'd first boarded, but he now felt he could navigate them in his sleep. Learning to travel from one point to another on the rig had been one of his top training priorities, and he practically had the place memorized.

"So she's doing ok in the Vancouver camp?" asked the housing overseer.

"Yeah. She's sick, but she's safe. That's all that matters."

"It's something else, her story," the man said, whistling through his teeth.

"Yeah. It's been a big weight off our shoulders. I feel like I've been able to focus a lot more on what's going on here since we got the good news."

"That's good. Focus is what we need."

The men passed a rectangular window looking out over a

tumultuous sea as a flash of lightning lit the distance, illuminating the dark clouds overhead for a brief second. Peter's eyes lingered a moment before catching a sidelong glance from the overseer.

"Should I be worried about that?" Peter asked, lifting his chin towards the bad weather.

"We'll see. The good news is, we're moving."

"We are?"

"Have been since noon. The entire convoy. Headed south, away from the storm, which seems to be curving up towards Texas now. Anyhow, I suppose I ought to brief you on the man you're about to meet," grunted the overseer.

Peter nodded, curious.

"Says his name's Bo Wharton. He came off one of the ferries last week, didn't have a congregation number. The brothers exercised caution as per directed by the branch, put him in his own little room between a couple of the overseers' cabins. They've been keeping an eye on him."

"Is he dangerous?" Peter asked.

The overseer shrugged. "Not too sure yet. No one's vouched for him. We don't know much about his story, only his name and city of origin. He's not far from where you and your wife came from–Cupertino, California."

"Oh, ok."

"Anyways, we'd like you to look after him for now. Maybe schedule some short study sessions around mealtimes, get him to know the friends in your congregation. Just exercise caution, you know?"

"He isn't studying?"

The overseer shook his head. "Not yet. He doesn't even appear to know about the study arrangement. I honestly think he just showed up out of the blue. Maybe he got one of our invitations. I haven't really had the time to sit and chat with him. But like I said, we know next to nothing about the guy. But from the looks of it, he's had a rough life. Maybe drugs, possibly prison time."

"Prison?"

The overseer nodded. "Just a guess. You'll see. Hopefully you'll get him to open up to you. Think you can handle it?" Although it was phrased as a question, Peter didn't think it sounded like one, and the overseer didn't wait for a response. They pushed through the swinging cafeteria doors and headed for one of the end tables, where a man with long, scraggly yellowish-gray hair sat with his back turned to them.

The men circled around the table as Peter's eyes took him in. He sat by himself, sipping from a paper cup, sucking the coffee through his teeth. His yellowed eyes gazed down into the cup, held in place by his wiry, veined hands. Peter knew instantly why the housing overseer had assumed the man had done time in prison. With the exception of his face, every square inch of his skin was covered in tattoos, and clearly not of the type drawn by the steady hand of a professional parlor artist. The markings were blotchy and uneven; some were half-finished. The dotted outline of a large cross crept up from beneath Bo's right collar, and Peter tried not to stare. At one time, perhaps, Bo Wharton's physique might've been muscular and intimidating, but now the sagging, wrinkled flesh hung from his skeleton like wet laundry. His red knuckles bulged, like the cheekbones on his face and the ribcage beneath the low cut of his stained V-neck shirt.

"Hey there, Mr. Wharton. This is Peter, the brother I was telling you about," said the overseer with a curt nod. Peter shook the man's hand and they exchanged pleasantries. Bo's eyes danced from one man to the other. Peter could feel himself being sized up.

"Yeah. Right. Yeah, I 'member," Bo said, slinking back down into the bench. His voice was rough and gravelly. The brothers sat on the bench across from him.

"So, Bo, what brought you to New Orleans? You have Witness family here?" Peter waited for the question to register in the man's eyes. Nothing. "So, did you get an invitation for the evacuation?"

"Invitation?" Bo asked, lightly wringing his wrists. Peter and the overseer exchanged a look and waited. "You two guards?"

"Are we guards?" Peter repeated.

46

"Yeah. Security."

"Oh. No, we're not guards. We don't have any guards here."

"No guards?" Bo asked, a faint glimmer in his eyes.

"No guards," the overseer confirmed.

"Huh." Bo's untrimmed fingernails danced on the laminate tabletop as he scrunched his face and stared up at the blank TV monitors. Peter could only wonder what all was going through the man's head.

"That yours?" Peter asked, pointing to a Polaroid camera sitting on the table beside Bo. He gave a slight nod.

"One of the few things that made it all this way with me."

Peter glanced over at the serving table, where several trays of pastries had been covered with plastic wrap and left out on small plates.

"Hungry?" he asked.

"Sure," Bo said. Peter walked to the tray and returned with a handful of bear claws and powdered donuts.
Bo snatched at them, stuffed a few bites into his mouth, and chased it down with the rest of his tepid coffee.

"So. How are you adjusting to life here on the rig?" Peter asked.

Bo shrugged. "Feeling cooped up, I guess."

"Yeah, my wife's been saying the same thing. It's to be expected, I suppose. There's only so many places you can go on a place like this."

"You married?" Bo asked.

"Almost fourteen years. You?"

Peter watched as a frown swallowed Bo Wharton's features. He shook his head slowly, said nothing.

"You, ah, like to shoot pool? I hear they've got a couple of tables set up on the lower recreation deck," Peter offered.

The corners of Bo's mouth wrinkled downwards. "Nah. No way I could keep my hands steady enough." He lifted his hands in the air. They trembled.

"Parkinson's?" Peter asked.

"Nah," the man said, his eyes suddenly wide, his stare boring a hole into Peter's head. "Withdrawals."

47

***

Stacy's red pickup labored up the interstate towards Vancouver. The roads were impossibly clogged with traffic, so much so that in some spots it came nearly to a standstill. Stacy and Joyce said nothing for most of the trip. News from the local radio stations clamored softly in the background, though nothing definitive had been reported about the Canada-US border. Joyce passed the time by alternating between massaging the kinks out of her neck and dozing off.

She'd debated calling Alvin all morning, ever since reuniting with Stacy. Stacy had the cell numbers of several brothers and sisters in her phone, so getting in contact with Alvin wouldn't have been a difficult thing. Still… Joyce knew her husband, knew how he'd react, how upset he'd be, how disappointed. It was better, Joyce decided, to call right before she arrived in Burrard Harbor, or to just explain things to him face to face in the privacy of their apartment. It wouldn't be long now. It wasn't a conversation she looked forward to, but in spite of that she missed him. She realized now just how isolated she felt without Alvin there. It felt like her against the world. Well, her and Stacy.

Stacy. Ever ambiguous and sarcastic, glass never half full. Joyce Tucker glanced over at the woman behind the wheel, the placid look on her face, the way she casually ran her fingernails through her hair and hummed some country ballad in her head, even as the possibility loomed over them that they would never be reunited with their congregation, with their *loved ones*.

Then again, thought Joyce, maybe that was just it. Maybe Stacy's cavalier worldview was her way of keeping others at a distance. Being alone meant nothing to her; in her world, loneliness was the comfortable option. Perhaps it was a coping mechanism?

Joyce gazed back out the window at the grey sky, thinking about how little she knew about the woman–the *sister*–next to her. They'd been in the same congregation for what–ten years?

Fifteen? And in that whole time, Joyce had never known Stacy to have a friend. So much of her life, really, was an enigma. She'd lived on the edge of town in that big, crumbling home all by herself–the one that had burned down. The only family Joyce had known about was the grandmother on her father's side who'd died years prior and left her the house. Joyce began to wonder.

"Tell me about your grandmother," Joyce said through a yawn. The weather wasn't helping her fatigue. Grey and dreary as usual.

"My grandmother? Why?"

"Why not? We're stuck in traffic, might as well talk about something. She died a while back, right?"

A few moments of silence passed; Joyce could sense Stacy weighing her options. Finally she gave in. "Lung cancer. The woman was a chimney. Had to have her two packs of Lucky Strikes a day, minimum. Three, if it was raining and there was nothing to do but sit out on the front porch puffing her life away."

"Sounds like a nice lady," Joyce said.

"Oh yeah. When she wasn't throwing rocks at my head."

"Throwing rocks at your head?"

"Yeah. She was old school. One of those 'kids should be seen and not heard' types. I mean, I was a brat too, I'm not gonna lie. Still, though. That woman had an arm on her. A temper, too."

"She actually threw rocks? At your head?"

Stacy tilted the top of her head down slightly towards Joyce and brushed away the hair, revealing a small, smooth stripe of skin. Joyce grimaced.

"How old were you?"

"Not really sure. Nine? Ten?"

"And when did she pass?"

"I think it was around '95, '96. I was in my twenties, I remember that. Was living in Oklahoma at the time. Had to come back and deal with all the paperwork with the house and the will and everything."

"Sounds like you two were pretty close," Joyce said, chuckling.

"Oh yeah, very tight knit family, us Owens."

"Huh."

Stacy shrugged. She flung an arm around behind the front row of seats and returned with a can of root beer. She pulled the tab and took a swig before mashing the can into a cup holder stuffed with coins and old receipts. "Thing one you need to know about the Owen clan is this: we're all messed up."

"Stacy, we all are, in this system," Joyce said gently. Stacy rolled her eyes with a smirk.

"Yeah? So, most of the men in your family have spent some time in the joint, then?"

"Well, no, not exactly."

"Any of your aunts schizophrenic?"

Joyce sighed. "No."

"Your dad ever try to hijack a police car?"

"My goodness, Stacy," Joyce said. She couldn't help chuckling, but it was an ugly sound.

"It's ok, you can laugh. It's the only way *I've* coped over the years. Gotta just laugh it off, otherwise the crazy will just seep right on in and take over. Bottom line is, our family was, is, and will always be jacked up. Maybe something in the gene pool. My mother once told me my cousins were inbred. I think she thought I was too young at the time to know what that meant, but I remembered the word, the ugly way her face went when she said it. Looked it up in a school dictionary the next day. Thing is, she was probably right."

"Geez, Stacy," Joyce finally said, bringing a hand up to massage the side of her head. "I had no idea. Sorry."

"Don't be. I've come to terms with it. You can't choose your family, can only choose who you become."

"Ain't that the truth," Joyce said, sitting up in her seat as the border crossing finally came into view. It was not a promising sight. The cars at the front of the line were going around the turnstile and creeping back down the interstate from where'd they'd come. The ones behind those were being approached by border guards with stern looks in their eyes. Joyce and Stacy exchanged a brief, worried glance and said nothing.

CHAPTER 5

Alvin Tucker sat for most of Sunday afternoon with his face in his hands, elbows planted on the cafeteria counter. There were no more tears to cry. He wasn't, in fact, particularly sad. Anxious–yes, there was that–but mostly just angry. Furious, even. He could feel it buzzing in his nerves just below the surface of the skin. Were Joyce to walk right in through those cafeteria doors, he wasn't sure how he'd react. Certainly not with wide arms and a welcome home hug. Leaving against his explicit directions was one thing, but it wasn't the worst of what Joyce had done in the last twenty-four hours. It was the lack of communication–the total inconsideration for his feelings–that really pushed him over the edge.

Alvin didn't mind Joyce helping others–he'd told her as much a million times over their twenty-eight years of marriage. Alvin knew it was part of what Joyce lived for, and everyone loved her for it, including him. But what really brought the frustration–the *pain*, if he was being honest–was the fact that of all the recipient's of Joyce's self-sacrificing attention, Alvin often found himself at the end of the line. After Joyce had doted on and cared for others, all that remained for her husband were the table scraps of her affection. Alvin had struggled to understand it for years and had yet to find a satisfying answer. Did she just not care about him as much as everyone else? Had the love somehow cooled in her heart? And if so, why? *What had he done wrong?*

Alvin sighed heavily as a thin hand settled on his shoulder. He looked up into the face of Paul O'Donnell and forced a tight smile. He'd known Paul and Debbie for years, long before they'd become special pioneers and eventually started in the circuit work. A year prior, just before the first evacuation letter had come through, Brother O'Donnell had been assigned to the Tucker's circuit, and since then the friendship had slowly been rekindled. The two were only a few years apart and their wives got along well, and sometimes Alvin wondered if, had things gone a little differently, his life would have turned out very similarly to Paul's.

Paul said nothing for a moment, just kept his hand there on Alvin's shoulder and squeezed for a moment before taking a seat beside him on the bench. There wasn't much to say, really. Alvin had called Paul late the night before, right after he'd found their Subaru missing from the lot.

The two sat there for a minute, saying nothing, grieving silently. A sister approached their aisle with a tray of plastic cups filled with Jell-O. Paul took two and thanked her.

"Had lunch yet?" Paul finally asked, sliding one of the Jell-O cups to Alvin's side with a finger.

"No appetite. Sorry," Alvin said.

"Still no word from Joyce today?"

Alvin shook his head. "There's talk of Canada closing their borders."

"Yes, I've heard."

"What then? What if she's stuck?"

"I really can't say for certain, Al. None of us can. We just have to take this one day at a time."

"I keep thinking about that Lot drama from a few years ago. Keep seeing that image in my head. But instead of that sister turning into a pillar of salt, it's…" Alvin's body shuddered, his shoulders rising as he struggled to contain the sobs. A few sets of eyes from the other tables struggled not to stare. Paul draped his arm around the larger brother's broad shoulders and squeezed.

"Don't give up hope, Alvin. Not yet."

"I appreciate you saying that, Paul, but the fact is that Joyce made a choice. She left the ark right before the door closed, and–"

"We don't know that, Alvin. Others are still on their way."

53

Alvin shook his head, a bitter expression seared into his face. "I *feel* it, Paul. It's too late. The door is shut."

Paul's frown deepened. His eyes went glossy and red for a moment and he bowed his head. "Jehovah will reward you for your faithfulness, Alvin. Hold on to that."

Alvin Tucker's eyes squeezed shut as the words blanketed him like fresh snow. He knew they came from a good place, but they seemed like a confirmation of his wife's fate, each syllable another nail in her coffin. He hurt everywhere, and in that moment he loved his wife and hated her. Yearned for her and was repulsed by her. Wanted to hear her voice, if only to scream back at it.

Alvin felt a buzzing in his pocket just as a soft pinging noise erupted from Paul's breast pocket. Similar phone alerts simultaneously erupted from various tables and corners of the cafeteria. The men retrieved their phones, looked at the screens, and then at one another.

***

Thiago spent his first night aboard the VLCC in a small cabin with Frank Henley, the man he'd met aboard the ferry. His daughter, Alyssa, had been somewhat fussy when they'd first entered the cabin, but had settled down after a bedtime story and quickly fell asleep. The two men had talked for another couple of hours before they retired for the night.

Initially, Thiago had dreaded the very thought of life aboard the VLCC: the constantly banking angles, the rollicking within his intestines, the endless sensation of instability beneath his feet. He could hardly picture himself being able to relax and think straight on the high seas. Once aboard the supertanker, however, his fears were quickly allayed.

Her name was *Valiant Alhambra*, and at three hundred and forty-five meters long, she was longer than most skyscrapers are tall. Normally equipped to carry two million barrels of crude oil per trip, the *Valiant Alhambra* was so large that she stood staunch and impervious amid the roiling, white-tipped waves slashing at her.

Thiago had been tired but hungry for details; there was much to be learned of the Witnesses and their intentions way out here on the sea in the middle of a storm. Thiago knew of the other evacuation camps, but it seemed that all were situated in similar coastal regions, or harbors, or islands. It was puzzling, to say the least.

Thiago had navigated their conversation carefully, asking questions while being careful not to arouse suspicions. It was difficult; it was clear to him now how much research he'd neglected. Frank threw terms around that Thiago struggled with. *Elders* was easy enough to understand, as was *congregation*, both of which he'd heard countless times in the last few hours. But as for *pioneer*, *circuit overseer*, and *faithful slave*, Thiago hadn't a clue. The terms were mentioned so casually that Thiago could guess they were common knowledge among the Witnesses, but he was unsure how to decipher them. He could only hope that none of this knowledge would be required of him in the next few days.

Thiago gazed up at the ceiling above his bunk, his fingers woven together on his chest, and mentally reviewed all of what he'd learned in the last few days. There were still so many questions, so many unknowns. The Witnesses, he'd observed, operated with military precision and efficiency, and their members fell right into line with few questions asked. The whole place had the aura, not of a refugee camp, but of an army barracks, everything tightly organized, no details left to chance. Everyone had an assigned ID number, and those numbers were associated with a congregation ID, and all of that data was stored in an easy-to-access computer system he'd been introduced to shortly after boarding the night before. Little was hidden, it seemed. But what was the motive, the *point?* Until Thiago could understand their intentions, he was ill-equipped to formulate a plan to finish his job.

And where were the security forces? That was another thing Thiago couldn't quite wrap his mind around. With such an enormous operation–thousands of evacuees from dozens of cities, hundreds of millions of dollars' worth of equipment and facilities on the line–surely the Witnesses had to have invested heavily in security. At the very least, this would include armed guards, (or, more likely for a populace of this size, an entire private police force), and obviously enough surveillance cameras to spy on a small city. But where was it all hidden? Since boarding the *Valiant Alhambra,* Thiago hadn't spotted a single firearm, and he'd been *looking*. No CCTV cameras, either. Strange. It was either the largest, most foolish oversight in the history of mass gatherings, or the Witnesses had something else up their sleeve, and given their acute attention to planning, Thiago suspected it was the latter.

That morning, when Frank had headed out for breakfast in one of the cafeterias with his daughter, Thiago had stayed behind to thoroughly search the cabin space. He needed a storage spot out of sight to stuff the more sensitive items in his inventory. Options were slim. The only storage space in the cabin was behind a row of cabinets with sliding panel doors. There were no locks on any of them. Thiago stuffed his clothing into a zippered waterproof pouch and stowed it in the cabinet, but he'd need someplace else to stash his arsenal.

He finally located a suitable spot about ten minutes later, above a network of pipes that ran atop a corridor not far from his cabin. He glanced up and down the corridor before reaching up, catching the pipes in his hands, and swinging himself into the tight crawlspace. It was dark and well out of sight, and the fine layer of damp dust around him told him that this was a not a place often visited by others. He stuffed the duffel of weapons into the crawlspace and snugged it down with an elastic cable.

Good, he thought. That was one problem solved. Thiago hopped quietly down from the crawlspace, his body sinking low into a crouch to absorb the sound of his rubber soles landing on the floor. Now it was time to explore.

Thiago had caught glimpses of the ship's deck maps during the boarding process the night before and his mind had since been compiling lists of questions. Most importantly, he needed a way to travel from the supertanker to Rig 7. Thiago wandered the lower decks, threading his way through hundreds of cabins like the one he was roomed in. The rooms, he noted, all seemed to have been built recently. The exterior walls and metal hardware attaching them to the inner hull of the VLCC appeared new, the nuts and bolts still shiny, free of corrosion. All of these units, Thiago realized, were intended to be lived in, though only a few appeared to be occupied at the moment.

Thiago climbed a stairwell to the next level to find an identical grid of cabins, and then another above that. How many people could this place hold? The corridors seemed to stretch on for miles, and if it weren't for the stenciled letters and numbers clearly specifying the sectors, rows, and columns, Thiago was sure he'd get lost.

So clean, he thought. That was odd too. Aside from the dusty crawlspace where he'd stashed his guns, the surfaces below deck were almost spotless. A faint, lemony trace of disinfectant hung in the air. Since he'd left his cabin he'd passed two small groups of cleaning crews in rubber gloves and aprons, their faces all smiles. What *was* this place?

Thiago finally entered the cafeteria just as the lunch lines were forming. He ate by himself in a quiet corner, studying the faces around him and gathering as much from the conversations as he could. He couldn't understand much of what they said, but almost everyone was discussing the same thing–an *announcement* that would be broadcast the following day.

***

They'd tried everything to reason with the officials at the border crossing: explaining, reasoning, even begging to be let in. Tears were in Joyce's eyes as she pleaded with the men with the stern looks in their eyes, inspection dogs sniffing circles around her feet, but nothing worked. Rules were rules, the guards explained, waving the women aside as the next vehicle stopped at the turnstile. Stacy had parked the pickup on the shoulder of the road and the two of them had approached on foot, thinking that it might make a difference, but it was becoming abundantly clear that words alone were not going to gain them passage.

Why? Joyce kept thinking. *Why now? Just hours after she'd left?* It was maddening, standing there just a few short feet from the country they needed to get into, all because of some stupid, imaginary line drawn in the dirt by men long dead.

"I need to call Alvin," Joyce finally said, her voice barely registering. Stacy said nothing as she handed the phone over. Joyce scrolled through the contacts and pressed her husband's name, feeling her heart flutter in her chest like a flock of angry, caged birds. He picked up almost instantly.

"Stacy?" came the voice on the other end. It was weathered and thick and exhausted, the voice of a man who'd spent the night in tears. It broke Joyce's heart.

"It's me, honey," she said, lips beginning to quiver.

"Joyce?"

"Yes. I'm with Stacy–"

"Joyce… Where are you? Stacy Owen? How? What happened?"

"I… I couldn't just watch Claire like that… I had to do something."

"You took the car. I went looking for you last night."

"I'm so sorry, Alvin. So, so sorry. I had no idea–"

"Where are you now?"

"We're at the border."

"How long till you get back? What's the traffic like?"

"I–I don't know about the traffic."

"What do you mean, you don't know? Aren't you on the highway?"

"Border's closed."

"Closed?"

"Closed. They say you need special government-issued permits to get through now. It just went into place this morning."

A long silence. "Oh, Joyce," Alvin groaned.

"I'm so scared, Alvin. I have no idea what we're gonna do."

"Oh Joyce," Alvin repeated, his voice soft and awful. "I wish you had just listened."

"I know, I know, I keep telling myself the same thing. I just

58

wasn't thinking. I just wanted to help the girl. You have to believe me, Alvin."

"I believe you, but it doesn't matter why you left. You didn't *listen*. Now look at the mess you've created," Alvin's voice was flat, tired. He was beyond anger and condemnation. The tone of his voice was much more painful to Joyce's ears. It was one of complete hopelessness, a total acceptance of loss.

"We received a message today, Joyce," Alvin said, his voice still cold and distant.

"A message?"

"An important announcement will be delivered tomorrow. It seems there's more to this evacuation than just coming here to Canada."

"What do you mean?"

"I'm not sure. The announcement is going to be broadcast tomorrow afternoon."

"Ok… Well, that's reason for hope, right? If you all are headed somewhere else, maybe Stacy and I can just meet you there? Right, Alvin?"

"I don't know. Maybe, it all depends on where we're going."

"Maybe you'll head back to the US," Joyce said, trying to sound hopeful. But Alvin said nothing.

CHAPTER 6

The crowd gathered in the cafeteria and fell silent as the hands on the clocks crawled their way towards three o'clock. The air was tinged with the sweet tension that had almost become a part of normal life in the last year. It was the evacuation letter all over again, Peter felt, except this time he was in the audience. All of the elders were. No one knew what was coming. At five to three, a digital countdown appeared on screen. Everyone took their seats, and the ensuing silence was dead enough to hear heartbeats in.

"Hello brothers and sisters, and welcome to this very special edition of JW Broadcasting. If you were obedient and fled with Jehovah's people on schedule, you are now surrounded by your brothers and sisters in one of our evacuation camps. How happy we are to know that many of you were willing to make great sacrifices and difficult decisions to be where you are today. Rest assured, the determination and obedience you've shown will be greatly rewarded."

The brother paused, a warm expression glowing on his face as the studio switched camera shots to reveal the large TV screen behind the studio's desk. As the station aired a brief montage with highlights from the upcoming program, Peter Burton felt his wife's hand rest on his arm and squeeze. He felt the goose bumps from her skin transferring to his and pulled her tightly into his side.

Peter glanced momentarily around at the hundreds of faces glued to the TV screens hanging from the walls of the cafeteria. As they watched the broadcast here, thousands more brothers and sisters aboard their rig huddled in training halls and meeting places and classrooms, all watching the same program. And beyond Rig 7, countless other friends would be watching along, all at the same moment, on rigs, supertankers, and ferries.

"Welcome again to our special broadcast. At this moment, millions of you are tuning in from the remotest corners of the globe, on six separate continents and countless islands. Thousands more of you are far out at sea. Today, history is being made. Never before have so many of Jehovah's servants attended the same spiritual gathering at the same moment. This is a first, but it certainly won't be a last!

"As we mentioned at the outset, many of you have made significant sacrifices to be obedient and loyal to Jehovah, and to the direction of the faithful slave. The governing body has received thousands of reports from overseers around the globe relating some of your experiences. It warms our hearts to know that so many of you let nothing get in the way of your obedience. Take for example sister Adalina Esposito from Peru. Note the challenges she faced when she learned of the evacuation notice…"

The brother paused as the screen crossfaded to a slow pan of snow-peaked mountaintops. An airy pan flute whistled a lilting tune over shots of llamas grazing on a steep hillside and round-faced women in straw hats and colorful garments with babies lashed to their backs.

"When I first heard of the letter regarding the evacuation, I was stunned," came the voiceover. *"I simply didn't think it would be possible for me to join the others."* The voice paused as a shot of a poor mountainside village filled the screen. The entire town seemed to have been sculpted by the dirt beneath it. None of the houses were of stone or concrete. Their roofs were of rotten, rust-bitten corrugated metal. Emaciated dogs roamed between the houses, their snouts sniffing hungrily at the ground.

"My village, Kygygy, is five hours from the main road and is accessible only by horse or donkey. The roads are rocky and bumpy, and in many areas it is necessary to get off and walk. But for me, this is impossible." For the first time, the scene cut to a shot of Sister Esposito. Her skin was dark and wrinkled, the hands on her arms like brown leather. On her face were a pair of

dark sunglasses, and her legs were missing below the knees.

"When I was just ten years old, an accident on the hillside required the amputation of my legs. Since then, I have been stuck in my village. I cannot travel by horseback, and no cars can reach my village. Five years ago, brothers came preaching in my village from a town ten hours away. I knew immediately that I had found the truth." The narration paused as the scene cut to the sister's hands gently stroking the cover of a well-worn Spanish *Bible Teach* book.

"A year ago, the brothers told me about the evacuation notice over the telephone. I was devastated! I simply did not see how I could be a part of such a thing. But they told me not to worry, that they would find a way to come get me. But I'll be honest, I didn't really believe them!" The sister laughed, her mouth opening wide to reveal a big smile in spite of the missing teeth.

"The brothers continued to visit me each month, as they always had, to provide me with the latest magazines and the meeting recordings, but for a long time they did not mention the evacuation, and so I thought that maybe they had come to realize that there was simply no way to get me out of this village. I was sad, but I knew that if I died in this system, Jehovah would remember me." Another smile, and Peter and Rachel exchanged a strained look, tears starting to form in their eyes.

"Then, two months ago, the brothers called again. They said that I should get all my things together and be ready on Friday morning, that someone was coming for me. I said, 'I hope that someone has wings, because there's no other way to get me out of Kygygy!' That Friday, I waited on the edge of my town, by the only dirt road leading into our village. My vision is not so good, so I kept listening for the sound of hooves, but there was nothing. I was very distraught until I heard something terrifying– a loud, booming noise! And it was coming from above me, from the sky! I wondered, had those brothers sent an angel?" A laugh rippled through the cafeteria; many of the friends were already dabbing damp eyes with tissues. On the screen, Sister Esposito looked up to the sky as a strong wind tousled her white hair.

"They sent a helicopter! The brother, who was a pilot, flew the helicopter over a hundred miles to get me in my small village. I couldn't believe it! Now I really know that Jehovah takes care of every one of his people! No one was left behind, not even me!" The camera slid back behind the sister, showing Adalina sitting in a bench on a hill overlooking a harbor, a sprawling grid of shipping containers out of focus in the background. Then the screen faded to black.

***

"As incredible as Sister Esposito's story may seem, she was by no means alone in her struggle to be obedient when the instructions came to leave. Many of you endured fierce opposition by your employers, teachers, peers, and family members. Perhaps many of these people felt that the decision to suddenly pack your belongings and leave was foolish and incomprehensible. The cry of peace and security was still ringing in their ears–"the end of terrorism," "open borders," "visa-free travel," these were all things touted by governments and the media, but how short-lived this period of peace proved to be."

Alvin Tucker felt a tight knot form in his stomach. His mind went to his wife Joyce, out there somewhere on the other side of the Canada-US border, alone and terrified. *If only she'd listened. If only he'd been there for her more.* He'd been shepherding so many others, and yet somehow he'd overlooked his own wife, the love of his life. Alvin squeezed his eyes shut, blocking out the pain, forcing himself to focus on the broadcast.

"But really, packing your belongings and leaving your homes, jobs, schools–and in some instances, even your own family members–was just half of the battle. For many of you, another trial came in the form of financially supporting those in need, and in donating surpluses to the organization. What faith and love it required for many of you financially well-off to part with your hard-earned wealth to support others in need! The spirit you dear friends manifested is in harmony with the Apostle Paul's words recorded at 2 Corinthians 8:13-15:

63

" 'For I do not want to make it easy for others, but difficult for you; but that by means of an equalizing, your surplus at the present time might offset their need, so that their surplus might also offset your deficiency, that there may be an equalizing. Just as it is written: "The person with much did not have too much, and the person with little did not have too little.'

"Rest assured, those of you who showed a spirit of generosity will be repaid bountifully! We remember that those showing favor to the lowly are lending to Jehovah. Yes, Jehovah considers it a gift given to himself. We can be confident that he will not forget this!

"Next, let's next travel to the state of Texas, in the United States, where one family's extraordinary generosity brought great blessings to our brothers in need..."

As the next segment aired, Alvin could think of nothing but his wife, the most generous person he'd known. Everything she'd done in the past few weeks had been out of selfless concern for Claire, and even if she'd been disobedient, surely, *surely*, Jehovah could read her heart and see her intentions? More than anything, Alvin wanted his wife at his side right now. He could just imagine her expressions of excitement and gratitude at watching this historic broadcast with her brothers and sisters.

On the screen, a couple in cowboy hats were explaining how they'd sold the family ranch–three hundred acres of land, beloved horses, and several hundred heads of cattle–and donated the funds directly to the organization.

"The hardest part was being ridiculed by our unbelieving family members," said the sister. *"They kept telling us that we were crazy for getting rid of the land, and crazier still for giving the money away to the brothers. But after simplifying our lives, we had such peace of mind. We hadn't realized how complicated our lives had been before. Suddenly, it was like we could breathe again. We had more time for the congregation, more time for the ministry, and more time for each other."*

"It was like flipping a light switch," the husband added. *"Suddenly, a lot of things got better. Our moods improved, our relationship became closer, the kids were happier. We decided to*

rent a small home closer to the Kingdom Hall and the entire family began regularly auxiliary pioneering together. We had never felt so good."

"At the time, our congregation was busy with distributing the tract Will You Come With Us? *To be honest, we were pretty nervous about joining the campaign–at the time the media was trying to smear the Witnesses' name. But we participated to the fullest, and were able to start two Bible studies. Both of those studies, along with their families, evacuated with us in January,"* explained the wife.

"There have been so many blessings in the last few months. We've really come to appreciate the words of King Solomon at Proverbs 10:22. It is absolutely the blessing of Jehovah that makes us rich. Material things just make us busy, but serving Jehovah brings real joy!"

The segment ended with the entire family seated before a picture glass window, high seas rolling in the distance, and Alvin momentarily wondered where they were.

"The Bennett family is convinced that their generosity was blessed by Jehovah. Many of you watching have no doubt experienced similar blessings as a result of 'not holding back in doing what is fine'. But where, exactly, did all of your donations go? In the following segment, note how the organization appropriated the funds to best serve the needs of our worldwide brotherhood..."

***

"When we were first approached by the Governing Body about planning a worldwide evacuation, I don't think any of us knew exactly how to react," said a grey-haired brother with raised brows and a smile cocked to one side of his face. *"Still, we got straight to work. And as we began the preparations, things started coming together and making more and more sense.*

"One of the first steps was to begin financial planning and start gathering funds. This meant scaling back many of our printeries. At the time, they were already producing less

literature than in times past, since things were shifting more and more to the digital side. And once the great tribulation began, aside from the production of the evacuation tract, there was no longer a need to print literature. In time, these properties were sold.

"Through letters from the branch, the friends were encouraged to simplify their lives as much as possible, also. We also knew we would need to sell most, if not all, of our Kingdom Hall properties around the world, which was organized under the direction of the LDCs. However, this was tricky, because the properties in most areas were used right up until the evacuation, so it required extensive planning and foresight. In many areas, the sale of property dates were just days before or after the friends evacuated.

"As the funds were being collected, branch offices around the world were tasked with finding suitable properties to construct simple evacuation centers, called camps. These camps usually held twenty to sixty-thousand Witnesses, though in some areas the numbers were much higher. The actual construction work was conducted under the oversight of the LDC, though many brothers and sisters from faraway areas were called in to lend assistance."

A time-lapse video showed the construction of one of the camps. The land was cleared first, followed by the laying of shallow underground pipe networks. Next came the paving of the ground, then the erection of cranes, which quickly stacked the shipping container pods into apartment blocks. Finally, walkways and stairwells were screwed into place.

"Because of the relatively low cost of materials used and the fact that, in most cases, the buildings were prefabricated, the camps were built quickly and with little impact to the environment. As with many previous building projects, the construction of these camps has proved to be a powerful witness, both to residents and businesses in the surrounding areas, and to contractors called in to help complete various tasks. In one instance in Europe, workers told our brothers that they'd recently finished a job in a refugee camp, and had expected

conditions in our camp to be the same. When they arrived, of course, they were amazed at how clean and organized everything was, and at the quality of the construction materials. One worker even jokingly asked, 'Do you have space here for me and my family?' The brothers placed invitations with the man and his crew, who then asked for extras to show their family members.

"In the end, we can say with confidence that Jehovah's hand was seen through the entire course of this project, right from the purchasing–or in most cases, leasing–of properties for the camps to the planning and construction phases. We truly believe that this direction was the right one, and we're excited to see what comes next!"

Thiago leaned forward on the cafeteria bench as he sipped coffee from a paper cup. He'd known, of course, that the Witnesses' evacuation was worldwide, but that fact had only loomed in the back of his mind, like a faint scent, secondary to the immediate task at hand. It hadn't mattered–still didn't, really–and yet he found himself absorbed all the same by the information pouring from the screens all around him in the cafeteria.

A hoax, perhaps? That was the most convenient explanation, the simplest one, and yet surely one that couldn't be sustained for long. A few phone calls would reveal the truth. And anyway, the Witnesses were a global organization. He'd seen their website when he'd been planning this trip, had seen the pictures from around the world, along with all the languages advertised on the site. And if they'd organized something so massive, so improbable, here in the United States–where the prices of construction materials were higher and the regulations far stricter than most places in the world–what was to say they hadn't managed the same thing elsewhere?

And so, if it wasn't a hoax, what was left? That all this was real? That people had donated homes and cars and millions of their own dollars to join some evacuation that placed them in the middle of the sea during a tropical storm? Thiago would've labeled it simple religious fanaticism–the last of its kind in a world that had practically been stripped of faith altogether–but

67

being here, in this cafeteria, it looked more like quiet compliance.

***

The segment ended, returning to the chairman sitting behind the iconic desk in the broadcasting studio. *"You dear brothers and sisters are to be commended for your generosity and obedience. Thanks to your donations, many of our friends in poorer countries were able to heed the evacuation notices in a timely and organized fashion. Your gifts helped to clothe them, provide them with transportation to the camps, and in many cases, made the construction of the evacuation camps possible in the first place. What a fine way to make use of our unrighteous riches!*

"As you may recall, in the letter from the branch that first detailed the evacuation process, the following point was made regarding our material support: 'Since all such money will have no value in the coming system of things, showing such generosity now is both loving and sensible.'

"Regarding the times we are living in, Ezekiel vividly prophesied that many would throw their money into the streets, and that once-precious things like gold and silver would become something abhorrent to them. Indeed, we are well aware that in the coming days, this system–including the financial sector–is sure to fail. At that time, things now considered to be signs of prosperity–impressive stock portfolios, retirement funds, large bank accounts–will be reduced to mere numbers on a slip of paper, digits on a computer screen. Thus, we again urge you, friends, to continue to use these financial assets generously to support our brothers and sisters. There is no better use for our material wealth, and no better time than now.

"Just imagine how angry it must make our adversary Satan, seeing his world crumble between his fingers as Jehovah's nation grows ever stronger, ever more united, and ever more blessed. In some lands, the volunteers who helped with the construction of our facilities were met with police harassment, angry protesters, and violent ex-religionists. We are certain that

all of you met with significant trials of your own. Still, you are here with us today–proof that Jehovah's helping hand has been with you all the way. How happy it makes us to announce that all facilities around the world are functioning as planned and on schedule, and that many of them are already nearly filled to capacity!

"Next, we'd like to address those of you who have not yet evacuated–those who will be watching in the days following this announcement, once this program is uploaded to our JW Broadcasting website.

"We are aware that there are many of you–whether brothers or sisters or Bible students, or perhaps others associated with the Witnesses for some time–who may be watching this and still coming to a decision about whether or not to leave. Perhaps family obligations have you feeling tied down. Perhaps threats from employers, coworkers, teachers, or peers have scared you. Maybe failing health or medical concerns have you feeling trapped. Maybe you are simply not sure if this is the right decision. Whatever the case may be, we sincerely hope you meditate on the video segments you've watched in this broadcast. We are convinced, beyond a shadow of a doubt, that Jehovah, the Sovereign of the Universe, is supporting our organization in these difficult last moments. On the horizon before us looms the end of this wicked system. The question, really is this," the camera inched closer as the brother paused to draw a breath, his eyes locking on to his audience as he raised a finger and pointed. *"...where will you be during the battle of Armageddon? Will your feet be firmly planted among God's people, or will they be intermingled with the remnants of this wicked system? Remember, during this final battle, there will be no middle ground. Which side are you taking? The choice is entirely up to you."*

The chairman paused for the words to sink into the ears and hearts of his audience. He wore on his face a stern expression, yet one that still conveyed the warmth of his invitation. It was an expression that implored his audience to take action, and Peter was not alone in thinking suddenly of Darren and Rita. He'd tell them to watch the broadcast, of course, and he was fairly certain they would, on that enormous 70-inch screen of theirs in the living room. Perhaps the look on the brother's face would be burned even more vividly into their eyeballs with the ultra high definition.

"Well, friends, what comes next? What events can we expect to see unfold in the coming weeks and months? Turn with me in your Bibles, if you will, to Jesus's words at Matthew chapter twenty-four…"

***

Numb. It was all Alvin Tucker could feel. Numb and hopelessly exhausted. The anger and frustration had passed, and the vacancy it left in his chest was a void he wasn't sure could ever be filled. As the brother on screen detailed the events soon to unfold, Alvin could hardly interpret them as anything but judgments against his wife. *Where will you be during the battle of Armageddon?* The words had echoed in Alvin's head over and over. Where *would* she be? *Will your feet be firmly planted among God's people, or will they be intermingled with the remnants of this wicked system?*

The faces in the cafeteria around him brimmed with expectation and excitement. Great signs in heaven. Possible celestial phenomenon. A global economic meltdown. Violence and anarchy.

Relief. That's what he was seeing on the faces around him. Relief that they'd gotten out in time. Relief that they'd be protected from many of the horrors soon to arrive on Earth. They'd done the right thing; they'd boarded the ark in time, and now they would wait as the rain and lightning fell from heaven and swept it all away.

They'd be protected. So would he. But not Joyce. No. She was still out there, stuck on a highway somewhere waiting for news of her fate, or perhaps wandering the streets back in Seattle, her only company an emotionally unstable sister who'd been just as disobedient. *Numbness.* It was the only way he could cope.

Alvin's attention snapped back to the broadcast as the

chairman for the program stood from behind the glass desk and buttoned his jacket. He moved wordlessly to the screen behind him, which had gone blank.

"Now that we know what comes next for this wicked system, what about us? What plan does Jehovah have in store for his people?" The brother paused as a map of the world faded in on the screen beside him. It appeared to be the same map used in old yearbooks, with each territory clearly labeled and demarcated by thick black lines.

"For centuries, worshippers of the true God have been separated. In some cases, this was the result of natural barriers– oceans, rivers, mountain ranges, and so forth. But more often than not, the boundaries were manmade. By pitting countries against one another and dividing lands and peoples, Satan has succeeded in creating a world full of prejudice and conflict. Humanity is more divided now than ever before! But not so of God's people. In these last days, Jehovah has united us, regardless of nationality, language, culture, or skin color."

As the brother spoke, the boundaries and names of countries on the map dissolved, leaving only continents, islands, and oceans. Alvin leaned forward.

"Of course, that unity has been primarily one of a spiritual nature–unity of thought, unity of spirit, unity of worship. At times, though, it has also been physical, as in the case of our international conventions, where tens of thousands of brothers and sisters from different parts of the world had the opportunity to worship Jehovah in the same place at the same time!"

"If you're like me, perhaps you've found yourself thinking, 'Wouldn't it be nice if we could always be together like this?'" The brother paused here, a small smirk lifting the corners of his mouth before speaking again. Beside him, hundreds of small red dots appeared on the map.

"The points you see here on the map are the locations of our more than four hundred evacuation camps. If you've been following the news on our website, you may have noticed that the majority of these camps are on the coast, or in areas accessible by sea. In fact, some of you tuned in right now are aboard large

71

boats–some even on cruise liners and supertankers! But why?

"The answer is that your evacuation to the camps was only the first phase in a large project that has been underway for some time now. It brings me great joy to tell you that soon, we will all be heading to a single destination! Our locations in proximity to the ocean is no accident. In the coming weeks, we will be disassembling the camps and loading everything onto large vessels, which will then take us to our final destination."

"Of course, this begs the question, where are we all headed?" Another pause, and then a large, white triangle appeared and hovered over the map. The red dots, in turn, were connected to the triangle via long, swooping red arrows. The triangle was located near the Southwest edge of the African continent. Alvin's eyes immediately went to the red dot in Vancouver, the location of his camp. The red line slipped down along the West Coast, past California, and cut eastwards through the Panama Canal before crossing through the Gulf of Mexico and then the Atlantic.

The map faded momentarily as a series of pictures appeared on the screen: A herd of elephants grazing at a watering hole. Powerful emerald waves crashing onto orange beaches. Sand dunes towering above a lush, tree-lined valley.

"Namibia, Africa, is a land rich in minerals and wildlife. Although in the last century it has been exploited to some extent, much of the land remains untouched, with a unique beauty found in few other places on Earth. Three years ago, our organization purchased a large plot of land here, and recently, a special agreement with the local government ensured that all of us, regardless of our national status, would be able to enter without the need of a visa, or even a passport. Although there is still much work to be done, with your cooperation we are certain that we will all be able to adapt to our new home..."

CHAPTER 7

Africa? This was the Witnesses' grand plan? Thiago surveyed the room around him, realizing he wasn't the only one here with questions. Several around him were whispering over their shoulders with concerned looks, and similar reactions seemed to ripple through the audience.

The questionable destination was just a part of the issue. What about the fact that they were being told to give money to this mysterious organization, which had, until now, succeeded only in planting them aboard a fleet of vulnerable-looking vessels right in the path of a storm? And had Thiago heard correctly? Were there really *four hundred* locations like this all around the world? How had this not been all over the headlines? There'd been plenty of coverage on the Witnesses, of course–late night monologues, political commentary, news footage–but that had centered on the Witnesses' evacuation, not the camps themselves. *Four hundred!* Thiago shook his head and closed his eyes. It was amazing what people would buy into these days. People looking for something to believe in, something to hold onto.

If they wanted to throw their money away, so be it. It certainly wasn't his problem, and he wasn't sticking around to witness the consequences. Because once they got to their destination–some *desert* in the middle of *Africa*–they'd riot, and Thiago, well, he'd be far away, back at his complex in Palo Alto, enjoying his three hundred grand. *Throwing money into the streets.* Yeah, right. *Knock yourselves out*, he thought, masking a snicker.

He tuned out for the rest of the program, which droned on

for another fifteen minutes. There was some hokey music video–a family packing up their car and heading down a highway, smiling all the way like they were going on some retreat and not actually throwing their civilized lives away. He could only shake his head and wonder.

When the program ended and the lights flickered back on, it was as if the crowd around him had been paralyzed by the news. And why not? Whatever notions they'd had when they first came out here, it was clear now that nothing about this was normal or sane. The men at the top of this organization were doubtless planning to take all the cash and run–to stash it away in some bank in the Caymans, like so many of Thiago's clients–while their parishioners wandered around in some remote country where they'd never be rescued, where they'd be far from legal assistance. It was a con of epic proportions. But then, Thiago had always believed that if someone was dumb enough to fall for a scam, they probably deserved it. Survival of the fittest.

That singular thought put a smile on his face. It was a reminder that he was a lion amidst sheep. There was nothing to fear here. They were in his den, now. No one would derail his plans, no one would interfere. Because the people here were simply incapable of comprehending the bad things in the world. These were the kinds of law-abiding, tax-paying, never-questioning individuals whom Thiago had only heard about, who had existed only in the peripheral of his world. But now that he was among them, he felt powerful. *Invincible*, even.

Thiago stood and stretched and walked to the edge of the cafeteria, where he grabbed a turkey sandwich and a bottle of juice from a shelf and looked for the checkout line.

"Can I help you?" asked a large woman in a hairnet and apron. She was wringing a rag in her hands and wore an eager smile on her red lips.

"Yeah, just looking for a place to pay for this," Thiago said. The woman chuckled and shook her head. When Thiago only stood staring at her blankly, she frowned and said, "This is free of charge, brother. Donation boxes are over there, though. They've got QR codes for online donations, too."

"Oh. Right," Thiago said, nodding once and returning the smile. He found an empty bench at the edge of the crowd and ate quickly. He'd nearly finished the last bite of his turkey on rye when a group of men entered from a door behind him and sat at the end of his table. They wore neon mesh vests with reflective tape on the shoulders and had two-way radios clipped to their belts. The men nodded in Thiago's direction and sat, spreading out a roll of papers on the table.

At first, Thiago ignored them, his mind still ruminating over everything he'd just seen play out on the TV monitors. But their conversation soon piqued his interest.

"…supply boats coming and going in this weather."

"It'll be a little choppy, sure, but it's not like we can just wait for the storm to pass."

"The forecast?"

"Strong winds through Monday. Expected to worsen on Tuesday. We could be looking at a tropical storm by then. They say we'll miss the worst of it, but it'll still be ugly out there."

One of the men let out a low whistle. "Let's pray it doesn't get that bad. That'd be real uncomfortable for a lot of people."

"Seems like now's our best shot at sending the boats, huh?"

"Brothers?"

Thiago shot them a sidelong glance. They were exchanging grim looks and nodding silently. "Make sure it's only the most capable seamen aboard those vessels. None of the new volunteers. If they're on deck, they should be harnessed and lit. No cutting corners on this. And if it's too sketchy to make the drop off, we send the boats straight back."

"Understood, Brother Mitchell."

The oldest of the group, a bald man in a white mustache and round glasses, rubbed at his creased forehead with three fingers, as if to iron out the wrinkles. "Carlton, you mind saying a prayer for us?"

Another of the men nodded as they all lowered their heads and Thiago heard nothing more.

***

"Still nothing?" Peter asked. His wife cradled her phone between her shoulder and the side of her head and reached for his glass of wine. It came from one of the two bottles they'd packed in the SUV. An indulgence, if they were being honest, but one they'd allowed themselves in lieu of everything else. But here they were, after an eventful, exciting weekend–finding Claire, for one, and that unforgettable broadcast back in the cafeteria, for another–and it only seemed appropriate to celebrate.

"Nothing," Rachel replied, dropping the phone into her hand as the call went to voicemail. Peter caught his wife's expression and smiled.

"Don't worry, hon. I'm sure it's nothing. Joyce is probably busy over there, just like we are. Or maybe she forgot to charge her phone."

"Yeah. You're probably right." Rachel's teeth released the corner of her lip and she allowed herself a sip of the wine.

"What a day, huh?" Peter said. He peeled his shoes off, stuffed them into a small drawer space beneath their bed and threw himself onto the mattress.

"Yeah. I think my brain is still processing everything," said Rachel, scooting onto the bed beside her husband.

"No kidding. Africa. Who'd have thought?"

Rachel's mouth fell open slightly as she gave him a feigned look of offense. "Are we forgetting what your wife predicted?"

"Don't tell me you're still stuck on Megiddo." Peter laughed. "Babe, that's like a couple thousand miles away."

"Same continent," Rachel said, shrugging. A web of wrinkles fanned out on Peter's forehead.

"You sure about that?" He stuck a finger in her side and she wriggled away.

"Fairly certain."

"How'd you feel about the rest of the program?" asked Peter.

"How did I *feel?*"

Peter nodded and gazed into his wife's eyes.

"I'm glad we did what we did," Rachel said finally. "I'm

grateful. Is that the right word?"

"I feel it too."

"Yeah?"

"Glad we sold what we could. It's too bad about the house, but it feels good knowing the funds we sent went to friends who needed it. That one segment, the one that showed those brothers and sisters from Africa getting loaded onto the evacuation trucks–that hit me."

"I noticed. I teared up too."

"How could anyone not? I mean, did you see those little kids? The looks on their faces–" Peter's voice caught, he shook it off. Rachel rubbed the side of his arm. "I keep thinking about Darren and Rita, though. That last part. I guess there are others."

"You mean other Witnesses who haven't left yet?"

Peter nodded.

"Makes me wonder how many there are," Rachel said.

"I guess it must be enough."

"Enough?"

"Enough to warrant a specific message just for them."

"I hope they watch it."

"I hope they do more than watch; I hope they listen."

The conversation was interrupted by a sudden rapping noise on the apartment door. Peter stood and opened it to find one of the department overseers on the other side.

"Evening. Sorry to bother you, but it looks like we're gonna need a hand. Grab a raincoat."

"Sure. Sure," Peter said, grabbing his coat from a hook on the wall, slipping into his shoes, and taking off after the brother.

"Can I ask what's going on?"

"Got a call from the supply department. They're sending boats tonight."

Peter glanced at his watch. "Nine o'clock at night? Don't they usually do shipments in the morning?"

"They're worried about the weather. Say it could get up to a category one."

"A hurricane?"

"Yeah, as of the six o'clock weather forecast."

77

Peter let that sink in for a few seconds, the exposed watch on his wrist still hanging in the air. He stopped walking, grabbing the overseer by his arm. "Wait. Are we going to be ok out here?"

"I don't have an answer for that."

"Mike, we've got tens of thousands of our friends here on the water. We're sitting ducks. If a *hurricane* blows through…"

"Peter, I'm worried too, but it'll get worked out. For now, let's focus on the supply boats. We need our crew on deck to haul the supplies in. We need *you*. You with me?"

Peter nodded, swallowed hard. "Yeah. I'm here. Let's do it." He shrugged into his coat and the two continued down the corridor.

***

Joyce stared up at the popcorn ceiling of her empty living room. She was pretty sure that in all the years she and Alvin had spent in the house, it was the first time she'd camped in her own living room, with nothing but a thin layer of carpet and a sleeping bag between her body and the floor. Stacy lay beside her, bundled in her own sleeping bag, both of which had come from the back of her pickup truck. Joyce was glad now that their house hadn't sold, gladder still that they'd left a spare key under the plastic rock in the back garden. They'd left it just in case of an emergency, if the neighbors had needed to get in for some reason, but she'd never expected to be the one to use it.

They entered the house and Joyce flipped on the circuit breaker in the garage and let the water heater run long enough to provide warm showers for the two of them. Next came dinner: several sleeves of saltines and string cheese, peanut butter, some beef jerky, and a couple bottles of water. While Stacy was in the shower, a call came in on her cell. Joyce saw Alvin's name and picked up.

"Where are you?" he asked.

"Back at the house."

"Our house?"

"Where else, Alvin?"

"I just figured you two would find a motel somewhere closer to the border."

"How? I've got no credit cards, no ID. Can't even pay for a payphone, let alone a hotel room."

"Stacy?"

"She didn't offer, I didn't ask. I don't know her situation," Joyce said in a low voice after confirming that water was still flowing in the bathroom down the hall.

"Maybe you should *find out* her situation," Alvin said, his voice flat.

"What would be the point of that? We're stuck together now, whether we like it or not."

"Does she even want to get back to the camp?"

"Of course she does, Alvin. She drove us all the way back up to the border, didn't she?"

"Just asking."

Joyce took a deep breath, let the tension subside. She could hear the clatter of plastic trays in the background of the call. "Where are you?"

"The cafeteria."

"Seems a little late for dinner."

"Yeah, we ate hours ago. The overseers had us get together for a meeting. I was just talking with some of the brothers."

"What's the upshot on the announcement?"

Joyce heard her husband take a deep breath, let it out slowly.

"We're headed to Namibia."

"Namibia?"

"Yeah. Africa."

"How?... When?"

"By ship, I'm guessing. Our meeting tonight was a preliminary training seminar. Walked us through how to dismantle the camp."

"*Dismantle* it?"

"Yeah. Apparently we're taking everything with us, I guess. As for the *when*, we're not sure. It sounded, from the way the GB worded it, pretty imminent."

Joyce clenched her teeth as the ground beneath her seemed to rock. She wanted to swear–or cry, scream, howl, tear her hair out–anything to vent the anger and frustration she felt building inside her like steam from a kettle. If only she'd thought things through. If only she'd *stayed*. If only if only if only. It killed her.

"What are we going to do, Alvin?"

A long silence. "I have no idea, Joyce."

"Have you asked around?"

"I've told a few people, yes, but it's not like there's a simple solution to this. The borders are closed. You can't drive in or walk in, and flying's out of the question, too. There's literally a wall between the two of us."

"Yeah, I can feel it."

"Joyce… Please. I'm not trying to be hostile, but what do you want me to say?"

"A 'don't give up' would be nice. Or even a 'hang in there.'"

"*Of course* I'm not asking you to give up."

"Really? Because it kind of sounds like *you* already have."

"No. I'm exhausted and I'm hurt. You leaving… It's like a knife in my heart, Joyce. I never thought you'd do it. Even as I ran, in the rain, Joyce–in the rain–to the parking lot, I just kept thinking that you couldn't have done it. Not my Joyce. No way. No way in a million years. Do you know what it felt like to find that car missing?"

"And what about how I feel? I'm terrified, Alvin! I'm stuck in our old house with nothing but memories and shadows and a sleeping bag wishing I'd been smarter, wishing I could take all of this back, but all I was trying to do was *save her*, Alvin. You don't see that?"

"It's exactly what I see. And it's Jasmin. All over again."

Joyce froze as an icy hand seized her by the heart. She felt its chill ripple through her veins.

"I know how much it still hurts. I know how much you wanted to save Claire."

"Don't…"

80

"But she's not yours to save. Her life isn't in any of our hands. You have to realize that, Joyce."

"I can't bear losing another one, Alvin. I can't."

"But…" Alvin began, then stopped. Joyce heard him draw a sharp breath on the other end of the line. "I think about her more than you know."

"It's like we lost her yesterday," Joyce said, her voice weak, barely audible.

"I can still smell her hair. You remember that strawberry shampoo she insisted on?"

"Barbie Bubblegum," said Joyce, a tear streaking down her face. She could hear Alvin's breathing begin to destabilize on the other end.

"Stuff was awful," he said, a chuckle slipping through his hoarse vocal chords.

"Like she had candy stuck in her hair." Joyce smiled. She remembered.

"She loved it though."

"Yeah. Kids."

"Kids."

"I can't wait to see her again."

"Won't be long now, will it?"

"No, I guess not."

"Yeah, I guess not."

"Joyce."

"Yeah?"

"I don't want to welcome her back alone."

The hand of ice in her chest became a fist. It squeezed the breath from her lungs and the blood from her heart. Her head dropped as tears streamed from her eyes and she wept.

***

Thiago pored over the deck map of the *Valiant Alhambra*. It hung on the wall of the cafeteria not far from where he'd overhead the conversation about the supply boats. If boats were coming and going from the VLCC to the rigs, this would be his best bet at ferrying himself through the seas. The only question was, *Where were the supplies boarded onto the supply boats, and how?*

Were it a smaller ship, Thiago could easily walk the exterior deck and expect to stumble upon teams of men loading containers onto boats waiting in the wings. But on a ship of this size–with a length of three football fields–and in this downpour, Thiago wasn't likely to stumble on anything but his own feet.

The map on the wall before him yielded no clear answers; he counted dozens of small storage spaces *per deck*. The only curious area he'd spotted was marked 'rail crane deck,' and judging from the diagram, it was a sizable space occupying two stories and thousands of square feet. It was located towards the back of the ship near the engine rooms. Thiago wondered if this could be it. There was only one way to find out.

From what he'd overheard, he knew the supply ships would be dispatched quickly and possibly wouldn't return until the storm passed. While Thiago didn't know everything about his client, Chad, he knew enough to determine he wasn't a patient man; if Thiago waited on the supertanker for a few more days as the storm passed, there was no telling how Chad might retaliate.

It was a thirty minute walk to the rail crane deck. Thiago ran into a few dozen people en route but hadn't bothered slipping into the shadows. No one seemed suspicious, no questions were asked. He'd even nodded and waved to a few of the particularly friendly ones. Thiago could feel his guard slipping. He'd been aboard this vessel for a full day now, and he'd spent the previous day observing these people. Two days surrounded by Witnesses was having an effect, and Thiago was assured that he had little to fear among them.

He would not enjoy disposing of the two men aboard Rig 7, of that much he was certain. Then again, Thiago had a long history of jobs he wasn't proud of; this would only be one more to add to the pile. One could only stay sane in this line of work by remembering that no one was really innocent, that even his marks–however clean they appeared to be on the outside–hid secrets. Secret pasts, secret sins. Saints no longer walked the

Earth. And if it was Thiago's hand that was chosen to bring about a reckoning, so be it. It was the way of life, the cycle of the universe. In the end, none of it meant anything, and all would be forgotten. The lives would be extinguished sooner or later, the result the same regardless of the means–particles would return to the soil and to the air and the next generation would breathe them, ingest them, and all would be reset.

A half hour later, Thiago found himself back in the crawlspace nestled among the pipes above his cabin block. He rifled through the items in his duffel bag, but it was difficult to know what to take and what to leave behind. After some deliberation, he finally settled on his climbing gear, his knives, a handgun, and nothing more. He stuffed the items in a small, black backpack and lowered himself silently back into the corridor and continued heading towards the rear of the ship.

Thiago heard the rail crane deck long before he saw it; the rhythmic grumble of machinery found his ears when he was still fifty yards away. It was intermingled with the shouting of men barking instructions to one another, the high-pitched whine of winches, and beeping forklifts. The room, which appeared to be some sort of warehouse, had an entrance large enough to drive a truck through. A tightly wound roll top door hung above it.

Thiago slipped into the shadows of the large room as workers whizzed around in forklifts and a half dozen hand operated pallet lifts. He snuck behind a wall of stacked wooden crates and watched. He gazed up at the ceiling; it rose perhaps twenty feet in the air and would provide a good vantage point, but there'd be no way to scale the walls without being spotted. His only option would be to navigate the maze of crates and shelves on the floor and hope not to be seen. Not that anyone was looking; the forty or so men and women in the room were near to frantic in their work. Thiago watched from a corner darkened by the shadow of a three-tiered shelving unit as the workers moved dozens of crates to the far end of the room, where a long, horizontal track spanned the width of the warehouse.

The noise level in the room shot up as the diesel engines roared to life. The outstretched arm of a crane slid slowly into view, a heavy hook block hanging from thick steel cables at its end kept steady by a man in an orange safety vest and a hardhat. He guided the hook to the crates as the crane arm telescoped out and pivoted slowly towards the load. The crane's arm came to an abrupt stop as two men connected the hook. More orders were barked, and the crane lifted the crates into the air with ease.

"Doors!" shouted a man at the center of the floor. He held a radio to his mouth connected to a funnel-shaped speaker at his side. Another man standing beside one of the walls gave a signal with his arm and pressed a button on a control panel and a new sound erupted, a guttural, metallic groan like a beast coming to life that seemed to come from the decks below Thiago's feet. He watched as a long vertical seam appeared in the wall. The wind screeched through the opening, a gust of cold rain and seawater carried with it. The workers pinched the brims of their hardhats between their fingers and lowered their chins, blocking their faces from the spray, and Thiago realized now that many of them had fastened tethers to their belts or else were wearing full body harnesses.

The seam expanded; it became a doorway, then a chasm. The entire side of the room had opened to the outside. Within a minute the ground was slick with rushing rainwater and sea foam. Several of the men fought back the tide with push brooms, where it was shooed off the edge of the deck back into the raging storm. Outside, the night sky brightened ethereally with flashes of sporadic lightning. The waves were oil black.

"Keep her coming. Load one!" yelled the man with the radio. More nods and signals from the men by the crane as its wheels began turning again, hoisting the load towards the opening in the wall. Thiago circled the warehouse to the opposite side. It wasn't difficult to move without being noticed; everyone's attention was focused on the loading of the crates. As the crane carried the first load, the second was prepared by the workers with the hand-operated lifts.

Thiago scaled a supply shelf against a wall opposite the opening on the side of the ship. From up here he spotted the crane operator: a man dressed in beige coveralls, neon vest, and blue hardhat with a control box slung around his neck. A cable connected him to a housing of machines and engines at the end of the track just below where Thiago was perched. From this vantage point, he could also occasionally make out the roof of a smaller vessel outside the sliding door. It rose and fell like a rubber bathtub toy in the waves.

It took the coordinated efforts of a dozen men nearly twenty minutes to successfully load the first batch of crates. The wind, the waves, the rain, and the load itself seemed to fight them at every opportunity. Once it was done, the team, now soaking wet, exchanged brief congratulations as the second load was prepared. Thiago observed their efforts for two hours, and in all that time, he heard not a single curse word, nor any arguments. What kind of people were these, to maintain composure under such extreme circumstances? And again, where were the guards? The guns? The surveillance cameras?

Thiago brushed the thoughts aside as he trained his focus again on the task at hand. Somehow, he needed to board those supply boats. It was now or never.

CHAPTER 8

Thiago stood on the outer deck of the *Valiant Alhambra* as the rain pelted the ground around him. He had few available options for getting himself on a supply boat. None of the men were boarding the smaller vessel from the VLCC, so impersonating a worker and sneaking aboard was out of the question. His second thought was stowing himself in one of the crates, but with no tools available, no way of accessing the crates slated for transport, and no way of knowing when and where the crate would be opened, it was an even riskier option than the first. Which only left one option, and it was the one least appealing.

Thiago approached the railing and gazed down at the agitated sea three stories below. As they slammed against the hull of the *Valiant Alhambra*, froth and green seawater splashed up the side. It looked thick and greasy. Thiago grimaced as he turned his attention to the small supply boat below. He walked a dozen yards towards the supertanker's stern, positioning himself just above the prow of the supply boat below. He estimated it to be roughly one hundred and fifty feet long, with two decks visible on the exterior–an upper and a lower–and likely a maze of corridors, storage rooms, and cabin below decks. Once aboard, Thiago would have no trouble staying out of sight. It was the boarding that would be an issue.

Using his night vision monocular, Thiago counted a dozen men at the stern of the supply boat positioning the crates with ropes and poles as they were lowered to the deck by the rail crane. No one was visible on the bow of the ship; all hands appeared to be focused on the loading process. Thiago took a few more paces, carefully aligning himself with the front tip of the supply boat. He took a quick glance around, ensuring that he was alone. Then he got to work.

He reached behind himself and unzipped a waterproof compartment strapped to his lower back. From it, he extracted a collapsible metal claw. He yanked back on a spring-loaded pin and the claw's fingers splayed open, ready for action. He fastened a thin metal cable to a metal hook at the back of the claw and fed out several dozen yards of cable in a neat coil on the ground beside him. The other end of the cable he hooked to a small carabineer at his waist. Then, grabbing the claw-end of the cable in one hand, he spun it like a lasso overhead and launched it towards the prow of the vessel below. Looking through his night vision monocular, Thiago saw that the grabbing claw had just missed its target: a web of suspension cables strung from the bow to the pilothouse. He swept the lens over the men on the other side of the boat just to be sure no had seen him, then he reeled the wire in and tried again.

On his fourth try, the claw found the suspension cables. Thiago pressed a button on a small device from his pack and the claw's fingers clamped shut. He tugged the wire and felt it go taut in his hands. At his feet, he estimated a good twenty yards of cable still remained. Sixty feet. It wasn't much, but hopefully it'd be enough. Thiago peeled off his raincoat and left it lying on the deck. Whoever found it would wonder, and maybe an investigation would even be held once he was discovered missing, but the conclusion would be seemingly obvious–man overboard, lost at sea–and he'd be forgotten.

Thiago leaned back, putting as much weight on the wire as possible. Satisfied, he checked that all of his pouches were zipped up, took several deep breaths, and climbed over the railing of the *Valiant Alhambra.* He fell silently into the sea as the waves rushed up to meet him. They sucked him under, the water frigid like needles of ice in his skin. He clenched his teeth against the shock and swam for the surface. Cold rain smacked against his face as he emerged. The water surrounding him rose and fell in black hills. Somehow, the current had pushed him much farther from the supply ship than he'd intended. He reached for his waist with one hand, checking for the wire, but it was gone.

Thiago glanced around frantically, looking for the line, but it was hopeless in these conditions. He saw nothing. He swallowed seawater and struggled against the panic rising in his mind like floodwaters. He was rising and falling with the waves, carried farther and father from the boats. He ducked his head underwater and cut through the water with his arms. His body wanted to flail and thrash, wanted to reel against the terror, but he stroked the water willfully, intentionally. *Just keep moving. Do not panic*, Thiago told himself. The bow of the supply boat inched closer. Thiago could now see the cable draped from the handrail like a thin black thread. He kept moving, kept fighting the numb sluggishness burrowing into his arms and legs.

The distance between himself and the supply boat closed. He continued to swim, his heart throbbing wildly in the cage of his chest, lungs aching. Finally, he felt it–the coarse, hard wire writhing in the waves in his arms. He sliced through them, brought the line up to his face, and held himself there, arms locked to his chest as the water tried to suck him under once more. He allowed himself thirty seconds of rest before slipping a hand into a pouch at his thighs and producing two cable grips, one for each hand. He fastened them onto the wire and made his way up slowly, excruciatingly. It took him nearly two full minutes to traverse the vertical distance from the waterline to the handrail of the supply boat. His arms shook uncontrollably. He shivered in the cold. Finally, his hands grabbed the metal railing and he slipped through them, slithering onto the deck like a dead snake. He lay there in agony for a few minutes before forcing himself to his feet to unfasten and collapse the grappling hook and load it, along with the cable, back into his pack.

Thiago flexed his fingers, the joints in his arms and legs, fighting the numbness. He was light-headed and having trouble thinking straight. He needed to head indoors.

***

Like so many of Silicon Valley's tech startups, the four-storied offices of Alphi Systems looked less like a professional office space and more like a trendy health club, just with computer monitors instead of exercise equipment. There were no cubicles or partitions to divide the place up, giving the sprawling space the open feel of a giant loft, with pop art graffitied on the brick-and-mortar walls, bright shag rugs strewn on the floor, and a coffee-and-juice bar. At one end, a handful of twenty and thirty-somethings alternated between tapping at their keyboards and chewing mouthfuls of pizza or deli sandwiches. At the other, a row of old cars cut in half and turned into sofas lined a wall next to a couple of ping pong tables, a ski ball machine, and two arcade units: Donkey Kong and Ms. Pac-Man.

Martin nodded a hello to a couple of software engineers as they slapped at a ping pong ball. He passed them and made his way to the end of the floor, where a long glass wall separated his and Chad's offices from the rest of the pen. They were the only walled-in offices on the floor and had thus earned the nickname 'the fishbowls.' Martin pushed through his glass door. He'd grabbed dinner out and was coming back for what was sure to be an all-nighter. Alphi was releasing a big patch for one of their apps tomorrow morning and the development team would be combing through it for bugs for at least another five hours. He threw his bag into the leather couch at the end of his office and took a swig from a Red Bull as he slid into his office chair and checked his emails.

He'd just begun skimming the first message when Chad barged in and plopped down on Martin's sofa. He lay down across it and flung his sneakered feet up on the armrests.

"Just make yourself at home," Martin said without breaking his gaze on the screen.

"It *is* my home."

"Thirty-five percent, anyway."

"Oh, that again."

"Just keeping you humble," Martin said.

"Is it working?"

"I guess not."

Chad spun around suddenly, planting his feet on the floor. "You get my note?"

"The napkin? 'Liar, liar, pants on fire?' that note?"

"And?"

"Poetry, man. Missed your calling. Could've been the next Ogden Nash," Martin said, only allowing Chad a glance. He could be as petulant as a child when he wanted to be.

"So why'd you lie?"

"Why'd you feel the need to go through my personal property?"

Chad shrugged. "Office door wasn't locked. Answer my question."

"Seriously, man. You crossed the line."

In the blink of an eye, Chad leapt to his feet and closed the distance between the two of them. He slammed his palm down on the surface of Martin's desk. The smack was loud enough to carry through the glass wall. Several interns sitting on the corner of a desk a few yards away turned and gaped.

"Geez, man, you scared the–"

"Answer. My. Question." Chad's voice was quiet, but it hissed through his front teeth as if his jaw had been wired shut like a chain link fence holding back a pack of snarling dogs. Martin blinked a few times and nodded slowly.

"Look, man. Just sit down, relax a little, ok?"

"I'm fine right here. Now talk."

Martin pushed himself back in his chair and stared into Chad's eyes. He didn't like what he saw. It frightened him. He'd seen his friend like this before, usually after he'd been drinking, but he couldn't smell any alcohol on his breath now.

"Where do I start?" Martin said, looking down at his desk.

"At the beginning. Tell me everything."

"Ok. I'm working on a zero day."

"I know that much. Why?"

Martin lowered his head, squeezed his temples for a second and drew in a deep breath through his nostrils.

"I was approached by a few other… guys… From the industry, a few years back."

"The industry."

"Software engineers, system analysts, digital security buffs, et cetera. At first they were all anonymous emails, only wanted to communicate through encrypted chat apps, yadda yadda."

"You didn't think they could be scamming you?"

"That's the *first* thing I thought."

"And?"

"It was clear these guys were from inside the industry. And they weren't trying to get me to send some money to a Nigerian prince or give over bank details. They were obviously trying to get me on board."

"On board what?"

"A coding project."

"A zero day worm."

Martin shrugged as he took another sip of Red Bull.

"Why, Martin? Why would you risk this company and everything you own getting tied up with hackers?"

"They weren't hackers."

"What?"

"They weren't hackers. At least, not in the usual sense."

"What's that supposed to mean?"

"They were all about preemptive measures. It was never intended to be used. Still isn't. To this day, the thing is caged up on someone's server. It hasn't hit the wild yet."

"Then why build it?"

"Like I said, preemptive measures."

Chad threw his hands up, but seemed placated compared to the ball of fury he'd been moments earlier. Martin breathed a little easier as his friend strolled back to the couch and sat down.

"Keep going."

"The NSA changed the game, you know."

"What game?"

"Digital security. Malware. The very nature of hacking."

"You're referring to Iran, I'm assuming?"

"A cyber weapon designed specifically to target industrial control systems. 200,000 infected computers, 1,000 machines caused to physically degrade. Nuclear centrifuges speeding out of control, exploding, scientists burning to death."

"We're not a nuclear facility, Martin. Explain what all of this has to do with us."

"Iran was the beginning, but now everyone's doing it. Did you know in the two years that followed, the Iranians developed a similar virus to go after the US banking system?"

"Scary."

"*Scary?* This is the stuff *nightmares* are made of. We're talking cyber arms race. Worse still, it's not just nation states dancing in the ring anymore, seeing if they can flip on and off each other's lights at night. It's corporate."

"Corporate."

"Sure. Why would it not be? If a nation can scrounge up a few million to hire some hacker kids to shut down the enemy's nuclear reactor, why can't a company do the exact same thing to go after a rival? Shut down their production lines and beat them to market, say, or cause a fire at a warehouse to get them tangled in a union lawsuit."

"Still don't see what this has to do with us. We're not in production. Our systems don't play with logic controllers."

"You're missing the point," Martin said, rubbing his temples again. Chad was a brilliant tech visionary, but he simply didn't have the mind for navigating digital security. "Let me put it to you this way. Let's say you build a mansion."

"I have."

"Great. And a top of the line security system, I'm sure. Alarms start blaring if an intruder walks in, right?"

"Obviously."

"So what happens if you find out that a notorious thief that's been prowling the neighborhood had your alarm code?"

"I change the code."

"Doesn't matter. He's got the master code, straight from the factory. It overrides everything else."

Chad thought for a second. "Where are you going with this?" he asked impatiently.

"You're stuck, right?"

"I guess."

"Now imagine you figure out who the thief is, finds out where he lives. Then you get the master code for *his* alarm system. Then you shoot him a message, let him know you've got it."

"And?"

"Now you're safe. He won't come after you now, because he knows you can go right back after him. This is the future digital landscape."

"A cyber weapons arms race."

"Basically, yes."

Chad locked his fingers behind his head and gazed up at the ceiling and cursed. "So let me get this straight. You met up with some guys who wanted to develop a zero day for the sole purpose of scaring off any would-be hackers or digital saboteurs. Is that it?"

"More or less."

"Doesn't add up. How do people know what we've got if everything's anonymous?"

"The programmers are anonymous, not the companies they represent. It's all on the dark web. People know who's vulnerable, who's protected."

Chad drummed his fingers on the back of his skull and narrowed his eyes. "Then why the bunker?"

"Excuse me?"

"If we've got our own... cyber weapon, or whatever, why are you still paranoid?"

"The worm is to protect the company, Chad. The bunker is to protect me."

***

"Feeling any better?" Alvin Tucker asked as he let himself into the small apartment. The subtle scent of unwashed linens caught his nostrils and he made a mental note to have someone from the laundry department come through to strip the sheets in the next couple of days.

"About the same," came the weak voice from the bed.

Alvin nodded in its direction without making eye contact. He unloaded a few meals in Tupperware containers from his backpack and placed them in the small refrigerator unit against the wall.

"Hungry, at least?" he asked.

"Barely," Claire said. Alvin grunted in acknowledgement and produced a thermos from his bag. He filled the cap with warm chicken soup and handed it over. Claire sipped from it gingerly as he waited.

"Everything ok with Joyce?" Claire asked, handing back the emptied cup. Alvin had avoided the topic for days. He'd been coming to drop off food since Sunday, three days prior, but had purposefully kept his visits brief.

"I don't mean to be pushy or anything. I really appreciate all you two have done…"

"But?"

"But I could really use a shower."

Alvin frowned.

"I need help."

Claire had been able to manage getting to and from the bathroom on her own, but Alvin hadn't even thought to ask if she needed help showering. Other, more pressing things, had weighed on his mind.

"Yeah. Ok. All right. I'll get one of the sisters to come by and give you a hand," Alvin muttered.

"Thank you."

"Don't mention it," Alvin said, refilling the thermos cap. He brought a chair over from the other side of the room and set the thermos down beside Claire's bed.

"And Joyce? Is she sick?" the girl asked, wide eyes blinking.

"She's… Been running around a lot lately," Alvin said, rubbing the back of his neck. "She, um… Sends her regards."

"Brother Tucker?" she asked softly. Alvin froze, his gaze lifting to meet her eyes. The skin on her face was white. The way it bulged at her cheekbones almost made it look translucent. And the way she spoke, that crystal quality of her voice, as if it had

94

echoed up to meet his ears from an icy cavern.

"Yeah?"

"I hope… I mean…"

"What is it?"

"I just hope I didn't say anything to upset Joyce."

"Upset her? What do you mean?"

"I've just been thinking. The last time I saw her, I'd just gotten off the phone with my sister and brother-in-law, and I was just so excited. My head is so scrambled, you know? And to have them there, talking to me, it was like a big piece of the puzzle fit back into place."

"Ok."

Claire nodded. "And I was just so happy about it, I felt so… so… *warm*. But I think I may have come across as ungrateful to your wife."

"Ungrateful?"

"Did she say anything? Was she upset after we last saw each other?"

Alvin's frown deepened. He leaned back against the desk by the wall and considered his options. He'd had his reasons for withholding the news of Joyce's departure from Claire but knew it was only a matter of time before she'd figure out the truth. And when that happened, whatever tension lay between them would only intensify.

"It was nothing you said," Alvin said, looking down at the floor.

"Oh. I see. Everything's ok, then?"

Alvin glanced up to meet the girl's eyes. He shook his head slowly. "Joyce left the camp." Alvin watched as the stunned look bloomed in Claire's eyes.

"She *left?* I thought none of us were supposed to leave."

"We aren't."

"Then… What happens now? Where is she?"

"Stuck in Seattle. The Canadian government closed the borders after all the terrorist attacks."

Claire's mouth fell open as the news hit her. She covered her mouth with a hand and brought her knees up to her chest.

95

"I… I can't believe it… I'm so sorry."

"Yeah, me too," said Alvin, his face blank, but his voice filling the air between them like a dense fog.

"What do we do?"

Alvin shrugged. "That's what I keep asking myself, but it doesn't seem now like there's much we can do. Just wait, pray. Hope something changes."

"Brother Tucker?"

"Yeah, Claire?"

"Please tell me she didn't leave because of something to do with me."

Alvin lowered his head again and grimaced at the floor. "It's not your fault."

"No," Claire moaned, dropping her face into her palms. Alvin watched as tiny sobs rocked her body. He let the grief run its course in silence.

"The thing about my Joyce is, she's got a stubborn streak." Claire looked up, wiped her eyes with the back of a sleeve. "As long as we've been together, almost thirty years now. Sometimes, it feels like she fights me just for the sake of it. She's always been independent. When we moved into our first house in Seattle, everything was a battle. I wanted to paint the living room walls eggshell white, she wanted blue. I wanted curtains, she wanted blinds. I wanted wood floors, she wanted carpeting. Every single thing." Alvin rubbed the side of his head. "Before she took off, we talked. I was clear. I reminded her of all the branch had told us about leaving. But it was too late. Her mind was made up. She left Saturday night.

"I should've known she was planning something."

"How so?"

"She took a blood sample from me on Saturday morning. When I asked about it, she said it was for testing. She'd had a strange look in her eye."

"Sounds like Joyce."

"I'm so sorry. I'm sorry for bringing all this pain into your life."

Alvin shrugged, brushed her away with a sweeping gesture.

"It was my wife's call, not yours."

"Yeah, but if I hadn't shown up in that hospital…"

"If you hadn't shown up in that hospital, that probably would've meant you were dead in the blast. Not something you should be wishing for."

"Yeah, but at least you two would be together," Claire said. Alvin turned away again. He felt the blood rush to his neck and cheeks. It was anger that had put it there. The feeling was sharp and intense, like a cold blade in his gut. He sucked a breath through his teeth slowly to calm himself.

The fact is, Claire had merely put into words exactly what he'd been thinking the last three days. *Yeah. If only you'd died in that blast, my wife of twenty-nine years would still be by my side. Instead, she threw her life away trying to save a near-total stranger who looks like she's about to die anyway. Thanks a lot for surviving, Claire.*

Alvin struggled to push the cynicism from his mind, but it sat there in the center of his thoughts like a wasps' nest–a million awful thoughts buzzing around noisily in his brain. His department in the camp had given him the last few days off to process things, time he'd spent alone in his apartment. But the isolation had only made things worse. He knew that now, but the diagnosis was easier than the cure.

"Do you remember Jessica Lanski?" Alvin asked, turning back to Claire and fixing his gaze on her. She frowned, looked down at the sheets, then back to him with a slow shake of her head.

"Sorry, I don't think so."

"She's about your age–twenty, twenty-one or so–jet black hair, dark eyes. She's mixed. Mom's Japanese, Dad's Polish."

"Wait, is that the girl we met at the gas station when we crossed over the border?"

Alvin nodded. "That was the first time you'd seen her, huh?"

"Well, yeah. You introduced me."

"Sure. Wasn't the first time she'd seen you, though."

Claire frowned again. "I don't understand."

"You two were apparently classmates. You had a reputation. She'd heard of you."

"What are you trying to tell me?"

The two stared at each other for a long moment before Alvin finally shrugged. "She didn't think you were a Witness."

Claire's lips parted as her mouth opened slightly. She looked as if she'd been slapped across the face. "You think I'm lying about having amnesia. Don't you?"

"The thought crossed my mind."

"Brother Tucker, I swear to you–" Alvin held up a hand, cutting the girl off.

"Easy. I believe you've got memory loss. It wouldn't make sense for you to lie to us this long. And I meant it when I said that it's not your fault Joyce left. That was her decision, the consequences of which are on her own head now. But that doesn't change the fact that she left because she was trying to save your life. So if there are things from your past that I need to hear…" Alvin trailed off, spreading his palms outward as if revealing a hand of cards.

"I'm trying," Claire said, eyes filling with tears.

"Try harder," Alvin said. He zipped his bag shut, and without another word left Claire's apartment.

***

"Tensions run high at the nation's capitol today after an emergency White House meeting was called by the President. Although the press secretary has yet to announce an official press conference, sources tell us that the emergency meeting was held in response to the closing of international borders on Sunday, which has led to mass chaos at airports and shipping facilities around the world. On the US-Canadian border in New York, protestors and Canadian border guards clashed in an armed conflict, leaving two protestors dead and seven others hospitalized.

"The Canadian Prime Minister issued a response this morning, stating: "In these particularly critical times, global

cooperation and understanding must be given key priority. Violence will only incite more tragedy. We must come together to end this senselessness. "

"In Atlanta, the CDC has remained mostly silent over the last two days on their latest findings in regard to the explosions that rocked a series of airports throughout the US two weeks ago. What was recently believed to have been a radiological compound is confounding the scientists and chemical experts brought in from around the globe to study it. Adding to concerns is the fact that seven of the nine hospitals treating patients from the blasts have been cordoned off by the US Army and the CDC. Although there have been no confirmed reports released, several hospital workers are claiming that the explosions contained contaminants now believed to produce contagious symptoms in victims. Reporting live from our sister station in Seattle is ... "

Stacy Owen shut down the streaming news app on her phone with a sigh. "Doesn't look like those borders are opening up anytime soon."

Joyce said nothing as she walked from the bathroom, a towel wrapped around her head. She'd hoped the hot shower would relieve some of the stress, but the look in Stacy's eyes put the pressure right back in her chest. She said nothing as she strode into the kitchen for a glass of water.

"People are going to start freaking out," Stacy said matter-of-factly. "The CDC should just come out and say something. Not just board those hospitals up like that. All those people in there. What was it like when you were there?"

"I told you, Stacy. It was bad. Like a war zone. Lots of soldiers, lots of scary-looking people."

"They're covering something up, aren't they? What do you know?"

"Why does it matter? This is the end. None of this is going to last."

"What, I'm not allowed to be curious?"

Joyce sighed. "Fine, be curious. But it's not like I have the answers."

"Well, they're saying it's contagious, now."

99

"Yeah? And?"

"So, what if you're infected?"

"Me?"

"You were working at the hospital with those patients, weren't you? And you took care of that girl in the camp, didn't you? And didn't you tell me she was still pretty sick when you left? So what if she's infected others? What if there's some kind of outbreak in the camp?"

"Geez, Stacy. Please."

"I'm serious, Joyce. I think it's a fair question, don't you? I mean, does your husband even know how bad this thing is?"

"My husband?"

"What, you don't think he'd like to know?"

"It's not that. I'm just wondering, since when do you care so much about what my husband and I talk about?"

"Look, whatever is going on between the two of you—"

"Between the two of us? Excuse me?"

"You used my phone. It's not like I was eavesdropping, but I couldn't help but—"

"Regardless of whose phone I was using, what's going on between my husband and I is none of your business."

"Lighten up, Joyce. I know you two are angry at each other. Big deal. Couples fight."

"And how would you know about that? It's not like you've ever been married! Or have ever had to care about anyone but yourself for a single day, for that matter!" Joyce stopped herself as a sudden pain flashed through her palms. She looked down at the heels of her hands, where her fingernails had left deep indentations in the skin. Stacy stared at her blankly, coolly.

"Look. I'm sorry. I… I shouldn't have said that," Joyce said, still looking at her feet.

"You said exactly what you meant."

"No, I didn't. I didn't mean that."

"Yeah, you did. It's ok. It's what everyone has always thought of me."

"That's not true, Stacy."

"It's all right, Joyce. I'm not mad. It's nice to hear some

honesty for once."

"You think people lie to you?"

"Maybe not intentionally, no. But I know a fake smile when I see one. I'm an outsider. Always have been. It's no big deal, you get used to it."

Joyce pressed her hair dry as she slipped into the sleeping bag on the floor. "Have you ever thought about... You know, getting tested?"

"Tested?"

"Sure. Maybe it's got something to do with social anxiety."

Stacy sighed. "I've tried putting a name to it, but what difference would it make? It's who I am. Not gonna change, not on this side of the system, anyway."

"But if it's something treatable, Stacy..."

"Then what? I take pills to become someone else? And what kind of honesty would that be? Then suddenly I'm the one with the fake smile." Stacy let out a sardonic laugh and shook her head. "I might not be comfortable in this skin, but at least it fits."

CHAPTER 9

Thiago woke with a head full of lightning. It thundered through his brain and his sinus cavities. His equilibrium was shot, helped none by the rollicking of the small shipping vessel atop the high seas. His throat and lungs throbbed in pain, his eyelids were sticky sandpaper against his eyeballs. He wanted nothing more than to be off this boat, off these cursed seas and back on hard, stable land, or better yet, a soft, horizontal bed.

He knew the risks jumping into that water, but at the time he'd been out of options. The only path forward was a plunge into the freezing black seas. Once aboard the supply ship, he'd located a tiny storage space behind the engine room, had entered and bolted the door behind him, and tried to warm himself. He pulled the dry change of clothes from a waterproof pouch lashed to his waist and struggled to change clothes in the small room as it spun around him. But even with the dry clothes he'd been much too cold, shivering uncontrollably, knuckles and lips as blue as corpse flesh. The diesel engines gave off some heat, which is why Thiago had searched out the location in the first place, but it wasn't enough. He folded his knees to his chest, wrapped them in his arms, and covered himself in a salt-encrusted plastic tarp he'd found below decks. He shut his eyes against the racking cold wondering vaguely if he'd be spotted before daybreak.

He wasn't. But the reason no one had wandered into this space during the night was now clear: it was a dusty, miserable place full of oil smoke and diesel exhaust. Thiago was dizzy, disoriented, and barely able to think straight. All he knew was that he needed to find a new place to hole up. He cleared his throat and hacked up a glob of greasy, soot-stained mucus.

First, breakfast: a couple of protein bars pulled from a zippered pouch. He ate quickly, eagerly. He'd need to find more food, but didn't think it'd be a problem on a boat with at least the twelve deckhands he'd counted from aboard the *Valiant Alhambra* the night before. Water. More than anything, he needed water. He knew he was dehydrated from the physical exertion the night before, and his skin's exposure to salt water during the swim had further dried him out.

He glanced at his wristwatch: 6:05 AM. Surely some of the crew would be up by now, but he hoped the decks would be relatively quiet, allowing him to explore with minimal risk of being discovered. Thiago peeked through a metal grating and could see no one.

Thiago crept from his hiding spot into the lower deck's corridor, listening at closed doors and keeping to the shadows as much as possible. In the end, there wasn't a need to; the lower decks were devoid of life. Satisfied that he was alone, Thiago began exploring the rooms behind the doors one by one. Most were storage areas filled with tools: drills and wrenches and welding apparatus, and cleaning supplies: buckets, mops, chemicals… But no food or water.

Thiago had only briefly glimpsed a diagram of the ship taped to a hallway on his way down the stairs the night before. He'd been moving quickly, with no time to memorize the map, but in the couple of seconds he'd spent studying it, he'd gathered that the galley and dining area was on the B deck, a level up from his current position, and situated near the crew's quarters. It would be unlikely that he would find the area empty, but he had no choice; the longer he waited, the more foot traffic the hallways would attract.

Thiago ascended the stairs cautiously, ears alert for any sounds of movement. Nothing. Perhaps the crew were still asleep. He approached the door to the galley and listened for a moment. It was odd, he thought, that even the cook would be sleeping–Thiago imagined he would be up at this hour preparing breakfast–but he heard nothing; no shifting of pots and pans, no rustling through shelved goods. Apart from the rumbling of the engine beneath his feet, the crashing of waves against the outer hull, and the creaks and groans of the listing ship, all was quiet. He opened the door slightly, a sliver of light spilling into the darkened space from the hallway lights.

He slipped in and quickly took a visual inventory of the space. There were stoves and a large oven, a swinging rigging of utensils, and shelves of plastic plates and bowls. He slinked further into the kitchen and located–*finally*–a pantry brimming over with canned foods, sacks of rice and potatoes, and bottled drinks. Thiago snatched several bottles of water along with a couple of cans of beans and granola bars and tossed them into a canvas sack folded on one of the pantry shelves. He needed enough to keep him fed and out of sight for a day or two while he planned his next move, but not enough so as to arouse suspicion.

Thiago turned and froze. There, standing not five feet from him in the entryway, stood a young woman staring at him with wide eyes.

***

Thiago's eyes burned as the overhead bulbs illuminated with a flick of the woman's finger. His head swam. What had been in those fumes coming from the engine room? His throat still stung, his lungs ached.

"Who are you?" the woman asked slowly, narrowing her eyes to study the tall stranger before her. Thiago did his best to think of an answer, but nothing was coming easily this morning.

"I–I'm James," he managed after some thought. He brought an arm up to shield his eyes from the burning light. As his sleeve brushed against his face, he felt heat radiating from his forehead. The woman only continued to stare, her frown deepening.

"I've never seen you before. How'd you get aboard this ship?"

"Last night. I boarded from the *Valiant Alhambra*. When your supply vessel made its drop off," Thiago explained, hoping this shard of truth would disarm the woman. Hey eyes widened by a fraction, but the expression of shock and confusion remained.

"You *boarded?*" asked the woman, incredulous. Her fists were on her hips.

"Yes, I… It's a long story, really. But I just came in here to get some water and some food," Thiago said, struggling to weave together a comprehensible story in his head. At the moment though, nothing made sense. This had all been too sudden. He needed to buy time to think. If only they'd let him sit and eat, he was sure he could work it out in his head. The goal was not to stay long aboard this ship, he reminded himself. He needed it only as a means of transit to Rig 7.

"You should come with me," said the woman, turning slightly to face the kitchen behind her. "The captain will want to talk with you."

"Yeah, sure. No problem," Thiago said, offering a smile.

The woman led him through the corridor he'd just snuck through and up a flight of stairs to the upper deck. It was fortuitous, Thiago thought, to be getting a guided tour of the place now. It would've been difficult to scope out this part of the ship on his own. He noted the captain's quarters and several other cabins. It was mostly quiet, but he heard voices ahead of him, on the bridge.

The voices fell silent as the woman entered; heads turned to gape at the tall stranger behind her. Their expressions were the same. Thiago felt anxious, but not threatened. He had worked for and against all types of dangerous men. Sensing threat had become second nature. He did not sense it here.

"Sorry to interrupt, brothers, but I just found this… man… in our galley," said the woman, shifting uneasy glances around the room. No one appeared prepared for this encounter. Thiago introduced himself as James and offered a handshake, which was accepted warily by the three men in the room.

"He says he boarded our vessel last night when we were loading the *Valiant Alhambra*. Says he's hungry. I found him in the pantry," said the woman, as eyes widened and exchanged

105

looks.

"What's that you got in the bag, son?" one of the men asked. Thiago placed him in his late fifties, with a head of greying curly hair and a gut that leaned eagerly over his waistline like the prow of a tugboat in the water. Thiago looked down at his hands and opened the mouth of the sack, showing those around the room.

"Just some food and water. I was hungry."

"Well, you should've just said so. Breakfast's in what, an hour?" asked the man, swiveling in his chair to face the woman. She frowned slightly and glanced at her wrist.

"Um, yeah. About," she said.

"Great. James can keep us company here on the bridge until we're ready to eat." The others nodded, if a little reluctantly. The man pointed at the sack in Thiago's hands and he turned it back over to the woman, who made a tight smile and disappeared back through the hallway.

***

Thiago leaned back on his stool, feeling the breakfast warm him from the inside out, edging out the cold that had leaked into his body from a night spent lying under a tarp on a damp slab of metal. There was no question that this was better than sipping from cold cans of stewed beans and chili. Still, Thiago found the hospitality puzzling. He was not one of these people, and he sensed that they knew this as well as he. Why were they treating him as one of their own, rather than chaining him to a pipe below decks and feeding him prisoner's rations? Where was the interrogation? Though he endured countless nervous glances as he ate quietly from a plate of scrambled eggs, fried ham, and oatmeal, there'd been hardly any questions.

Maybe, he thought, it was because they had too many things on their mind at the moment to deal with him. After a brief discussion of a Bible verse and a prayer, the group began analyzing the weather.

"So, how's this storm shaping up?" asked one of the men,

slathering a slice of toast with marmalade.

A woman sitting directly opposite of Thiago answered. "Well, it's official. As of four thirty this morning, it's a category one hurricane." The group mulled over this silently as they chewed.

"How's its path looking? Any changes since yesterday?"

"I've been monitoring the reports, and it looks like it started arcing northwards early this morning. If it keeps on its current course, we should be through the worst of it soon. As it is, we're just skirting around the southern edge of the storm. It'll be close, but we should be ok."

"That's good," said a thin man with thick glasses at the other end of the table. "Last night was pretty rough. This ship wasn't meant to sustain weather like this."

"You couldn't sleep? Man, I was out cold after loading all those crates!" someone exclaimed from the end of the table, eliciting a wave of chuckles.

"You really have gotten your sea legs, then. Not bad for a city boy," said the older man with the grey hair at the head of the table, the captain. "How's everyone else holding up?"

There were nods and half smiles around the room. Everyone seemed ok, although several sets of eyes were drawn towards Thiago with curious looks. Someone finally spoke up.

"So, I'm just going to come out and ask it. Are you an angel?" asked a young woman. Several of the people around the table chuckled, but it was an uneasy sound. Thiago said nothing, struggling to gauge their feelings before forming a response.

The woman continued: "I mean, you just appear out of nowhere after the night of a bad storm. Sounds sort of angelic." Most of those around the table had stopped eating now. All eyes were on him.

Thiago shrugged with an easy smile. "My name is James. I'm from the *Valiant Alhambra.*"

"The *Alhambra*? You mean the VLCC we loaded last night that nearly sunk us?"

"Sunk?" Thiago repeated.

"Those were some of the worst seas I've ever seen. Not the

107

kind of thing you want to be facing on a boat this size, let alone loading items onto a monster vessel ten thousand times your tonnage. We could've been crushed out there. Easily."

"But we weren't," the captain followed up quickly. "You all worked hard out there last night, and everything went as smoothly as could be expected. As Susan said, that should be the worst of the weather. We actually changed course last night– we'd been waiting on a few of the last ships to join us and they arrived at around two this morning. One of them is a cruise liner. The decision's been made for her to be the main support vessel out here, so she'll be running the supply lines from here on out."

"A cruise liner?" asked the man in the glasses. "How's that going to work?"

"The brothers decided that rail cranes are a little too risky on the open seas. As you all saw last night, they can be awfully temperamental and dangerous in wind and high seas. Having a larger ship do supply runs means they can approach at a better angle, string a gangplank across, and just wheel the supplies over on hand trucks. Much easier, much safer."

"Makes sense," said Susan. "What about maneuverability, though? How's a big cruise liner going to go back and forth between the rigs and the VLCCs?"

"The brothers want the entire convoy in a line, rigs at the front, VLCCs and other storage ships at the back. So it's a straight shot for the cruise liner to go from a supply depot to any of the rigs. And to go back, it doesn't need to turn around and realign itself, it can just kill the engines and idle off to the side as the convoy catches up. Like leapfrogging on a freeway." Thiago watched as the group nodded in understanding. *Of course*, their eyes said. *Why didn't I think of that?*

"And get this: the cruise liner's had a whole section of one of the decks remodeled to serve as a kind of hospital."

"But aren't there already clinics on most of the rigs?" someone asked.

"Not a clinic, a fully-functioning hospital. They've got a full staff of brothers and sisters aboard: nurses, doctors, psychiatrists, the whole works. So if someone can't get the treatment they need in one of the clinics, they can be ferried to the liner. It also means that moving personnel around just got a whole lot easier."

"Well, we can't compete with that," said the man in the glasses.

"Yeah, so do we get a new job, then?"

The captain gave a slow, knowing nod and smiled. "Security patrol," he said.

"Security?"

"Our job will be to circle the fleet and keep an eye out for anything suspicious on the seas."

"Like what?"

"Pirates, I'd suspect. As we near the African coast, we'll be in waters frequented by pirates from Nigeria, Guinea, Ghana, Senegal… Practically every country on the West African coast has reported incidents of maritime attacks."

"And how are we supposed to stop them, if we run across them?"

"We'll be installing a series of high-powered lamps outside the compass bridge and on the transom. We'll keep them lit all night and start patrols as soon as we get to open seas. There will be more detailed instructions to come from the brothers, of course, but the main thing will be to keep an eye out and stay sharp to protect the friends."

"Sounds kind of exciting," said Susan, and the others nodded in agreement.

***

When Peter finally rolled out of bed on Tuesday morning, it was nearly eleven o'clock, and still he was exhausted. The muscles in his neck, arms, and back were torn and twisted. He'd pulled an all-nighter the night before helping the loading crews haul crates aboard their rig. Yesterday afternoon's drizzle had gradually turned to sheets of rain, and by midnight the crews were drenched. Peter's job hadn't been complicated–operating a hand-truck hauling crates from point A to point B, but the high seas and strong winds made operating the cranes and keeping the cables straight an incredibly difficult task. Once the crates had been brought indoors, they then had to be opened immediately and inspected for water damage. Fortunately, the brothers in the Supply Department had been smart: the contents had been double-wrapped in plastic sheets and sealed with packing tape. Still, Peter and the crew had been tasked with opening everything, checking the items one by one, and organizing it in the storage areas of the lower decks.

Peter found Bo Wharton just where they'd met the last time, in the corner of the cafeteria, sipping from a paper cup of what he presumed was coffee, red eyes jittery and scanning the crowd. Bo didn't notice Peter at first, and Peter took the opportunity to join the lunch line for a sandwich and a cup of strong, caffeinated joe. He took a seat across from Bo and managed a smile and a cordial greeting. Bo studied him for a long moment before nodding. His lips formed a thin smile.

"Looks like someone ran you through a rain puddle," Bo chuckled.

"Yeah, that about sums it up," Peter said.

"What you been up to, then?"

"Long night. They needed help on the loading docks. Only got about four hours of sleep."

"Out there?" Bo asked, looking back over his shoulder. He shook his head, whistling. "You all are crazier than I thought."

Peter just smiled.

"You should'a just slept in."

"We had an appointment. I wanted to honor it."

"An honorable man, is that it?"

"I try. We all do."

"Yeah. I've noticed. You're good people. Honest, clean." Peter scanned Bo's eyes for signs of sarcasm but found none.

"So you knew about the Witnesses before you joined the boarding parties in New Orleans?"

"Course, man. Who doesn't?"

"I mean personally. You have Witness family?"

Bo grimaced. "Not that I know of. Then again, we don't

really keep in touch, family and me."

"Oh? Had a falling out?" Peter surprised himself with his directness, but it seemed to come naturally, just as it had the first time he'd laid eyes on the man. There was something about him that made pleasantries seem superfluous. Or maybe he just didn't want to waste time getting to the details. Bo was, after all, a self-proclaimed drug addict sharing a confined space with the sheep under Peter's care.

"Falling out? Wouldn't say that. It implies there was a time where I was once *in*, which I don't ever recall. Nope. Family and I've been strangers long as I can remember."

"Where are you from?"

"Mississippi, originally. Not far from here, actually. Something poetic about it all, don't you think? Born in Mississippi, die in the waters off its coast."

"Oh? You think we're going to die out here?"

"I'd say it's a strong possibility. We're on a floating raft facing a hurricane head on. Like rats on driftwood, man. Those sound like good odds to you?"

"Then why join us?" Peter asked.

"Like I say, you're good people. Figured I could use the change of scenery."

"Not used to being around good people, then?"

"Drug addicts, rapists, couple'a murderers. Those are the types I spent the last ten years of my life around. So no, not exactly what you'd call the cream of society."

Peter looked down at his sandwich. It was still wrapped in plastic and he'd suddenly lost all interest in eating it. He realized how unprepared he was for this conversation. "Prison, huh?" he asked, trying to seem nonchalant. Bo lifted his eyebrows, nearly matching Peter's feigned expression, then stuck a finger in his mouth to pick at something between his teeth. Peter handed him a toothpick from a tray at the center of the table.

"Six years in a Mississippi pen before I got moved to the good ol' sunny state of California."

"Cupertino, I heard."

"That's correct. So I finished a four year stint there. I'd just

111

made it to the outside when I got one of your pamphlets. A pretty little thing showed up on the porch of my buddy's trailer and I couldn't say no." Bo laughed, but it was an ugly sound that did nothing for Peter's appetite. He struggled to smile.

"And that's how you knew about the evacuation."

"Like a message from the Lord himself," Bo said, making a praying gesture with his hands and giving the ceiling a penitent gaze. Peter found the man difficult to read and could only wonder at his intentions.

"So that was that, then? You got an invitation from one of our sisters and decided to leave it all behind to make some new friends?"

"That's more or less the gist of it, sure. There a problem? Thought your invitation said all were welcome."

"They are. *You* are. We're glad to have you. But we do have a responsibility of caring for everyone aboard these vessels, and to do that, we prefer to know everyone's background."

"You're saying you know all of these people's backgrounds?" Bo asked, dragging a dubious glance over the crowd seated in the cafeteria around them.

"Not me personally, no, but those of us serving as overseers are assigned systematically to care for everyone."

"Huh. Thought you told me the other day you weren't a security guard."

"I'm not."

Bo shot Peter a droll look.

"Look, Bo. Put yourself in my shoes for a moment. We've got thousands of people aboard this rig, and that's not to mention the thousands more on the supertankers out there. There's got to be a system in place to make sure everyone's safe and to assure that it all runs smoothly. So while it's true we're welcoming to people of all backgrounds, we require that everyone abides by the same rules. Without some kind of standard, it'd be anarchy."

"Sounds like my old warden."

"You really think this feels like a prison?"

Bo grinned and made a see-sawing motion with his hand.

"No one was forced to board. No one's being forced to

stay."

"And if I change my mind about being here? What happens then? I walk a plank and they throw me a life vest and point to the nearest shore?"

Peter stared at Bo blankly for a moment. He had no answer. Leaving his brothers and sisters, abandoning the evacuation that he'd sacrificed everything for was a scenario he'd simply given no thought to. "Well, if you change your mind, we'll both get to find out."

Bo chuckled at this, and Peter breathed a little easier. "All right. Ask your questions," said Bo.

***

John Morales scratched his chin as he stared pensively out the pilothouse windows and over the bow of his supply ship. It was a great relief to see the dark storm clouds receding to the North, but just as one problem had resolved itself, another had fallen directly into his lap. He swiveled back around in his chair to face the four souls he trusted most on this ship. That he'd known two of the other brothers–Carl and Ned–less than a month mattered not. They were experienced seamen and mature overseers and had quickly become his friends and confidants. The other two were sisters; Lisa Regan, Carl's wife and a capable sailor with an exhaustive knowledge of their supply ship, and Susan, the ship's meteorologist and navigator and the wife of the captain himself.

"All right. What's everyone think?" The captain had expected a barrage of suggestions, but the group appeared speechless. Most of the eyes were staring out at the waves or gazing blankly at the terminals.

"Someone will need to talk with him," Ned finally suggested. "You know, get the full story."

John nodded. "That's my plan, too, but I don't want to go in there blind."

"What, do you think he's dangerous?" Susan asked, looking concerned.

113

"I honestly don't know what to think, Sue," John told his wife.

"He didn't deny it this morning," Carl said.

"Deny what?" asked John.

"You know, being… an angel."

The room fell silent as eyes turned up to gaze at Carl.

"We can't rule it out. There are plenty of precedents for this kind of thing–Biblically, I mean. And even modern day stories of people seeing things, or being prevented from seeing things. We know the angels are active. Why wouldn't they be even more visible this close to the end? We're all going to see them at Armageddon, right?"

"But what's the point? Why here, aboard our little supply boat?" John asked.

"You'd have to ask him," Carl replied.

"There's something that doesn't fit with that theory, though," Lisa said. The others turned to look her way. "When I found him in the galley, he was rifling through things in the pantry, as if he was looking for something. The way he was acting… I dunno. It wasn't like someone who had a right to be here. It was like he was sneaking around. A stowaway. And you saw the items he had in his bag."

"Okay, but how? How on earth could anyone have gotten aboard this vessel? Lisa, you know this ship inside and out. Is there any way he could've managed it?"

Lisa wore a staunch look. "No way. Not in that storm. And if he'd been here for a while, he would've been detected. The cleaning crew goes through every part of the ship every couple of days, and then there's maintenance, not to mention our daily inspections. He had to have arrived recently, in the last twenty-four hours, say."

"At the peak of the storm? How?" Susan asked.

"Still, that fits his story of boarding from the *Valiant Alhambra*," John said.

"No. No way," Ned said. "You all saw those swells. We could barely keep abreast of that carrier. There's no way someone could've boarded from her. Impossible."

"Well, not for an angel," Carl said.

"But what about his sickness?" Lisa said. "He's obviously not well, he looks feverish. How does that work?"

"Maybe it's a ruse," Carl suggested. The others looked at him questioningly.

"Well there's some precedent for that too, right? The angel that wrestled with Jacob was obviously only using a fraction of its strength, right? It was a test. And maybe that's what this is. Maybe it's our response that's important."

CHAPTER 10

Peter had nearly made it back to his apartment when a hand caught him by the back of his sleeve. He turned to find Ron Feldman, his old neighbor and evacuee tagalong, standing behind him. He'd trimmed back his hair and beard, and in doing so had shed a good ten years. Peter thought he looked a lot healthier and stronger than he had in the years he'd known him, and he was slowly putting back on the weight he'd lost after his wife's death.

"Hey, Ron," Peter said, turning to face the man with an easy smile. Though the two had only been in close company for a few weeks, they'd quickly become friends. Despite working with different crews, they studied together as often as possible and Ron's progress had been remarkable. Being in close association with the brothers day in and day out hadn't hurt, of course. Ron was quickly finding his place in the organization and seemed to be thriving. Peter found it almost difficult to remember the man he'd been before.

"Hey Peter. Just wanted to make sure we're still on for later this afternoon?" Ron asked. Peter gave him a blank stare before bringing the heel of his hand to his forehead.

"Ron. I'm so sorry. It slipped my mind."

"Oh, right. No worries, Pete. You look pretty beat. Everything ok?"

"Yeah. Pulled an all-nighter."

"I heard a bunch of crews were called to the loading bay last night."

"Yep. That was us."

"I can only imagine what that was like in this weather. The work ethic here is just incredible. Never seen anybody work this hard, and with smiles on their faces the whole while."

"You've been pretty busy yourself. I keep hearing only good things from the kitchen crew."

Ron beamed with the bright eyes of a small boy. "Yeah? They're good people. Really good people."

Peter gave him a warm smile. "I've said it before, Ron, but I'm so glad you're here with us. I know it wasn't easy getting on that ferry–even Rachel and I had our concerns–but you did the right thing. And now you're part of our family."

"Yeah, well... Speaking of concerns, you think we ought to be worried about this storm? They say the winds are approaching hurricane speeds and the thing keeps changing direction."

"We'll be ok, Ron. Jehovah brought us all the way out here, he's not going to abandon us now. You check out that movie I told you about the other day?"

"The one about the Christians leaving Jerusalem before the Romans attacked?"

Ron nodded. "I did. Looked up the history on Wikipedia, too. Pretty interesting stuff."

"When the Romans destroyed Jerusalem, only the Jewish Christians who'd followed Jesus' instructions and fled were safe."

"Like us."

"We've been obedient, and the result is that we're safe in Jehovah's care. That doesn't mean it'll always *feel* safe. Those Christians fleeing in the first century probably had their fears– they might've worried about wild animals attacking at night, or falling victim to robbers, or running out of food and water. Some may have been sick, some pregnant. But regardless of how things would've looked from a human standpoint, they *were* safe."

"And you think we are, too."

"I do. It simply wouldn't fit Jehovah's personality to bring us out here and then let us die in a hurricane. Think of the reproach that would be brought upon his name. The world is watching us, you know."

"Ok. I've got another question for you," Ron said finally.

"I'm all ears."

"This evacuation was open to the public, right?"

117

"That's right. You saw the invitation."

"So just anyone could show up?"

"Just about."

"Well, then what prevents someone boarding who has ill intentions? How do they get weeded out?"

Peter mulled over this for a moment before explaining. "Again, that's where our trust in Jehovah comes into play. But really, it was the same back when we met in Kingdom Halls for meetings. Those were public events; anyone could attend. We didn't do background checks on people before they walked through the front doors. We had to trust that they were coming with pure motives. The Bible tells us that love 'believes all things', so we try to assume the best."

"But there had to have been instances where people slipped through the cracks, right?"

"Well sure, not everyone has pure motives. I remember a few years ago, a brother in our hall started studying with a homeless man. He came to meetings, started reading the Bible, had his hand up all the time for comments. Really seemed to be progressing. Later, though, we found out that the brother and his wife were giving the man money out of their own pockets each week. So the elders sat down with the brother and recommended that instead of giving his student money, he try to help him find a job to care for himself."

"What happened?"

"Wasn't long before he stopped studying. He wasn't ready to give up his life on the streets and apparently he wasn't really interested in spiritual things. He just wanted handouts."

"So you're saying that over time, motives become clear."

"Usually they do. But even if the real motive of a person never comes to light, Jehovah sees the heart and that's all that matters. He does the judging. So even if someone's been around the truth for years just to take advantage of the brothers and sisters in a congregation, in the end they'll be judged for it, and we can be assured that Jehovah will recoup any of the losses the congregation incurred in the meantime. So really, it's nothing to worry about. Besides, I tend to think that in the case of these evacuations, few people would consider entirely abandoning their lives just to join us on some oil rigs in the middle of the sea on the off chance that they might gain something from our hospitality. The cost would far outweigh the potential gain."

"Yeah, I suppose. But then what about that guy you were talking to at lunch today?"

"Bo?" Peter asked, surprised at Ron's question.

"I don't know his name. But I recognized those tattoos."

"Tattoos? What about them?"

"That stylized cross on his neck with the two skulls. It's a gang tattoo."

"Really?"

"Back when I worked construction, I'd see those guys around from time to time. One of my coworkers knew some things about them, told me one day. He said a lot of them get recruited while in prison, where they learn how to work the system when they get out. Very violent, very dangerous."

"We'll keep an eye on him. Thanks for mentioning it, Ron."

"Yeah, no worries. Just doing my part, you know?" A smile worked its way onto Ron's face and lingered there as his eyes dropped to the floor thoughtfully. Peter reached across the table and gripped Ron's arm. His presence in their evacuation party had been a powerful encouragement to him and Rachel. Being able to assist him kept them focused when so many distractions had been vying for their attention. He wondered if Ron even knew how important he'd been to them. He'd tell him, one day, when the time was right.

"You know what I keep thinking?" Ron suddenly asked.

"What's that?"

"I keep thinking how Doreen would've gotten such a kick outta all this," Ron said softly. His eyes glistened with her memory. Peter said nothing, only nodding his head gently. "She always liked you two, you know. I remember once when we were driving past the Kingdom Hall, she said we ought to stop in sometime, see what you two were up to in there. I refused, made up some excuse. I keep thinking about that day, you know? Keep wondering how things might've been different had I not been such an old fart."

Peter chuckled lightly with a shake of his head. "You're here now, Ronnie. That's what counts."

"Yeah, but… she's not. Maybe, just maybe, if I'd had an open mind, more like her…"

"It was the cancer that took her life, Ron. You had nothing to do with that. You couldn't have known. And even if you'd known, there's nothing you could've done."

"Yeah, my brain knows all that, Pete, but still."

"Well, just think of all the stories you'll get to tell her the next time you see her. I hope you're taking good notes."

**

After breakfast that morning Thiago was offered a small bed in a vacant cabin on the lower deck not far from where he'd spent the previous night. The space was a little cramped, but he didn't mind. His head was still throbbing and his body ached, and he wanted nothing more than to be off of this ship, off of these awful waters and back home. It was a lot of money to walk away from–three hundred grand for this job–but he was willing… *Almost.*

The fact was, it wasn't just about the money–his reputation was on the line. And frankly, he wasn't sure what his client might do if he failed at his task. Chad was smart and conniving, with seemingly bottomless pockets. Thiago's experience told him just how dangerous of a combination this could be. Chad was not a man to be trifled with.

On the other hand, his misgivings about this mission were only increasing with each passing day. Chad had painted a dark picture of these people–a dangerous, brainwashed cult who'd kidnapped his wife and son. But none of this was matching with what Thiago had witnessed aboard the docks, the ferry, the VLCC, and now here, aboard the small supply ship. While he found it impossible to subscribe to their beliefs about an impending doomsday, they clearly cared for one another like family and were neither violent nor dangerous. If anything, they were far too trusting. The fact that he'd been able to get this far with so few questions asked of him was a testament to their naiveté.

Still, a job was a job, and letting morality play into the equation was a sure way to sabotage things. *No one is really innocent*, he reminded himself. *There are only varying shades of guilt.* Thiago needed a clear head to focus and complete his task. He pressed his eyes together and tried to will away the pounding between his temples and the ache in his bones. A soft rapping on his door echoed through the cabin, followed by a gruff voice:

"You in there, James?"

"It's unlocked," Thiago responded, summoning what felt like the last of his strength. He sat up as the door creaked open. The captain entered with a steaming thermos.

"Here. It's one of those Theraflu nighttime teas. Honey lemon, I think," he said. Thiago accepted it gratefully and took a sip. The captain sat and gazed out the cabin window as Thiago waited for the scalding tea to cool. For a few minutes, the creaks and groans of the ship and the din of engines churning at the cold salt water beyond the hull were the only sounds.

"The name's John Morales," the man finally said with a polite nod in Thiago's direction.

"James."

"Right. James. You've got the whole crew pretty curious."

"Curious?"

"Sure. It's like you fell out of the sky."

"In a manner of speaking, I did," Thiago said, smiling. This was the truth. In the time he'd spent laid out in the cabin waiting to be questioned, he'd formed in his head what he thought would be the most convincing explanation possible. He was a stowaway, yes, but only trying to make his way to one of the rigs to reunite with his estranged daughter. In spite of some of the fuzzier details, it was not a difficult story to believe, and Thiago expected that his hosts would give him the benefit of the doubt. Who knew, they might even take him straight to his mark? It was his best chance.

But the look Thiago's comment triggered on the face of the

121

captain told him that perhaps things would not be so easy. The man turned to peer at him carefully, his body going rigid.

"So," John said, his voice catching. "You're saying it's true, then?"

Thiago bit his tongue as his mind raced. He wanted to ask for clarification, but his gut told him otherwise. There was something here he could use; he could sense it, if only it manifested itself. He relaxed, letting his expression soften. The captain would reveal more if he only let him.

"May I ask why? Why here? Why us? This little ship seems so insignificant when compared to the rest of the fleet."

Thiago kept quiet, his mind sifting through each of the captain's words, desperately searching for clues. He stalled the conversation with a long sip of tea. Most significantly, he thought, the captain's demeanor had shifted. He was no longer keeping his distance. Whatever suspicion he'd been holding had seemed to vanish. And then it struck him–a snippet from the morning's conversation around the breakfast table.

"You are *not* insignificant," Thiago said, his voice calm, reassuring. The words had an instant effect on the captain, whose eyes suddenly brightened. Thiago nodded with a warm look, playing the part as best he could, all the while wondering just how long the ruse could possibly last. He knew nothing of the Witnesses' religious beliefs and thus nothing of their concept of angels. He would need to say as little as possible.

But now he had the upper hand.

***

The tension between Joyce and Stacy grew with each passing day. For Joyce, being around Stacy was like traversing a minefield; she never knew what topics would turn into an argument, but they seemed unavoidable. Almost every discussion carried the potential to devolve into a fight. Perhaps it was better to just keep quiet altogether.

They'd spent the previous day sitting around the living room watching the news on Stacy's phone. There'd been no updates on the Canadian border situation, but there was no shortage of news on hospital conditions where the infected from the blast attacks were being treated. Private investigative reports were revealing more and more about what was happening behind closed doors, and the picture being painted grew uglier by the day. In Atlanta, the CDC was being hounded by protestors demanding answers, many carrying blown-up photos of their dead and missing on placards and poster boards high above their heads. Things were no better in Seattle and New York.

Late that afternoon, the two piled into Stacy's pickup for a grocery run. They had no idea how long they'd be stranded in Seattle and had decided to stock up on supplies. After nearly a week outside the camp, Stacy's provisions were beginning to dwindle.

"I'm sorry about last night," Joyce said, finally mustering the courage to speak again after nearly a day of silence.

"What for?" Stacy asked.

"It was wrong of me to judge you."

"It's fine."

"No, it's not."

"Joyce, stop it. Look, we judge each other every day of our lives. We judge people as soon as we see them. We make a choice in our head and that's that. First impressions last forever. That's people."

"But we're supposed to be better than that."

"*Supposed* to, sure. But are we? Really?"

Joyce bit her lip. There it was again–that maddening, dogged negativity that stained Stacy's entire worldview. Why couldn't she just try to see things in a different light? Why did everything have to be tainted by her pessimism? Why could the glass never be half full?

"Do we have a grocery list?" Joyce asked, deciding it was best to just change the subject altogether.

"We're running low on everything. Might as well get regular groceries as well. Maybe we can, like, eat a real meal tonight."

Joyce grunted an acknowledgement but didn't like the

feeling that was creeping up from her gut. She didn't want to get comfortable here; she never intended to stay this long.

They found a spot at the edge of the Wal-Mart parking lot and approached the building as a sharp, chilled wind blew dust and leaves across the pavement. Shoppers emerged hauling cases of items similar to the ones Stacy and Joyce would be looking for. They exchanged uneasy looks and quickened their pace.

The super center was a madhouse. Long lines had formed at the cash registers, where the din of shoppers arguing amongst themselves and with cashiers filled the air. Many of the shelves were sparsely stocked; items were strewn haphazardly on the floor of the aisles. Joyce stepped carefully around an open bag of sliced bread, its contents smeared on the Linoleum.

"Did we miss something?" Joyce asked Stacy without turning to look at her.

"People panic. That's what happens whenever there's a crisis," Stacy said, trying to sound nonchalant. The women stepped aside as a couple dressed in army surplus camouflage rushed past them to the exit, newly purchased gun cases cradled in their arms like children.

"Probably has something to do with the borders, too," Stacy continued under her breath. "Highways are all blocked up, maybe the trucks can't drop off their shipments, so people are stocking up while they can."

"On guns and ammunition?"

"Good ol' 'merica," Stacy said with a feigned twang and a shake of her head.

"We should stick together. It'll be safer that way. This place is a zoo," Joyce remarked. A woman ran past with a screaming child in her arms. The child's face was covered in red splotches.

They navigated the chaotic aisles carefully, scavenging what they could of canned items and bottled drinks. They placed their items hurriedly into plastic shopping baskets slung over their elbows. Dozens of shopping carts sat abandoned in the aisles–much of the supermarket's floors were covered in fragments of scattered goods, making the wheeled carts useless.

It appeared that the employees had given up on the task of cleaning and were instead doing their best just keeping order at the registers. As it was, customers were pushing through the lines, trying to sneak out the doors with lifted goods under their coats, or else hurling threats and insults at the staff.

"I have a real bad feeling about this place," Joyce said anxiously, tugging at Stacy's sleeve as she began to head towards the frozen food aisles.

"Me too, but we're out of options. This is the biggest supermarket in the area; if Wal-Mart is like this, I can only imagine what the other places will look like."

"Let's forget cooking tonight, Stacy. I mean, just look at this," Joyce said, gesturing towards the register, where a knot of women were working themselves into a screaming match over a box of diapers. Stacy watched them for a few moments as the voices climbed. A man in a blue employee vest approached the women to try to calm them and was nearly clobbered by a swinging purse. He dodged the attack but lost his balance and toppled into a rack of magazines and scampered out from view.

"Ok, fine. Let's just check the meat section and–"

"No, Stacy. We have to go *now*," Joyce said, planting her feet firmly and giving the woman an adamant look.

"Joyce, we barely have enough between us for another three days *at most*. And then what? If this place looks like this now, there's no telling what'll be left in another few days."

"We'll figure it out. We need to get out of here. It isn't safe, Stacy!"

Stacy gave her a long look before finally complying with a shrug. "Fine. But I'd better not hear you complain about not having salami with your crackers."

Joyce said nothing as she turned abruptly and headed for the nearest checkout counter. But as she did, the store erupted in a wave of panicked gasps and screams.

The power had gone out.

***

Chad Harkett emerged from his office and glared silently at the dead rows of overhead bulbs hanging from the ceiling.

"What is this?!" he shrieked at someone sitting at a nearby desk. They ripped the earplugs out of their head and followed Chad's finger stabbing up at the lights.

"Power outage?"

"You think?"

The young tech shrugged sheepishly and broke away from Chad's stare.

"How about going and figuring out why our backup generators aren't kicking in?" Chad said, scowling at the young man, who darted from his desk and out an exit at the back of the room. Martin emerged from his office moments later from behind Chad's shoulder.

"What's going on?" he asked.

"Power," Chad said without turning to look at him. "Right when I was in the middle of writing a long email, of course."

"Backup generators?" Martin asked, already making his way towards the back of the room where a stairwell led to the utilities room.

"Sent someone to check it out. If those generators are faulty, I swear I'll file a lawsuit against that company for lost wages."

"I'm sure the generators are fine. We paid top dollar for those. They're supposed to be failsafe."

"Hence the lawsuit."

Martin ignored Chad's comments and gazed out the windows of their complex. Employees from companies in other buildings were gradually gathering on the sidewalks and in the outdoor courtyards, clearly enjoying their unscheduled break. These were tech companies; without power, there was nothing to do. Martin frowned. He dug a hand into his pocket and retrieved his cellphone, glanced at the screen, and felt his pulse quicken.

"Chad, you got a sec?" Martin asked, his voice low. Chad turned to look at him, still sneering.

"What now?"

"In my office. We need to talk."

Chad followed Martin in, closed the door behind him, and watched as Martin began pacing wildly.

"What's your problem?" Chad asked.

"Check your phone," Martin said. Chad did, shrugged.

"You getting a signal?"

"No."

"Me either."

"So what? It's a power outage. The cell towers must be down, too."

Martin shook his head. "No, man. Not out here. The cell signal for our campus comes from a direct satellite feed. Totally unconnected to the land power grid."

"And? What are you implying?"

Martin said nothing, letting his expression express his anxiety.

"What? You think this is some kind of... attack?" Chad asked derisively. He walked over to a small fridge unit beside Martin's desk and removed a bottle of water. It was still icy cold. Chad wagged his head as he wrung off the cap and began drinking.

"It's a possibility. They've been talking about it for a while. "

"Who's been talking about it?"

"People. The ones who prepare for this kind of thing."

"What, survivalists? Those nuts who build bunkers to stash Geiger counters and non-perishables?"

"I'm just saying it's a possibility."

"More like a fantasy."

"What's that supposed to mean?"

"Martin, the people out there predicting this stuff have nothing else to live for. They're psychotic ex-military fanatics with cash to blow and too much time on their hands, so they start burrowing. How do you not see that?"

Something like the spark of rage flickered in Martin's eyes, but he smothered it quickly and smiled with a shake of his head. "Not all of them, Chad."

"How do you know? Have you actually spent any time

with these people outside of some internet forums and the YouTube comment section?"

"Look, Chad, I'm not asking for your permission. I don't need it. I just wanted to, I dunno, give you a heads up. This world is a ticking time bomb, man. But there are always signs, signs before it really hits the fan, you know? And this–" Martin paused to hold up his phone, "–a dropped satellite signal at the same time as a blackout? This is *huge*. You might have your doubts, but this is what a cyber attack looks like."

"You're paranoid."

"Yeah, maybe. Doesn't mean I'm wrong, though," Martin turned briskly away from his friend and business partner to scoop his laptop and a few miscellaneous items from his desk and throw them into a messenger bag.

"So what, that's it? You're just leaving?"

"I can catch up on the rest of work at home. You need me, you know where to reach me. Anyway, I want to make a few stops before traffic starts piling up out there."

"Seriously, Martin? This is Silicon Valley. The companies sitting on these couple of acres alone will lose millions if that power stays off for even a couple of hours. I'd be surprised if the lights aren't back on by the time you reach the parking lot."

Martin glanced down at his phone again and frowned. "Yeah, well, I didn't set up a shelter just to be far from it if something bad happened. If nothing else, call this a dry run." Martin slung his bag over his shoulder and pulled as many bottled waters from his fridge as his arms could hold. "Like I said, you know where to find me."

Chad shook his head in disbelief as Martin walked briskly through the darkened office and out of sight.

***

Stacy cautiously threaded her pickup over the roads as she and Joyce made their way back home. The panicked scene at the grocery store had dissolved instantly into chaos after the blackout. In the end, Stacy had thrown the last of her cash at one of the employees as she and Joyce bolted from the store and back to the safety of their vehicle. Most of the other shoppers had seized the opportunity to leave without paying, and some of the more opportunistic ones had even restored to looting. The wheels of Stacy's pickup had screeched against the parking lot macadam as they fled the scene, a cacophony of panicked screams and animalistic screeches of joy close on their heels.

The scene beyond the shopping center was slightly more subdued, but no less disorderly. The power outage had effectively disabled all traffic lights, turning the roads and intersections into a series of knotted vehicles, horns blaring, their drivers cursing and threatening one another in frustration.

"I wonder where all the police are," Joyce said softly, unable to keep the fear out of her quivering voice.

"They're probably at the main intersections. Traffic will be a lot worse there," Stacy said distractedly, motioning to the digital clock in the dashboard. It was just before six o'clock.

"Rush hour," Joyce said, bringing the back of a hand to her forehead. "It'll be a nightmare."

Stacy was quiet as she eyed her mirrors.

"Can I borrow your phone?" Joyce asked. "I forgot to call Alvin this afternoon. I'm sure he'll be worried. I wonder if they've lost power as well?"

Stacy said nothing, fishing her phone from her back pocket and handing it over.

"That's strange," Joyce said a moment later.

"What?"

"No signal. Is the reception usually bad on this road?"

"Not that I recall," Stacy said, shrugging.

"Guess I'll have to wait till we get home. I can't forget to call Alvin. Not looking forward to that conversation, though," Joyce said, forcing a chuckle to lighten the mood, but Stacy was silent. Joyce glanced at her and found her squinting at the rearview mirror.

"What is that?" Stacy said, turning to look through the glass window behind the cab. Joyce turned. Several miles behind them, a dark cloud was forming, sealing out the light of the setting sun.

"A storm front?" Joyce suggested, her voice barely a whisper.

"Not like any storm I've seen. There's no… *features*. It's just black. Like a wall of ink."

"Well, we have been having some pretty freakish weather lately, and–" Joyce paused as the ground trembled slightly beneath them, rocking the pickup from side to side like a small boat upset by the ripples of a passing ship. A low reverberation followed, stirring the loose change on the dash. Joyce held her fingertips to the surface of the glass window, feeling it buzz as if a low voltage current was passing through it. The two women felt the hair on their arms and the backs of their necks stand on end for a moment. Stacy slowly raised her fingers to her jaw as a pair of metal fillings tingled against the nerves of her teeth.

And then the lightning struck.

In the instant it blazed from the sky, it bathed its surroundings in a dazzling purple light. It was crisp and perfectly defined, as if drawn in the sky by a painter's brush. Another bolt exploded several hundred yards in the distance, narrowly missing a tree and leaving a smoldering spot in the blackened grass.

The honking stopped, along with the bickering of passengers. Everyone, it seemed, was entranced by the sudden freakish storm.

"You ever seen weather like this?" Stacy asked. But her voice barely registered in Joyce's ears. The women watched as purple flashes of light illuminated the undersides of low lying clouds off in the distance. They felt the rumble of thunder gently rock the pickup truck as the sky continued to blacken.

"We need to get back to that camp," Joyce finally said.

Stacy gave her a look before nodding slowly. "But how?"

"We won't be able to cross the border normally. And if the power stays out, these roads will only get worse. We need to think of another way."

Stacy bit her lip. Black clouds were quickly thickening and spreading above them, forcing many of the drivers to turn on their headlights. "I might have a way," Stacy finally said. "But you're not going to like it."

CHAPTER 11

Darren Hughes stood transfixed behind the picture glass window of his living room as lightning streaked through the skies. The warbling sirens of fire engines and police cars wailed in the distance. He fumbled his way to the kitchen, where he opened a drawer and removed a shrink-wrapped set of dinner candles. He lit a handful of them, but the light did nothing to calm his buzzing nerves, did nothing to stave off the dread in his stomach.

Darren nearly jumped from his skin as another bolt of lightning stuck. Thunder shook the walls of the house, jiggling the glass windows. *That one was much closer*, he thought uneasily as he carried the final candle to his wife's bed.

Rita was just as he'd left her hours ago when he'd delivered her lunch: bundled in a knot of blankets and pillows and watching some sitcom on her tablet. With the shades drawn and her earphones in, Darren doubted she even knew about the storm beyond the walls of her room. He set down a candle beside his wife and sat on the corner of her bed waiting to be acknowledged.

Rita finally shut down her device, rubbed her eyes, and glanced at the candle. "What's that for?" she asked.

"Power's out," Darren said.

"Oh. No wonder my device isn't charging. Thought it was another bad cable," Rita said. She worked a hand beneath the neck of her shirt and scratched her back. "What time is it? I'm getting hungry."

"Almost seven. I'd suggest ordering something out, but I don't think many places will be open."

"Because of the power?"

"Among other things," Darren said, walking to the side of the room where he drew back the curtains. He watched his wife's expression twist as her mouth fell slightly ajar. "You really didn't notice anything?" Darren asked.

"Not really."

Another purple flash of lightning blazed through the premature night, casting its otherworldly glow against the dead trees in the Hughes' backyard.

"Freaky," Rita said.

"Never seen a storm like this before. Especially not during the Winter. Something about those clouds, too. Just doesn't seem right."

"Probably just more climate change stuff. Did you try the pizza places?" Rita asked. Darren stared blankly at his wife before shaking his head. "It's worth a shot. Maybe they have generators or something."

"Yeah, maybe," Darren said, gazing back out at the sky. "This storm, though. It's kind of got me thinking." Rita lifted an eyebrow at her husband but said nothing. "You remember the last time Pete called?"

Rita shrugged. "Sure."

"And he mentioned that they were all aboard the rigs, and that they'd watched a special announcement."

Another shrug.

"I saw part of it this morning. It was on the website."

"And?"

"Well, it mentioned stuff. You know, all that great tribulation stuff."

"Ok…"

"One of the things they mentioned were signs in heaven. They said it could be, you know… literal. Like, stuff people could actually see in the sky."

Rita smirked with the slightest shake of her head. "You think this is part of that?"

"Jesus did say that the sky would be darkened."

"Darren, it's nighttime. The sky tends to do that at night."

"No, this is different. I saw the clouds coming in with my own

133

eyes, Rita. They weren't like regular storm clouds. They were solid black, completely blocked out the sun. I've never seen anything like it."

"So, what are you saying?"

"I'm saying that… I mean, just hear me out, but… I'm saying that maybe we should think about joining Pete and the others."

"In New Orleans? On some oil rigs? Are you serious?"

"What if they were right about all this, babe? What if this is it?"

"If this is it, then we'll be fine, Darren. It's not like we aren't Witnesses just because we didn't join a bunch of people on some evacuation. If this really is the end, I'm sure we'll be protected."

"But what if that's just it, Rita? What if that *is* the protection—being out at sea while everything goes crazy here?"

"Darren. It's a *power outage* and some *lightning*. This isn't the end of the world. Relax."

"I'm not sure. I'm just not. I mean, have you been watching the news lately? Chemical warfare right here in America? Nuclear weapons pointed straight at us? What if that's how it all ends? What if Jehovah just lets all these people wipe each other out and then he steps in and finishes off the last of them?"

"Stop it Darren, you're scaring me."

"Maybe you should be scared."

"Don't, Darren. Don't you dare put this on *me*. We *both* agreed that joining that evacuation was out of the question."

"I'm not blaming you, Rita. I'm just saying that maybe we need to reconsider."

"And what, abandon the lawsuit? After everything that company did to us?"

"You really think our attorneys are any better?"

"At least they're fighting for us."

Bitter laughter erupted from Darren's mouth. "Are they? Or are they just trying to squeeze a bigger settlement from the company to make more of a profit? So they can buy whatever Rolls Royce or luxury yacht they've got their eyes on while we get buried in medical bills. I mean come on, it's obvious they're in it for themselves. I hate to say it, but I'm beginning to regret ever signing that contract with Schucker and Dial."

"You won't say that when the settlement check is signed."

Another crash of thunder shook the Hughes' home as the sky lit with pale, ghostly light. The couple gasped as the large tree in their neighbor's yard was shorn apart by a blade of lightning. Bright yellow embers burst from the destruction and sprayed into the air, scattering along rooftops, catching in gutters filled with dead leaves and burrowing into the dried grass on the ground. Small flames began to spread as Darren leapt into action.

He dashed into their garage to collect a bucket and then sprinted to their backyard, screaming over the fence at the top of his lungs to get his neighbors' attention. He yanked furiously at the garden hose and unwound several coils before turning on the faucet. But nothing happened. Only a few stray droplets of water leaked from the end of the hose.

"WHAT ARE YOU DOING?! PUT OUT THE FIRE!!" Rita screamed from behind the window of the bedroom, slapping her palms against the glass.

"Water's off!" Darren said, heart racing. He looked back over his shoulder, where the flames fed quickly on the dry grass. More flames were trickling out of his neighbor's rooftop gutter. He ran over to the grass and attempted to stamp the flames out with the sole of his shoe, but this only seemed to worsen their spread.

Darren charged back into the house to check the indoor faucets, but they were all the same. An idea struck him; he ran into the bedroom where his wife still stood at the window, watching as the fire crept across her lawn. She clutched her phone in one hand with a puzzled look.

"I tried calling the fire department, but there's no—"

Darren ignored her as he ripped the sheets off of the bed.

"What are you doing?" Rita demanded.

"Putting the fire out!"

"Not with my brand new sheets you aren't!"

Darren said nothing as he charged out of the room, white sheets trailing behind him. Rita screamed after him.

In the bathroom, Darren removed the lid of their toilet tank and soaked as much water as possible into the sheets before dashing back outside to battle the flames. Nearly half of the yard was blackened by flames. Though the fire flickered only a few inches tall, Darren could feel its heat through his sweater. His lungs stung with the acrid scent of burnt grass.

Darren did his best to contain the fire, to keep it from crawling its way to the house, but the wet sheet was quickly dried out. Darren abandoned the sheet as it began to singe and burn, opting to kick dirt onto the fire. When that didn't work, he tried to extinguish the flames with a case of bottled water from their garage, and then soda, and then beer, and then an expensive case of wine they'd purchased the year before in Napa.
But by now the wooden fence had begun to burn. His neighbor was still nowhere in sight, the flames engulfing his rooftop gutters and slowly feeding on the shingles. It was only a matter of time, Darren knew.

"We need to leave," he said as he returned to their bedroom and gave his wife a defeated look. Her face was contorted with anguish and disbelief as she stared at their backyard and fence slowly being consumed by fire, her eyes glossy with tears. For a long moment, the two said nothing, struggling to hold on to the last few moments with their home.

And then they began to pack.

***

For Alvin Tucker, the last few days had been a maelstrom of activity. Shortly after the special broadcast from the branch, the overseers of Burrard Harbor ordered that everything in the camp—from the suspension cranes and electric trams to the residence pods, every pot and pan and grain of rice—was to be immediately disassembled and transported onto an incoming fleet of supertankers, trawlers, and cruise ships. Many of the ships, it turned out, were purchased overseas at just a fraction of their value during the South Korean and Chinese economic crises, and had been moved from port to port ferrying tens of thousands of Witnesses from islands in Southeast Asia and the Pacific Ocean westwards to Japan and Korea, where several branches in

Asian territories would be responsible for caring for the brothers until further directions were received.

The first vessels of the fleet emerged from the thick Vancouver fog just as the camp's docks were reaching full capacity. Specially built bridges and gangplanks were fitted into place by cranes and tugboats, greatly expediting the process of evacuation. In just a couple of days, two whole supertankers were loaded to capacity with thousands of passengers, dozens of vehicles, and over thirty-thousand tons of construction equipment, supplies, and food.

It was an almost unbelievable feat, even to Alvin, who had been closely involved with many of the logistical details. Still, time was of the essence. There were dozens more vessels lined up just outside the harbor, and everyone and everything was to be loaded within a one week window. Alvin could hardly imagine how it would be accomplished, but he knew it would. It was good, of course, to be busy. Anything less than the breakneck speed of his life these last few days would've just led to more distressing days spent staring out the window at a bleak sky, wondering what would become of Joyce. The anger had faded somewhat, but it had left a lonely, painful void in its place. In spite of it all, Joyce was his wife, his flesh, the love of his life. Losing her was an unbearable thought.

Alvin stood on the raised platform suspended over one of the gangplanks, surveying the moving crews as they hauled the last items by forklift into the belly of a cruise ship. They would hit their target of another three ships loaded by the end of the day, but the end wasn't yet in sight. Alvin pressed his eyes shut and slowly sucked in the clammy, frostbitten air of the harbor. It wasn't a pleasant smell, but he'd grown accustomed to it over the weeks since his arrival. Sometimes he tasted the sea in his dreams.

"Heard the news?" came a familiar voice over Alvin's shoulder.

"Tell me they extended the evacuation deadline, Paul."

His friend chuckled. "Not so, I'm afraid. There's been a blackout."

"A blackout?"

"Not here. Our generators are still going, and most everything else runs on diesel. But the city grids are down."

Alvin turned and lifted an eyebrow. "In Vancouver?"

Paul shook his head. "Whole West Coast."

"What?" Alvin said.

"See for yourself," Paul said, raising his chin towards the opposite side of the bay, where the entire landscape lay submerged in blackness.

"How do you know it's the whole West Coast?"

"A couple of brothers just arrived with news from the branch. They told us to be extra cautious, that these are the kinds of conditions that could lead to outsiders raiding our camps, looting food and gas. We're putting extra brothers on night patrols. Cell towers are down, too."

Immediately, Alvin pulled his phone from his jacket pocket and stared at the screen. A spinning wheel confirmed that the network was down.

"Do they know what caused it? Or how long it'll last?"

"No official word on that yet."

"No official word from the organization or from the government?"

"Neither. We're in the dark. From what little we've heard, the government just keeps telling people to stay calm. You know it's bad when that's all they'll say. Pretty amazing timing if you ask me. Just as we're about to head out of here."

"Yeah. Amazing."

***

The two women sat on the harbor as a salty, icy wind washed over the pickup truck. It had taken them nearly two hours to come to the decision to be here, and hours more to navigate the congested roads. It was now well past midnight. The harbor around them lay plunged in darkness, though generators aboard a handful of yachts moored nearby kept their lights on.

"Have you ever known a blackout to last this long?" Joyce

138

asked, glancing at her watch. "It's been over fourteen hours now."

Stacy ignored her. She was too preoccupied steeling herself for the task at hand as she nibbled nervously on a sleeve of crackers.

"So, which of these boats belonged to your grandfather?" Joyce asked, glancing up at the row of yachts. Stacy frowned.

"It's a little ways from here. We can go over and check it out in the morning, when it's light."

"And you're sure you can operate it?"

"I'll do my best. I was out here a few months ago. It's in good shape, so that shouldn't be a problem. I'll need your help, though. Tomorrow we'll go aboard and I'll show you the ropes." Stacy leaned forward in her seat to gaze up at the dark night clouds. The moon and stars were nowhere to be seen; the sky was pitch black.

"What is it?"

"Just hoping for clear weather tomorrow. I can't sail in a storm." Stacy lifted her cellphone from the dashboard. The battery was nearly dead, and still there were no reception bars onscreen. No way to check the weather forecast.

"So, if the weather's clear, we sail tomorrow?"

"That's the idea," Stacy said.

"And how long will it take us to get from here to Burrard Harbor?"

"It all depends on the wind conditions. Best case scenario, we'll get there by late tomorrow night."

"A whole day of sailing out there," Joyce said, looking out at the black sea.

"I don't like it either, especially in Winter, but we're running out of options. And if they're packing up camp in Vancouver and heading somewhere else, we need to act quick. It's now or never."

"So we just sail right into the harbor? There won't be any sort of border guards or anything?"

Stacy shrugged. "Might be Canadian coast guard patrols, but my guess is that with everything else going on, they'll have their hands full and we'll be able to slip right in, undetected."

"Is that even legal?"

Stacy turned to give Joyce a scornful look. "Seriously?"

"Well, yes. I don't want to be caught doing something illegal and then have the two of us hauled away to a cell someplace. That would only make things worse."

"Look around you, Joyce! This entire area has no power, and for whatever reason, cell towers aren't working. It's going to be absolute chaos here in another day or two. You were there at the grocery store today, you saw how that went down–and that was before the storm! No one is going to be paying attention to two women on a little old sailboat cruising into some shipping port."

"I just don't want to do anything *illegal*," Joyce said. "It's the principle."

"Well, you're welcome to stay here. Or maybe you can hitchhike back up the interstate on foot and see if the border police will let you through. Of course, without any kind of identification, you won't be able to prove who you are, or even what country you're from, but hey, be my guest."

"My goodness, Stacy, you don't need to chew me out for raising a simple concern! All I was saying was–"

"I know *exactly* what you're saying, Joyce. I know you're trying to play this all according to the old rules. But those rules are already crumbling all around us. There will be nothing left of any of this. I can see that clearly now. I made the wrong decision when I left the camp, but *you* made that same decision. So don't preach to *me* about right and wrong. We both made mistakes, and now we're facing the consequences. You are no better than me here."

"I didn't mean to make it seem like I was better than anyone, I just–" "Please, Joyce, please! *Enough*. We're here. That's *that*. We need to just get through this. I don't want to fight. We both need clear heads. We've got a long day ahead of us and we're going to need our strength, so let's let this drop. Please."

"I... Ok... Fine," Joyce relented, turning away from the other woman and discreetly brushing a tear from her face.

Thiago smiled smugly to himself as he leafed through the small booklet. There was little in these pages pertaining to angels, but it hardly seemed to matter now. The captain and the others had taken his claim at face value–had practically assumed it from the beginning, in fact. It had been almost too easy.

And to top it all off, they'd expected him to deliver a message, one that hadn't taken him long at all to think up–he needed to be safely delivered to Rig 7. Why an all-powerful angel wouldn't just be able to fly over on his own power, Thiago didn't know, and the staff of this ship didn't ask. They merely nodded with solemn, awestruck faces and vanished from his quarters. They were not fearful, and not particularly reverent, but certainly respectful and obedient, which was all Thiago required to keep the wheels of his plan in motion.

He couldn't help feeling as if he'd taken a big step in the right direction. What had seemed like an impossible task only days before was now a feasible reality. Thiago did not believe in fate; he was a man perpetually in control of his own destiny. Still, he wasn't about to refuse a serving of serendipity.

Thiago slipped the booklet below the covers of his bed as footsteps approached outside his cabin.

"James? You in there?" asked a woman's voice.

"Yes. Just resting," he replied. *Did angels need to rest?*

"We're approaching Rig 7 now. We called ahead; they're all ready for you. Be there in about ten minutes."

"Right. Thank you, Susan."

There was nothing to pack. The few items Thiago had brought with him aboard the supply ship had either been lost or damaged at sea. He would leave with no more than the clothes on his back.

Thiago rose and tidied up the room and emerged into an empty hallway. He ascended the stairwell to the main deck, eliciting respectful nods from crew members as he passed. He spoke as little as possible. The image in these people's minds was powerful enough to convince them of his identity.

Superfluous words would only risk destroying that image.

Thiago found himself a few minutes later on the aft deck, looking up at a grey sky as the brooding silhouette of a massive offshore oil rig loomed overhead. It appeared unmoving, as if the half dozen pillars supporting it were anchored to the sea bed far below.

"Lowering passenger cage," crackled a voice over a walkie-talkie strapped to someone's side. Thiago turned to see the captain pull the radio to his lips and confirm. He stretched out his hand and smiled warmly.

"James. On behalf of my entire crew, it was a pleasure having you with us," the man said, shaking Thiago's hand.

"Thank you. You are all doing a fine job," he said. A woman approached from his side, a brightly colored life jacket and hardhat in her arms.

"You, um, probably don't need this, but... Well, rules are rules," she said.

Thiago smiled and slipped into the jacket. The group was pushed back by several pairs of arms as the cage approached from above. A dozen hands steadied it as it came to rest safely on the deck. A lever was pulled and the metal cage door whined open. Thiago ducked his head and stepped in. The metal door clicked shut as the captain gave him some final instructions.

"The brothers aboard the rig will take care of opening the cage door for you. Try to keep yourself centered while inside; it'll keep it balanced, prevent it from rocking around too much. Just sit tight and enjoy the ride. I'm assuming you're not afraid of heights, right?" the man said with a wink.

"I'll be fine. Thank you, Captain," Thiago said, returning the wink.

"Door shut. Cage ready for extraction," said the captain into his radio. A moment later, the floor lurched from beneath Thiago's feet. The transom of the small supply ship, the surface of the sea, and the handful of faces that had come to see him off slowly dropped away.

The rocking and rollicking of the sea vanished, replaced by a new sensation, one of drifting weightlessly in the air. Thiago closed his eyes and savored it. Up and away the crane pulled him, through the air and above the sea as the boat shrunk beneath him. He watched as the engines of the supply ship fired up, white water churned from its propellers, and it headed off to some new destination.

The mechanical whirring noise of the crane's engine grew as Thiago neared the surface platform of Rig 7. He felt the cage sway to one side as the arm of the crane swung him gently over the deck. There was a jolt as the ascension stopped suddenly and the gears reversed themselves. Thiago looked through the metal grating of the cage between his feet as he was lowered onto a large, white circle painted onto the deck. Several men in hardhats stared up at him as he descended.

Once the crane had settled on the deck, an arm reached through the cage and unlocked the gate. It groaned open and Thiago was helped out. He studied the expectant faces around him. It was clear that they had been told about him.

"James, I presume?" said a large man with an outstretched hand. His round face wore a wide grin. Thiago gave his hand a firm shake.

"Indeed. And you are?"

"My name's Ted. Ted Watkins. Good to have you aboard Rig 7."

CHAPTER 12

This is all some kind of nightmare, Darren thought as he gripped the steering wheel and made his way down the highway. He could hardly fathom how quickly things had come apart. In those final moments in their home, scrambling to scrounge up as many boxes of legal documents and medical records as possible before the flames climbed into their bedroom and began filling their home with smoke, all that Darren could remember thinking was how surprised he was that his wife had the stamina and the strength to help pack their SUV.

They'd sat in their car for some time, just watching with tears in their eyes as the fire slowly climbed the walls and chewed through the roof of their house, eventually spilling over into the neighbors' properties. Within two hours, much of the neighborhood was in flames, with residents gathered numbly in the streets or scrambling to move as much of their furniture and belongings as possible into their driveways. Some were manic and hysterical; a few began fighting.

By midnight, the Hughes could stand the suffering no longer. Darren wiped the tears from his face, cranked the engine of their 4Runner, and slowly made his way over back roads towards the nearest freeway, heading south, farther into the valley in search of a hotel.

They would soon discover that the fire that had been sparked in their neighborhood was hardly an isolated incident; similar blazes seemed to burn everywhere Darren and Rita drove. The air was thick with sour smoke that hung in the black morning sky reflecting orange flames. People wandered the streets in confusion, or else tried vainly to douse the flames with bottles of water, soda, and beer. Some sat hunched over on curbs, faces buried in their hands as they wept. Others expressed grief through anger, screaming at one another, searching desperately for someone to blame.

The Hughes finally made their way to the edge of town, where the residential sector gave way to industrial parks and tech villages, neighborhoods bleeding into the arteries of highways. This is where the hotels and motels were, and with no friends still around to house them, it was their only option.

Darren pulled their black 4Runner up to the carport of a Holiday Inn. The lobby was dark; not even the stray beams of flashlights could be seen through the sliding glass doors. Darren exited and tried to pry the doors open as a perturbed face materialized from behind the glass.

"We're closed," yelled the man. He wore dark slacks and a white dress shirt. He had on a pair of rubber gloves and was covered in what looked like grease and sweat.

"Closed? Not even one room available?" Darren asked.

"Closed! NO guests!" said the man, smearing the sweat on his face with the back of his arm before disappearing again into the shadows.

What was going on? Darren wondered. How were the lights still off after so many hours? Surely California had some sort of backup grid? And what about private generators? Why weren't they up and operational? What was happening here? Why them? Why now?

"What did he say? Can't they let us in?" Rita demanded when Darren climbed back in the SUV. He simply shook his head, frowned, and pointed the car towards the next hotel. But they were all the same. Every Motel 6, Days Inn, and Ramada had the same set of locked doors concealing dark interiors and eerily quiet corridors.

By two o'clock that morning, Rita and Darren had exhausted every motel and hotel they could find. Darren grimaced at the fuel indicator on the dash; they were nearly red-lining it now.

"We need to find a gas station," Darren grumbled under his

145

breath as their SUV crept onto the freeway. Perhaps a few stops down on the interstate things would be different, Darren thought. Perhaps the blackout was isolated. But as they descended the ramp to the next exit, it was clear that this was wishful thinking. The lights were dead here, too. And just like back home, small fires could be seen in the distance.

"This is unreal," Darren thought aloud.

"What are we going to do? What if we get stuck out here? You didn't grab an extra carton of gas?"

"An extra carton of gas? What are you talking about?"

"Don't you, like, keep extra gas in the garage in a plastic container? For the lawn mower or whatever?"

"I didn't have time."

"But you had time to stuff all these papers and files in the car," Rita quipped.

"I got the files for *you*, Rita. And it's not like you mentioned anything about a gas container when we were packing."

"Yeah, well it kind of seems like an important thing now, don't you think? Please tell me that you at least thought to pack some food."

Darren said nothing, turning away from his wife as she seethed.

"You didn't pack any food? What were you thinking!"

"I was *thinking* that if we didn't get out of the house, we'd burn to death, Rita."

"Great. So now we'll get to starve to death. Much better."

"Would it hurt you to just be thankful for once? After all I've done for you. After all I've put up..." Darren stopped, bit his lip, and turned abruptly away.

"What? Say it. Go on. After all you've put up with, right? Wasn't that what you wanted to say? Well, I really apologize for being sick, Darren. I'm *so sorry* that's been so inconvenient for you."

"Rita. I didn't mean it like that. What I'm trying to say is–"

"No, forget it. Just stop."

For a moment, Darren was temped to put up a fight, but for

146

what? This argument had played out hundreds of times in the past and there was never a winner. There was nothing left to say, nothing left to defend. There were only fresh wounds and old scars. There were bigger problems on the horizon than marital strife and they both knew it. Darren kept silent as he stared numbly at the town below as the embers spread.

Peter had been right. They should've never stayed behind.

***

Chaos. Total chaos. Chad Harkett gazed down at the dark valley and fumed. All of this was unheard of–first a major, statewide blackout, then total cell coverage failure, followed by a freak lightning storm. There were too many factors out of his control, leaving him with a feeling he found infuriating.

Back at the office the day before, he'd been forced to end the work day early and send everyone home; employees had been in a frenzy when it was discovered they had no means of contacting their families. While he'd put up a fight in the beginning, he finally relented when someone threatened legal action, and the offices of Alphi Systems emptied within minutes. In the end, no one had figured out why the backup generators hadn't kicked in, though it apparently wasn't an isolated incident. The entire block's tech campus was experiencing a similar phenomenon, with only the grids running on pure solar generating even the barest of power output. But with the sudden storms blackening the skies, even that didn't seem like a long term solution.

And so Chad went to the one person whom he suspected might know something, his friend and business partner, Martin Landretti: the man with the bunker and the conspiracy theories. *Who knows, maybe he's been onto something after all*, Chad thought as he hauled a case of beer from the trunk of his Mercedes and rang Martin's doorbell. Martin let him in, but only after a long, suspicious look over his shoulder and down the driveway.

"You sure no one followed you?" Martin asked as he

bolted the door behind them.

"Only a couple of guys in suits and sunglasses," Chad said, eliciting a quick, frantic look from his friend. "There was a saucer, too, I think, with the illuminati logo on the underside…"

Martin shook his head, clearly annoyed. Chad laughed it off.

"This is serious stuff, Chad," Martin scolded. "The West Coast hasn't ever experienced a major blackout like this."

"West Coast? How do you know it's that extensive? You somehow getting internet in here?"

Martin shook his head. "My signal is as dead here as it was at the office, but I've got some other tech, older stuff, that's helping fill in the gaps."

"Older tech? Care to elaborate?"

"Maybe in a bit," said Martin obliquely. Chad's eyes narrowed. Martin wasn't one for keeping secrets, especially from him.

"All right, so do you have any explanations for what's going on out there?"

"I dunno man, I really don't. Obviously my first suspicion was that it was a cyber attack. That would explain the downed power grids, cell signals, satellites, et cetera. But this weather. I just don't know. I mean…" Martin trailed off as his gaze wandered.

"What? Go on," Chad prodded.

"Look. Controlling the weather sounds crazy and all, but the fact is that governments have been experimenting with it for decades. If they can seed clouds to force it to rain, I don't see why they couldn't charge the atmosphere somehow to cause a lightning storm."

"And the point of that would be…"

"Who knows? To spread terror? What's the point of most attacks?"

Chad was shaking his head. "This is crazy."

"The *world* is crazy. This is exactly what I've been saying. Something was bound to happen like this sooner or later."

"Well, at least we've got this to help ride it out," Chad said, raising his hand with the six pack.

Martin shook his head without looking up. "I don't think this is exactly the time to be drinking, Chad."

"Really? You seen how it looks out there? Seems like the perfect time to take the edge off. C'mon, man."

Martin took a deep breath as his head sunk lower between his shoulders. "I don't know, man. Maybe another time." he said softly.

"Dude. Martin. I think you're taking this all a little to seriously. I mean first it was bunkers and conspiracies, but now you're really freaking me out. I mean look at you–you're a mess. Next thing you know you're gonna be making foil hats and trying to find number patterns in static."

Martin pretended to laugh as he threw several items from his countertop into a backpack. "That's always your way, talking down to people, trying to play it cool like you're the one in charge."

"Excuse me?"

"You act like you have a handle on this, Chad, but I can see that look in your eyes. You're scared. Even as you're making fun of me. You are genuinely *scared*."

"Scared? You think a little thing like this has me scared?"

"Yeah, I do. Why else would you have come here? You're just looking for a place to hide. You've got nowhere else to turn, so you come here, to try to get into my bunker."

Chad lifted his palms in the air and scoffed. "All right, Martin, I admit it, I'm genuinely scared–I'm scared that you've straight up lost your mind. At first I thought you were just being cautious, or maybe just into some new weird hobby, but this– man, this is paranoia."

"So you mean to say that you didn't show up here just for the bunker?"

"Martin, it's a power outage. Not a nuclear holocaust."

"I have preparations to make, Chad," Martin said, brushing past him.

"So what, you're telling me to just leave? Just like that?"

"Well, you just said you didn't want to get in the bunker,

and that's where I'm headed. You're welcome to stick around the house if you want, but–" Martin words were cut off by a loud banging. It came from the front door. The two men fell silent and exchanged an uneasy look.

"Expecting someone?" Chad asked. Martin shook his head and walked cautiously to the front door.

"Who is it?" he called out.

"Your neighbor–I live down the street. I need help!"

Martin reached for the door, but Chad's voice stopped him. "Don't open that door," he hissed. "Figure out what he wants."

"What kind of help?" shouted Martin through the door.

"It's my kid... I think she's hurt. Might've broken both her ankles, I'm not sure. She's in a lot of pain. Look, my wife's got the car and I can't reach her, and there's no way to call an ambulance! Please!"

"Sorry, I don't see how I can help," Martin said.

"I just need a ride into town. That's it, just drop us off at the hospital. It's my kid, man. She's only ten."

Martin turned back to glance back at Chad with a pained look, but Chad was shaking his head. Martin ignored him, opened the door. A man in a green A's baseball cap and leather jacket stood on the other side. His eyes, like the look in his face, were dark and desperate.

"I'm sorry," the man said, "but I really need your car."

"I'd be happy to drive you, but I can't, not right now," Martin said, trying his best at diplomacy.

"Then I need to drive it myself."

"Excuse me?"

The man fumbled for something behind his back and produced a small, black handgun. Martin's hands shot into the air. "I'm sorry, man, but I need that car. I'll bring it back, I swear. I just gotta get my kid to the hospital." The gun trembled in the man's hands as he talked. Martin was frozen.

And that's when the sound of a gunshot rang out. For a moment, the two men wore an identical look of shock. The stranger had not meant to pull the trigger. He stared at the gun in his hand in confusion, and then down at the small, dark hole in his chest. He gasped, stumbling backwards as a sharp pain seized his body and the gun dropped from his hands. He staggered into the driveway. Martin could only stand there staring at the man in confusion, until he turned back.

Chad was standing there, his arm still outstretched, holding a smoking gun.

***

Joyce slid her face out from behind the wool blanket she'd bundled herself in the night before. It had been a cold, miserable night of restless sleep, a night that apparently hadn't yet passed. The digital clock on the dashboard of Stacy's truck read 7:35, but Joyce knew that had to be wrong. She gazed over at the East horizon, back towards the city, where everything laid in darkness. Buildings' windows and streetlights were still without power. Stranger still, the hazy blue outline of dawn was nowhere to be seen.

Stacy woke fifteen minutes later and the two women peeled the lids off of cans of beans for breakfast. They were cold, hard, and bland, but not a word of complaint was uttered. By the time they'd finished eating, it was past eight, and still the sun had yet to rise.

"What do you make of this weather?" Joyce finally asked.

Stacy shrugged. "It is what it is."

"Sun should be up by now. It was up yesterday by this time. It's still pitch black out there."

"At least we'll have power on the boat," Stacy said, motioning towards the harbor. As far as the eye could see, the lights aboard the ships were the only electrical things not affected by the power outage.

"You sure about that?"

"Only one way to find out," Stacy said. She started the engine and drove from the public parking lot onto a pier surrounded by smaller sailboats.

"Still here," Stacy said as she brought the pickup truck to a stop. "You were afraid it wouldn't be?" Joyce asked.

151

"There was always a chance. You saw people at the grocery store and on the roads. It won't take long till things descend into complete chaos. And when people find out that these boats have power and lights, it won't be long before they show up. And most of these sailboats aren't locked up like homes, with a security system and dead-bolted doors. Usually it's just a couple of padlocked latches and that's it. Easy to snap off with a pair of bolt cutters. The only thing really protecting these boats is the fact that most people don't know how to sail them."

"I've been meaning to ask about that. I never knew you had a sailboat."

"It's been in the family for years. My dad used to take me sailing when I was little. He's the one who taught me. When he died, one of the stipulations in his will was that the family maintain the boat. Not cheap. The moorage rate alone is almost three hundred a month. In the end, pretty much all of the money he left the family went into this stupid thing." Stacy shook her head with a tired look.

"Well, maybe it'll all pay off in the end," Joyce said hopefully.

"Yeah. Maybe."

The women exited the red pickup and made their way to the slip, where Stacy tugged at the mooring ropes and hopped aboard. Joyce, who had no experience with such things, had some difficultly imitating the maneuver, and nearly toppled into the water. She chuckled at her own lack of coordination, but drew a stern look from Stacy.

"Watch it. This water's ice cold. You fall in here, bad things happen. Always keep your hands on the lines," Stacy scolded, demonstrating with a firm grip on a thin braided wire that threaded through metal posts around the perimeter of the boat's surface.

"Ok," Joyce said. "Anything else I should know?"

"Plenty. Originally I wanted to sail today, but on second thought, I think we've got at least a day of preparations before we can head out there. Once we hit open waters, it'll just be me and you, and those winds could be strong. You'll need to know how to handle yourself."

"So we can't leave today?" Joyce said, disappointed.

"No. Too dangerous. It's not worth the risk. You need some basic training first."

Joyce lowered her chin as a cold wind blew over them. She dug her hands in her jacket pockets as Stacy fiddled with a combination lock on the hatch leading down to the cabin. It came loose and Stacy slid the doors back, revealing a narrow room lined by two beds and a tiny cooking area. It smelled of old wood and sour, sunbaked vinyl.

"Floor's still dry. That's a good sign," Stacy said offhandedly.

"Why? Does this boat have leaks?" Joyce asked uneasily.

"All boats have leaks. It's a constant battle, keeping them seaworthy. Like I said, our family spent a fortune keeping this thing afloat."

Joyce said nothing as she descended the wooden steps and sat on one of the beds. For the next hour, Stacy scurried silently about the boat, flicking on lanterns and flashlights, checking batteries and propane tanks and stored foods, seeing to one thing after another as Joyce watched on in curious silence.

Joyce had only been sailing once before in her life. It had been during a vacation years ago. It had been a rocky time in Joyce's and Alvin's relationship. Jasmin had died only a few years prior and Joyce was still reeling from shock. Alvin did all he could to keep their marriage from disintegrating completely. He knew Joyce had always wanted to go to Hawaii; the tickets were a surprise. Looking back now, that trip had probably been a turning point in their marriage, the moment when she knew they'd make it, the moment she realized she could look into her husband's eyes without seeing her dead daughter staring back.

She hadn't especially enjoyed the sailing. The winds had been strong and frightening, and despite the captain's constant reassurance, she was sure they were powerful enough to capsize the vessel, leaving them stranded in the middle of the ocean.

Joyce gazed out the circular porthole of Stacy's sailboat

and ached for the memory. Alvin's embrace, his thick arms wrapped around her, the warm splash of crystal water in her face and the Hawaiian sun beating against her neck. They were sensations from another life. The wind here was cold and jagged, the sea air stale and clammy. A bitter feeling swelled in Joyce's stomach as Stacy shook her by the shoulder.

"Hey, get that hatched closed, would you?" Stacy said, pointing. Joyce turned and snugged the doors and hatch tightly shut as Stacy flipped on the space heater. The small space slowly began to warm.

"Well, that's a bit of good news," Stacy said, sounding relieved.

"What is?"

"Looks like everything's in sufficient shape. We've got some leftover food that isn't expired, and there's power. I wasn't sure if there was going to be any juice left in the batteries."

"This thing runs on a battery?"

"Yeah, same kind that cars run on."

"Does that also run the boat's, um… engine?" Joyce asked.

"The outboard motor runs on standard gasoline. There should be plenty for us to get out of the harbor. And when we get to Burrard Harbor, well… We'll see how that goes."

"You don't sound too sure."

"I'm not sure about anything," Stacy said as she lifted one of the bed pads, opened a hatch below it, and extracted a couple of life vests. She handed one to Joyce and showed her how to wear it.

"Rule number one–you must wear one of these at all–"

Stacy was cut off by a loud noise. The women fell silent and turned to look out of one of the windows, towards the direction of the noise. A car pulled into a parking spot in the harbor and two figures emerged. They walked up and down the pier, their features hidden in the darkness. A large yacht caught their attention; they peered into its windows and spoke quietly between themselves. The lights on the upper deck windows of the yacht were on, but there didn't appear to by any movement inside.

"Hey! Anyone in there? Open up!" yelled one of the men from the car. He pounded his fist against the hull. The vessel remained quiet for another moment before a figure silhouetted by the cabin lights approached one of the upper deck's doors and edged it cautiously open.

"What do you want?" barked a large man. The two men on the pier below him stepped backwards and raised their hands in the air when they spotted the shotgun in the man's hands.

"Easy there. We don't mean you any harm. We're just looking for a ride outta here."

"A ride?"

"Yeah, we got family up in Broadview. We were planning on driving up, but the roads are a nightmare. We thought going by boat would be best, made our way here and saw your lights on."

"Yeah, looks like you got enough space in there. It's only the two of us," the smaller of the two men chimed in.

"Sorry, I'm not taking passengers," said the large man, lowering his shotgun a few inches.

"We're not looking for handouts, man. We'll pay you."

The man considered this for a moment. "How much?"

The men on the dock shared a brief look before one dug into his jacket pocket and dangled a ring of keys in the air. "My Acura's right over there. Only a couple years old. I'll even let you test drive it first if you want."

The man on deck was silent for a moment as he leaned over the railing to gaze at the car. "Where you say you two were headed again?"

"Broadview. It's maybe what, twelve miles from here? It's usually like a half hour drive, but with these roads…"

"And you're willing to just hand over your car?"

"We're in a rush, ok? Our mom–she lives up there–she's got a heart condition, you know? We haven't been able to contact her with the phones down. Without power in the house, anything could happen. We need to get up there and make sure she's ok."

"You two are brothers?"

155

"Yeah. Name's Tim, this is Corey." Corey lifted a hand in the air.

"Broadview. Right. It'd be at least a couple of hours to get out there. Not sure if there's a place to dock, though. Just beaches out that way. How do you plan to get to shore?"

"You let us worry about that. We'll swim to shore if we have to. Just gotta get to mom."

"What d'you say, man? An Acura for a couple hours of work?"

The captain thought it over for another moment before finally setting his firearm down on the deck and descending a staircase behind the pilothouse. He flipped on the lights on the lower deck and the two men climbed aboard and vanished.

"You hear what they said about the roads?" Joyce said, turning to Stacy with a look of dread. Stacy nodded slowly.

"It'll only get worse. Like I said, by sea's the only way. And we need to get moving, because it'll only be a matter of time before people start figuring it out for themselves, and then this place will turn into a circus. People are nice now, trying to bargain their way for safe passage, but in another couple of days–"

A sharp crack echoed over the surface of the harbor's waters. The two women turned back to the yacht where the men had just boarded.

"I sure hope that wasn't what it sounded like," Joyce whispered. Stacy said nothing as she reached for a switch in the cabin and killed the lights.

***

The whisky swished around in Martin Landretti's glass as his hands trembled. He never drank the stuff straight, never had the fortitude for it, but now... Now, even the glass and a half that he'd downed in the last hour hadn't seem to do a thing to take the edge off. His adrenaline burned right through the alcohol. His eyes found Chad on the far end of the bunker, where he stood huddled over the weapons locker.

156

He'd shot a man. Just like that. No questions, just *bam*.
And apparently he'd hit him right in the heart; he'd stopped
breathing within minutes. Even if the cell towers had been up
and they'd called an ambulance, there likely wouldn't have been
time. *DOA*. That was that. A life ended, right on Martin's front
steps. His head spun as another wave of nausea swept up from
the pit of his stomach. He scrabbled off of his couch and into the
bunker's restroom, sticking his face into the metal toilet bowl
just in time to watch his body expel every ounce of whiskey he'd
just ingested.

When the wave of agony passed, he crawled back to the
couch and tried to sleep. At least they weren't in the dark down
here, he thought with some relief. Installing a Faraday cage and
stocking it with car batteries had been a smart move, even if it
hadn't been a cheap one. The batteries would keep the lights and
ventilation system working even if the entire national power grid
was down.

The entire grid. God.

Martin hoped that wasn't what was happening here.
Hopefully this was all just temporary, a snag in the system, a
hiccup that'd be sorted out in a few days–a few weeks, max.
Worst case scenario, they'd go to State of Emergency and the
National Guard would be called in. Because in spite of all of
Martin's thorough preparations, an end-of-the-world scenario
was never something he'd hoped for, not like some of the gun-
loving survivalists that populated the bunker-builder forums and
survivalist blogs. He was not one of those nuts, even if he'd
taken a few pages from their books. This was never supposed to
happen. His head spun again as he pressed his eyelids tightly
together and heard Chad's approaching footsteps.

"Hey, Martin, so you should probably fill me in on some
stuff," Chad said. Martin didn't reply. "Look, I went over your
stockpile in here, and there's some stuff you aren't stocked up on.
I'm just gonna go back to your place, grab some things, and be
right back. But I need the door code to get back in, so if you
could just tell me–"

"Why did you shoot that man?" Martin asked.

157

"What?" Chad asked.

"My neighbor. Why did you shoot him?"

"You're sure he was your neighbor? You'd seen him before?"

"No, but that's not the point. You… You just *killed* him. Like it was *nothing*."

"He would've done the same to you, Martin."

"You don't know that."

"The gun was loaded."

"That doesn't mean he was going to pull the trigger."

"So what should I have done? Exactly how long should I have waited before doing something?"

"We could've talked, figured out if there was another way."

"*Another way?* He pointed a loaded gun at you and was trying to steal your car. He wasn't open to another way."

"What about his kid?"

"You believed that little story?"

"I don't know. But if it's true? What if his kid is waiting for her dad to come, and… Oh god…" Martin's head rocked again as he pressed his fingers into his eye sockets.

"If it's true, then that man was an idiot. He should've thought of the consequences of leaving his kid home alone while trying to commit an armed robbery."

"How can you be so *cold*, Chad? Do you even realize that you took a man's life today?"

"How can you be so soft? Look around you–you've spent all this money, all this time, to build yourself a little apocalypse bunker, stock it with weapons, and you can't even pull the trigger when someone's threatening you at your own front door? How do you expect to survive?"

Martin was silent. On some level, Chad had a point. It wasn't the first time that Chad had chided him for his lack of ruthlessness, for not being able to steel himself to do difficult things. Through years of department mergers and layoffs and arguments with investors and partners, Chad had always been right at the helm. At times he'd almost seemed to enjoy the conflict, to thrive on the savagery of office politics. One disgruntled employee had even branded Chad Harkett the Sociopath of Silicon Valley. Martin had enjoyed the joke then, but he wondered now if there wasn't a kernel of truth in there somewhere. What, exactly, *wasn't* this man capable of?

"If anything, Martin, you ought to be thanking me for saving your life," Chad said with a sneer.

"I don't mean to be ungrateful, Chad... I just wish there was another way. There's a corpse lying in my driveway, man."

"Yeah, I've been thinking about that. That's one of the things I want to take care of while I'm out there. We don't need someone stumbling on that and coming down here to look for us."

"Wait, what? What are you suggesting?"

"I'm not asking you to help. I don't think you have the stomach for it, but..." Chad lowered his voice as he knelt by Martin's side until his friend turned his head and looked him in the eye. "...I mean this as a friend, but you need to toughen up. If things get nearly as bad as you used to think they might get, this is only the beginning. Survival of the fittest, right?"

There was something about the way he said it, or perhaps it was the twinkle in his eye, the curled smile on his face, that brought Martin an odd and indescribable relief. Because in that moment, he realized just how much he needed his friend. Chad Harkett was someone who wasn't afraid of getting his hands dirty.

"All right, Chad. I'll give you the code."

***

"So, how've you been the last couple of days?" Peter asked as he finished off the last bit of his sandwich. Bo Wharton sat across from him polishing off a slice of apple pie with a cup of coffee. He smiled with the corner of his lips and shrugged one of his knobby shoulders without meeting Peter's gaze.

"I noticed your hands are looking more stable," Peter said.

"It's just the caffeine," Bo said with a grunt.

"Caffeine helps with the jitters?"

"Guess it gives my body the hit it needs to settle the nerves.

Or something. I'm not a doctor."

Peter tried to smile hopefully. "So the withdrawals are getting a little easier?"

Bo snorted. "Spoken like a man who's been clean all his life." Peter said nothing, waiting for Bo to continue.

"Look, it's like this, man–withdrawals aren't a thing that ever really go away."

"Oh?"

"I know guys that were clean for weeks, even years, thought they were totally over it, when *BAM*, one day the itch comes back hard and heavy as ever. Next day they wake up in the back of some alley, a stranger's apartment, behind a bar. People that say they've 'sobered up' or 'gone clean' or whatever are lying to you. There's no going back. There's only trading one drug for another." Bo lifted the Styrofoam cup of coffee between gnarled fingers and winked. The web of wrinkles on his face rearranged themselves to form a smirk.

Peter smiled graciously. He'd been studying the *Teach Us* book with Bo daily since the two had been introduced a few days prior. The organization had mandated that all evacuee tag-alongs begin an immediate study program with experienced brothers and sisters and that they be assigned shortly to a work detail. The program, while rigorous, was intended to acclimatize them speedily to their new surroundings. With Bo, however, Peter was unsure of how well any of this was working. They were already a third of the way through the book, and while Bo was able to answer the questions correctly, it was impossible to determine what was going through his head.

"Get any good shots lately?" Peter asked, gesturing to the Polaroid next to Bo's cup of coffee. He glanced down and shrugged.

"Not lately, not in this weather."

"I'm surprised they still make film for those. How old is that thing, anyway? Looks like it's been around the block a few times."

"Yeah, well… It was one of the few belongings I had on me when I was locked up. Stuck with me all these years, doesn't feel right tossing it out."

"Interesting. You don't strike me as the sentimental type," Peter said through a grin. Bo looked away.

"So, what's all this I hear about losing contact with the mainland?" Bo asked.

"Come again?"

"Been overhearing some people talking about it the last couple of days."

Peter raised his eyebrows. In an effort to avoid a panic, there had been no public announcement of the loss of contact with the branch. As for the loss of cell phone coverage, many simply assumed it was a result of being so far out at sea.

"Well, I–" Peter was interrupted by a hand on his shoulder. He turned to see the familiar face of one of the overseers staring down at him with a puzzling expression.

"Sorry to interrupt, but you're needed on the top deck," the man said to Peter. Peter said a brief apology to Bo before standing and following the overseer out of the room.

"What's going on?" Peter asked in a hushed voice as the two of them left the cafeteria.

"We've got a visitor. A representative from the branch."

"Do they have news about why the communication has stopped?"

The overseer gave Peter a sidelong glance and a slight nod. "That, and then some," he said.

Ten minutes later, the two men found themselves on the top deck of Rig 7. While the hurricane had skirted past them two days prior, the sky remained grey and streaked with storm clouds. Farther off in the distance, the skies were even darker, and Peter was thankful that their convoy had evaded the worst of it.

Dozens of brothers had gathered on the top deck, where they'd apparently been summoned from their respective departments. Whatever news was to be learned from their visitor, Peter thought, it was obviously of great importance.

"He came by air," the overseer beside Peter said, motioning with the gloved hand towards a raised metal platform. Its surface had been painted black with a large, white "H" at its center. A

161

gleaming blue helicopter sat atop it. Beads of rain trickled down its shiny hull as its pilot checked items off a clipboard from behind the controls.

"You think they flew through the storm?" Peter asked the overseer, who didn't hear the question.

"Follow me," he said, gesturing for Peter to move in the direction of one of the trailer offices at the far corner of the rig, near one of the loading cranes.

Inside the office there was standing room only. Peter was squeezed against a wall as the lights shut off. At the far end of the room, a TV screen was turned on and connected to the brother's phone. He stood on a raised platform beside the monitor, called on one of the overseers to offer a prayer, and began his presentation.

CHAPTER 13

"As you've all likely heard by now, communications networks have been down for the last two days," the brother said, his eyes scanning the room. "That includes cell phone signals, phone landlines, the internet, and most radio communications. From the information the branch has access to, this appears to be due to a massive solar flare." The brother paused to raise his phone and swipe at something on the screen. The TV monitor beside him projected a high definition, red and yellow close-up of the Sun.

"Astronomers have actually been warning for years that something like this could happen. It was feared that if a solar flare was severe enough, the radiation hitting the Earth could permanently disable a lot of the technology we rely on and send us back to the Dark Ages. Judging from the way things are going on the mainland, that seems to be exactly what's happening."

The speaker paused for a moment as a wave of gasps and hushed conversation spread through the room.

"It gets worse. Unfortunately, it's not just the communication networks that have suffered. Power grids are down, and with them, running water and natural gas. As you can imagine, things are starting to get pretty chaotic, and fast."

The speaker's hand flicked again, and the image on screen showed a dark hillside dotted with bright fires. "This image was taken not far from Patterson, New York. In spite of the snow, fires have begun to spread due to lightning strikes. Without phones, residents have been unable to call the fire department, leaving them to shovel snow onto the fires in an effort to extinguish them. They've only been partially successful."

The next image appeared on the wall: a black sky punctured by daggers of purple lightning. The room gasped again. "This image was taken in Florida by a brother volunteering at the facility our helicopter departed from, but it's apparently not an uncommon scene in many parts of North America. Some seem to think that it's the result of the increased magnetism and radiation in the atmosphere, while others..." the speaker's voice trailed off, eliciting a wave of uneasy laughter in the room.

"One thing we can be certain of that's not a result of the solar flare, however, is the darkness." The brother paused as a motion of his wrist triggered a new image on the TV. This one was a video. In the background, the noisy thud of helicopter rotors hacking at the air and the high-pitched whine of powerful engines blocked out all other audio. Lights and electronic readouts from the helicopter could be glimpsed as the camera panned back and forth, along with the pilot's grimace of concentration as the cockpit rocked in the turbulence.

"This video was taken only a couple of hours ago on my phone. We were about a hundred miles out to sea at this point."

The eyes in the room remained glued to the video image as the sky began to lighten. The blackness in the air seemed to lift away, as if a curtain had been pulled back. A dark mist whisked away, revealing the same cloudy skies seen just outside.

"As I'm sure you can all tell by that video clip, this is not a normal storm. I can tell you from being on the mainland that the darkness in the sky is like nothing I've seen before. It's thick and impenetrable, and seems to be getting worse by the hour. Even flashlights and headlights barely seem to be able to penetrate it.

"Now, given the extraordinary nature of these events, combined with their timing just after the last of the evacuations, the branch believes that we could be seeing a literal fulfillment of Jesus' prophecy at Matthew twenty-four."

The brother flicked his wrist again, bringing the verses just mentioned to life on the monitor.

"As you can see, these current events seem to harmonize with the sun being darkened, the stars not giving their light. Additionally, due to the high magnetism in the atmosphere, some

164

areas reported seeing red and orange auroras before the darkness set in—some described it as a blood moon.

"Of course, we can only be precisely sure of any of these prophetic meanings looking back, after the fact, but the branch wishes to communicate once again its warm commendation to your brothers heeding the orders to flee. We'll do our best, given the circumstances, to keep you in the loop. Now, I'm sure you brothers will have questions, and I'd be happy to field as many as I can before my helicopter leaves for the next convoy."

A smattering of hands poked through the crowd.

"How are the brothers at headquarters?"

"Doing well. As you know, they were the last ones scheduled to evacuate, wanting to be sure that all evacuations around the world were conducted according to schedule. We're happy to report that they were, with very few exceptions. As was previously announced, the branch facilities will be shut down and locked up as the remaining Bethel family sails to Africa, but they wanted to assure the friends that they are not planning on abandoning the facilities forever."

Another hand was called on: "If communication lines are down, how come we can still communicate between rigs?"

"A good question. As far as power grids are concerned, the official word is that systems were overloaded due to the swell in subterranean electrical current. That means that anything on land that wasn't protected—say, surrounded by a non-conductive material like rubber—was totally fried." The brother paused a moment as a small smirk crept onto his face.

"Here's the amazing thing: that same electrical current was present in the oceans and other bodies of water, of course, but it wasn't nearly as concentrated, since water doesn't conduct electricity nearly as well as solid matter. For the most part, this means that boats, rigs, and cruise liners—the very places that most of our brothers and sisters around the world are located—were unaffected. As for communications, that one's a little harder to explain. The government is saying that most communication satellites have been severely disabled, and the magnetism in the atmosphere is interfering with normal radio signals even now.

165

But since that's atmospheric, it should have the same effect on land and sea. So frankly, why you're still able to communicate with one another via radio is a mystery. Kind of like how it's a mystery that the darkness on land doesn't seem to be affecting the weather out here. Of course, all of this strongly suggests a... *supernatural* element at work."

Another hand darted from the crowd and was selected by the speaker, who was grinning as the energy in the room began to spike. "Has anyone drawn the parallels between this and what happened in Moses's day, with the ten plagues?"

The speaker's smile widened, though he took a diplomatic tone. "That possibility has been presented, yes, and you can be sure that your brothers at headquarters are watching these events with great interest. However, it is not our objective now to speculate, but to keep in mind the task we've been given–to stay with these convoys, to stay with our brothers and sisters. Whatever this turns out to be, it's clear that Jehovah is maneuvering things to keep his people protected, and when the final attack comes, we can be sure of our continued safety."

***

Joyce was going on her fourth hour huddling in the dark of Stacy's sailboat, shivering as much from the cold as the fear. Her afternoon plans of helping to prepare the boat for travel and learning how to sail the vessel as Stacy's shipmate had been largely derailed by the events of that morning. It was difficult even now to fully process what she'd witnessed–two men hijacking a stranger's yacht, murdering him in the process.

For all her effort, Joyce could not erase the sight from her mind: the large, lifeless body of an innocent human being hefted like unwanted garbage over the railing of the top deck and slapping onto the waters below. Joyce was no stranger to injury and death–in fact, her job demanded a certain desensitization to certain horrors–but never before had she witnessed firsthand such a cold act of violence, and it shook her to her core.

The power had been out now for what, a few days? And

166

already people were turning into savages and killing one another. What would happen if this were to continue for another week? *A month?* At least the men in the yacht had gone, had apparently not noticed that Joyce and Stacy had been witnesses to their crime. A crime, Joyce thought with sickening realization, that was perhaps repeating many times, over and over, in these tense, gloomy hours.

Joyce jumped as the hatch slid open and Stacy climbed inside, closing the small door behind her. She carried in her arms the remainder of the supplies from her pickup. Joyce simply stared; she couldn't remember Stacy leaving.

"Change of plans," Stacy said abruptly, dumping the items onto the bench opposite of Joyce. There were a few odds and ends they'd managed from their fateful trip to the supermarket the day before, plus an assortment of other items that Joyce could hardly imagine a use for: a half empty bottle of motor oil, spare rags, and plastic bags.

"What do you mean?" Joyce managed. "What change?"

Joyce wiped her face with the back of her hand and sat heavily on the bed. "People are starting to show up out there, going to the boats with lights on, trying to figure out why they've got power. I knew this would happen. Word will get out, pretty soon this place will be flooded with desperate people. It'll get dangerous."

"Like those two men..." Joyce said.

"Just the beginning. I've seen this kind of thing before, Joyce, and I'm telling you... It's only going to get worse. We need to move."

"But what about all the training I was supposed to go through? Don't I at least need to learn a few things about sailing?"

"Sorry, no time. The waves in the bay aren't too bad right now. We can putter around out there for a while and I'll show you what I can. But sticking around here, that's just asking for trouble."

"What about food and water?"

Stacy surveyed their rations with a dismal look. "We'll have to work with what we've got. It's too risky to go anywhere to try to get more. Anyways, it's not a long trip back to Burrard Harbor. So long as, you know…"

"So long as what?"

"We don't get lost."

"Is that a possibility?" Joyce asked, shocked.

"My plan was to keep the shore within sight of us so we could just follow the coast northwards. But without any lights on land, and without any sunlight during the day, that's going to be a challenge. And whatever's darkening the sky out there, it seems to be thickening."

"You don't have some navigational system here? Like a GPS?"

"Checked it already. It's not getting a signal. It's useless to us."

"So how on earth are we supposed to get anywhere?"

"We'll play it by ear. Once we get out to sea, we'll have a better idea of what we're up against. Maybe it won't be as dark as it is here. I just don't know."

Joyce buried her face in her hands. She felt as if she ought to be sobbing from the anxiety and frustration, but she was too tired to cry. Distant sirens passed across the bay.

"Ok, fine," Joyce finally resigned. "Let's get out of this place."

***

Alvin Tucker watched the harbor slide past as the supertanker's foghorn let a long, mournful bellow into the dark fog. He'd stayed back as long as he could, all the while holding out hope that Joyce's face would be among the faces of latecomers. He'd passed up several nights of sleep just to keep the night watchmen company, his eyes glued to the roads, waiting for their Subaru to make an appearance. It never showed up.

Those who did arrive in those final days after the blackouts seemed to be clinging to the very last of their sanity. Their eyes were sallow and dark, pupils wide from lack of sunlight, skin pale and trembling in the cold. They told harrowing tales of the crimes they'd witnessed on the roads and highways; armed motorists opening fire, women attempting to sell their bodies in exchange for rides home, bodies frozen on the side of the road. Horrors upon horrors, Alvin was told. Everything was falling apart.

Still, he would've stayed behind. He'd have gladly given his pod to a replacement couple if it had meant taking a later tanker, sticking around for a few more days to see if Joyce would arrive. But it wasn't his call. There was a system in place, and besides, there were nearly a hundred other Witnesses with similar circumstances, waiting at the gates for family to arrive. Without internet and cell phones, there was no way to communicate, no way to know their fate. Hope wore thin.

And so Alvin left.

Black water churned and parted beneath the ship's prow, tufts of mist illuminated by the deck lights as they swept past. The darkness was as thick as an oil stain.

"Hey," came a soft voice from behind Alvin. He turned to find Claire seated in her wheelchair, bundled in a down coat and wool hat.

"Hey," Alvin grunted.

"Mind if I join you?" asked the girl. Alvin shrugged. She maneuvered herself closer, wheels butting against the railing. They watched the harbor disappear together; it didn't take long. Whatever this darkness was, it seemed to engulf everything, as if it possessed the power to swallow light.

"This weather sure is freaky, huh?" Claire said.

"Nothing we didn't expect," Alvin muttered.

"What do you mean?"

"Jesus foretold that during the great tribulation the sun would be darkened and that the moon would turn to blood. We suspected that some sort of phenomenon like this might happen."

"You think this is happening worldwide?"

"It's possible."

"So... Have you heard anything from Joyce?"

Alvin stiffened as if shielding himself from a sudden

wintry wind. He gave his head a shake. "Phones are down."

"Oh, geez… I'm so sorry, Alvin. I wish there was something I could do."

"Yeah. That's life."

"It just doesn't seem fair. She was just trying to help. Jehovah has to know that, right?" "He still requires obedience."

"I wish I could change places with her. I don't deserve a spot on this ship, you know. She should be the one here with you."

Alvin bit his tongue. The girl had a point and they both knew it. There were no words of solace or reassurance. More than all else, he was tired. He wanted to just lay down and sleep until it was all behind him.

"I'm sorry, Alvin," Claire said, placing a hand on the large man's jacket sleeve.

"Yeah, you've mentioned that."

"I mean it."

"I know you do, Claire, but the fact is that Joyce wanted you to be here. This is the hand we've been dealt, it's up to us to do our best playing it."

"You think she'll be ok?"

"She's resourceful. I'm sure she's doing her best to find a way across that border. Only problem is, once she does, she'll find out we're not there anymore."

"But someone is."

"Only a few more days, and then Burrard Harbor will be nothing but a huge empty lot. She's running out of time."

"Well, for what it's worth, I'm praying for her."

Alvin turned to look down at the girl in the wheelchair, her green eyes beaming in earnest. The color had returned to her cheeks. The bruised skin was returning to normal, the cuts and scrapes on her face and neck nearly fully healed. She was looking better every day. *Joyce would be relieved to know that,* Alvin thought.

"Thanks, Claire."

"I wish I could do more."

"Yeah, me too."

The two fell silent as the foghorn bellowed once more into the night air and the sea gathered their ship into its arms.

***

Chad gazed disdainfully at the shriveled man on the sofa, blithely sleeping the morning away while there was work to be done. Important work. *Vital* work.

Chad had made use of his time the night before; he'd even refused himself a glass of bourbon, if only for the reason that it would lead to another glass, and then another, until the entire bottle was drained and he was dealt unconscious just like Martin. But no. As much as he craved it, now wasn't the time.

Chad now knew the layout of Martin's shelter well. Everything had been stocked and inventoried only a month prior, shortly before he'd been led into the underground shelter the first time–which had only been two weeks ago. It felt like much, much longer.

Time had slipped through their fingers and down through the cracks of society where everything else was headed. Maybe Martin's paranoia hadn't been so far off after all; it certainly hadn't been without its benefits. Sure, Chad would've been ok on his own for the first few days, holed up in his mansion, locked up in his gated community, but even his lavish pantries weren't stocked to hold out through a week without power. Martin's bunker, on the other hand, had enough in the way of canned goods and dried fruit to keep them comfortable for at least a couple of months.

Chad shook his head at the thought. *Two months.* Why was he already thinking like this? What had caused him to lose hope so quickly? Surely the power would come back on, and the storms would clear. Surely this was all just a temporary scare, and things would return to normal as they always had.

Yeah, sure. Chad couldn't shake the feeling in his gut that told him that this wasn't like those other times. This wasn't just a major disaster–some earthquake or wildfire sweeping through the area. There was something else at play here. He could sense it when he closed his eyes, could sense it ebbing like a dark current below the surface. Maybe it was the way those clouds had looked when they blacked out the sky, or the radiant purple lightning flashes. Whatever this was, Chad felt, it was a *culmination* of something. A perfect storm of chaos.

Martin Landretti mumbled something in his sleep as Chad wandered to the back of the bunker to inspect the weapons locker. He hadn't managed to get it open–he'd need another code to get past the combination lock–but that didn't keep him from staring hungrily through the thick metal mesh. Martin had prepared a bit of everything: there was a shotgun, two rifles, and a couple of handguns, not to mention the stacked crates of ammo and pepper spray. It was enough to survive an all-out assault and then some.

Of course, none of it would be to any avail if Martin didn't have the guts to pull the trigger. Chad shook his head again as he recalled the look of disbelief on his friend's face after Chad had shot the intruder. It was a good thing he'd grabbed the gun from his trunk and kept it with him. It would never leave his side again. There was no question in Chad's mind of what needed to be done when that man had pulled his gun. Chad had been ruthless in his business dealings and this was just an extension of that. He'd had no qualms about doing it, and he knew without a doubt that he'd do it again if the need arose. *Martin, on the other hand...* Only time would tell.

Chad snatched a can of beans from the wall and dumped the contents into a pot on the stove. He cranked the burners and let the beans warm as he located a set of bowls and silverware. He was surprised to find Martin sitting upright on the sofa when he set down a bowl for his friend on the coffee table and sat.

"Eat up," Chad said dryly. Martin said nothing, taking the meal between his hands and eating voraciously.

"Geez, slow down. There's plenty more," Chad said.

"What day is it?"

"Friday morning. Almost eleven."

Martin nodded slowly as he surveyed the small space. "You sure found your way around the place."

"Not much else to do."

"Power's still out?"

Chad nodded. "I took a walk around the premises this morning. Got a few more things from my car, and some stuff from your house. Paper towels, garbage bags, odds and ends we might need."

"Run into anyone out there?"

"Yeah, couple'a zombies. Shot 'em."

"Very funny," Martin said. "Seriously, though, you see anyone? My neighbors?"

"No one. Maybe they've got bunkers like yours."

Martin shrugged as he spooned the remainder of the beans into his mouth.

"Anyone else know about this place?" Chad asked.

"Maybe. Had a lot of earth movers in here when we installed the septic tanks and dug the holes. Hard to keep something like this a secret."

Chad frowned.

"Why? What's the matter?"

"Just that it increases the chances of people turning up here looking for handouts."

"What, like you did?"

Chad scoffed. "Give me a break. I saved your life back there. You need a bodyguard, I need a place to hole up till this blows over. Our symbiotic relationship continues."

"Yeah, maybe."

"I just don't get you, Martin. Why buy all those weapons and ammo if you aren't going to use it?"

"I'll use it. When the time comes, I'll be ready."

"So you know how to load and fire each of those weapons."

Martin nodded proudly. "I have a membership on a firing range."

"And? Did you actually go?"

"Yeah, a few times. I'm guessing you frequent those places too. I didn't even know you owned a gun."

Chad smirked, nodded, and pulled the handgun from behind his back, letting it glisten in the low light of the bunker. Then he glanced up at the LED bulbs and frowned, puzzled.

173

"How've you still got electricity in here?"

"I've got backup generators and solar panels hooked up to a chain of batteries."

"So what? We had generators at the office, they went down with the blackout."

"Could be the Faraday cage."

"Come again?"

"A Faraday cage. It's a shielding used to block electromagnetic fields. I had it installed with the bunker; it houses the generators and all of the sensitive electronic equipment. Maybe whatever's causing the blackout was EM-based, like some kind of electromagnetic pulse weapon."

"I thought you said it was a zero day attack?"

"That's just one possibility of many. The sad fact of the matter is that it could be a number of things. Our infrastructure isn't as failsafe as you might think. There are a few things that could bring it crashing to a halt."

"All right. So the generators in here are working. That's good. And you've got batteries. So how long will the power in here last?"

Martin made a thoughtful face for a moment. "How's the sunlight looking out there?" he asked.

"Not great. Whatever this attack was, the clouds are thick out there—if you could even call them that. It's almost like a thick black smoke out there. It's blocking most of the light. Your solar panels won't do a lick of good."

Martin frowned. "That's a problem. I've got enough backup fuel in here to keep the generators running for a couple of weeks if we use them sparingly—LED bulbs, heaters, ventilators, that kind of thing. If we're not sure about solar, though, I'd say we should drain their battery reserves first. They'll bleed power if we're not using them anyhow, might as well make use of the electricity we've got stored."

"How long will the batteries last?"

Martin shrugged. "No idea. I just had them installed. If they've been charging properly, maybe four or five days."

"So we're looking at less than a month of power with what

we've got?" Chad asked.

Martin nodded.

"What about water?"

"That shouldn't be an issue. The reservoir tank has over one thousand gallons, enough to last us months. Plus, the drains are all hooked up to a filtration system, so the water gradually recycles. If we run out of anything, it won't be water."

"You thought of everything."

"Tried to. Like I said, this was my passion project for a while. I researched as much as I could and did my best to foolproof the place."

"Too bad the internet's offline."

"I've got books."

"Books?"

"Sure," Martin said, reaching under the sofa and extracting a plastic crate full of paperbacks. He slid it across the floor, where Chad stopped it with his foot. Chad sifted through the contents, reading the titles aloud.

"*Doomsday Preparedness. Surviving a Nuclear Holocaust. Zombie Bunker.* Are these for real?"

Martin nodded seriously. "Most are written by ex-military buffs. These guys have been through everything, they break it all down, one thing at a time."

"They've been through zombie attacks?"

"Oh, yeah, that one's a little far out there, but you know... The strategies are still sound. Principles are the same."

"Right," Chad said, shaking his head as he fanned through the pages.

"Regardless of the circumstance, the most important thing is—"

Martin's words were cut off by the crackle and pop of static. It hung in the air for a second before transforming into a high pitched electronic squeal. Martin shot to his feet and bolted to the back of the room, where he flung open a heavy metal door. Chad followed him into the small room, where a smaller hinged door was inset into a rectangular wire mesh cage. The Faraday cage. Martin unlatched the cage door and squeezed in, seating

175

himself at a narrow wooden table. Below it sat the two generators. The linked series of batteries Martin had just mentioned hung from a pegboard beside the table, all of it neatly organized and well within the confines of the cage.

Another burst of static shot from two small, black speakers on the table as Martin sat and fiddled with a series of dials and sliders on a metal panel. Between the static suddenly came snippets of garbled words. The two men strained to make sense of the sounds.

"...*repea... enti...... blackout.... unab........ conta.... copy?...*"

The air filled with static whine as the line went dead.

"Weird," Martin said, rubbing the back of his neck. My signal here is usually crystal clear. I've got an antenna on the roof of my place that's wired to this room–I've gotten broadcasts all the way from Kansas."

"Is this a government broadcast we're getting?"

Martin shook his head. "Nah, this frequency is for amateur radio users. If I could hear his call letters, I might be able to figure out who it is, but..."

Another punch of static. "*Anyone........ chaos.... canno... copy?...*"

***

Darren Hughes stirred awake to a loud, hacking cough. Rita was crumpled over in the passenger's seat, clutching a half-emptied bottle of water in one hand and a wad of tissues in the other. Her cheeks and neck, lit only by the interior dome light of their SUV, were bright red.

"Oh my god, Rita, you ok?" Darren asked. Rita glared at him frantically, gasping for air and unable to get a word out. She made a motion with her hand to her lips. *Her inhaler*, Darren realized.

He flung open his door and ran to the back of their vehicle, where he'd thrown armfuls of pill bottles and assorted medicine into a plastic bin just before they'd evacuated. Darren dug through its contents with both arms, struggling to see in the low light. Had they even packed a flashlight? It had all been so sudden, so crazy. He couldn't remember if he'd grabbed her inhaler. It had all been a blur.

Darren raked through the contents of bin after bin. *Please, Jehovah*, he thought. *Please tell me I didn't forget the inhaler.* Rita continued hacking, noisier now than before. Darren pulled several of the bins from the back of the car and snatched at a box behind them. This one was mostly medical and legal paperwork, but he recalled tossing in some other items from their kitchen table. He flung away the manila folders, the X-rays, the paper clipped photocopies of blood tests and spinal taps and who knew what else. Why them? When was all this going to let up? After all these years of sickness and grief, one symptom after another, when would this tide ever turn?

Rita had fallen silent. Darren glanced up. She doubled over, hands on the dash, unable to draw a breath. He'd seen this before and it had terrified him. It was an asthma attack.

Darren's teeth ground together, his face flushing in anger, fear, and uncertainty. He tossed the second box aside and grabbed for a third. He dug his hand in blindly, clawing at the bottom and sides of the cardboard with his fingers, searching desperately for the plastic device. And finally, he found it.

Darren raced around the back of the SUV to the passenger's side door, where Rita's face had turned purple. She snatched the inhaler from his fingers, her eyes wide with panic as she jammed the device between her sweating lips and pressed down on the pump.

The effect was immediate. She took a second pump and slowly her breathing returned to normal. Darren placed a hand behind her head and gently stroked her hair. She felt hot and damp.

"You all right, baby?" Darren asked. Rita's head bobbed slowly, her eyes glassy from tears of exertion and fear. She slumped forward against her husband's chest and sobbed.

"I can't take it anymore," Rita said between breaths. "It's too much. Too much."

"We're gonna be ok," Darren said, finding it difficult to muster the confidence. He was starved of hope, a useless consoler. Here they were, on some lonely highway, sitting on the shoulder of the road in pitch black. It was 10:00 AM and the sun still wasn't out. It was enough to drive a man mad, Darren thought uneasily.

He pulled out his AAA highway map from the glove compartment and found their location after a few minutes of careful study. He hadn't used a paper map in years. He'd taken so much for granted about his normal life, simple things like sunlight, running water, Wi-Fi. And now none of it was left. No way to call for a tow if the car broke down out here. It was only him and Rita and an eternal black road slithering aimlessly through an endless night.

"What are we going to do?" Rita said softly, her voice trembling.

"We just take it one step at a time, until we reach New Orleans."

"New Orleans… Darren… We'll never make it."

"Can't talk like that, baby. Just gotta keep positive. We'll get there, and when we do the others will be waiting for us. Peter and Rachel, Marcus and Vivian, they'll all be there. We just gotta stay focused. We can do this."

"And then what? So what if we find them? We'll have to live in some camp with who knows how many other people. It won't be our home, Darren. It won't be our life. And what happens when my medicine runs out?" Rita asked, wiping tears away with the back of her sleeve.

"All that is gone now, Rita. The house, the stuff. That old life is history. We just have to keep looking ahead. Keep our eyes on the prize, right?"

"What prize?"

"I'm talking about the future, Rita. Beyond the camps, beyond the great tribulation. We're so close, babe. We gotta, you know, see with eyes of faith!"

Rita cast her husband a derisive look before turning to gaze out the windshield into the darkness. "I just want my old life back."

CHAPTER 14

Thiago helped himself to a second plate of roasted chicken and mashed potatoes and returned to his spot at the cafeteria table. His time aboard Rig 7 had been surreal. First, his incredible luck at being introduced to one of the men he'd been sent to find, and no sooner than he'd touched down on the rig's deck: Ted Watkins. He was a large man with a muscular build, but Thiago had been trained to size up his targets from a quick glance; he wasn't intimidated. For all his size, Ted wasn't a fighter. Thiago had felt it when he'd first shaken his hand, had sensed it in the way Ted's feet were placed–unbalanced, too close together. He had no sense of his center of gravity; he had no anticipation of being attacked. He would not pose a challenge.

As for his other mark, a man just a few years older than Ted named Peter Burton, Thiago had yet to make visual contact. He was aboard this vessel somewhere–he'd gathered as much from his nonchalant conversations with some of the crew. Perhaps he was one of the higher-ups in the organization, possibly even with trained bodyguards. It would make things more difficult, but not impossible. Thiago had seen it all.

If anything here aboard Rig 7 was posing a real challenge, it was simply keeping up appearances. As word spread aboard the rig, Thiago could feel his presence drawing more and more attention. Posing as an angel–still such a ludicrous idea, he thought–had been a means to an end, and a successful one at that, but it had not been without its consequences. Thiago only hoped that it would not jeopardize his mission too much.

Of course, taking out the two men was only half of the job he'd been contracted for. The other half, and perhaps the more difficult part, would be the extraction of the woman and child. He had their names and their faces burned indelibly in his mind, but locating and securing them would only be the first step. Getting them off of the rig would be the real challenge.

"Mind if I join?" said a voice from over Thiago's shoulder. *Speak of the devil*, he thought. Right before his eyes stood all six feet four inches of Mr. Ted Watkins.

"Not at all, Ted," Thiago said, smile beaming.

"Wow, good memory. You must've met like forty brothers right after stepping off that lift. But then, I guess I shouldn't be all that surprised, right?" Ted said, chuckling nervously as he rubbed his hands together. "I was kind of curious about the conditions aboard the other boats. You were on the *Valiant Alhambra,* I heard?"

"Conditions?" Thiago asked, careful with each word.

"Yeah. I mean, are they doing ok on supplies and everything?"

"Supplies are holding out. Conditions are much as you would expect, really."

"Well, I only ask because of the news we got the other day. You know, about the blackouts."

Thiago had no idea what the man was referring to but was careful to maintain his expression. If he waited, the information would reveal itself.

"I mean, since the blackouts, they said that the shipments coming in from the mainland to the ships are going to decrease a lot, so we're gonna be rationing everything. I was told this'll be the last meal like this. We really have to rein everything in from here on out to make sure supplies last. I was just wondering if the tankers are doing something similar."

So the blackouts were happening on land, not aboard the ships, Thiago thought.

"I'm sure, whatever happens, that everyone will be taken care of," Thiago said calmly. It seemed to be the right answer; the tension in Ted's expression seemed to lessen by a degree. But Thiago needed more information. How extensive were these blackouts? And how bad could they possibly be that shipments from the mainland were being interrupted?

"These blackouts you mentioned. When did you brothers first receive news of them?" Thiago asked.

"Just yesterday. We stopped getting broadcasts from the branch before that, though. Finally found out that it was all linked to that solar flare that took out everything: electrical, phones, internet. They say things are totally falling apart back home. But I guess you probably knew all that, huh?"

Thiago merely nodded again, but found that it was much more of a struggle to continue smiling now. Phones were down too? And the internet? Now how was he ever supposed to leave this rig? Or get in contact with his client, for that matter. It had been nearly a week since the two had been in contact.

"Anyways," Ted continued uncomfortably, "if there's anything that you need help with while you're with us, I'd be happy to lend a hand if I can. Just let me know."

Thiago thanked him. "Actually, come to think of it, there is something I could use your help with," he said suddenly.

"Sure. You name it."

"I have a message to deliver to a sister aboard this rig."

"A message. Wow. Ok," Ted said, leaning forward with an intent look.

"Perhaps you can help me deliver it to her."

"Absolutely. I can check the database and have her meet you. What's the name?" Ted asked, already removing a small spiral notebook from the inner pocket of his jacket.

"Angelica," Thiago said. "Angelica Parry."

Ted's expression froze, his pen still poised above the paper, as he slowly looked up. "You're looking for Angelica?"

"Yes. I'd like to speak with her and her son."

***

Peter sat behind his laptop at the tiny apartment's desk, looking over the latest information from the branch. Along with news from the mainland, the courier had arrived with a thumb drive packed with instructions, diagrams, manuals, and letters from the branch to be distributed to each of the departments. Most of the information concerned their destination in Namibia, which they were scheduled to arrive at in another seven weeks. It was a long time to be at sea for Peter, a man who'd scarcely set foot aboard any kind of boat prior to New Orleans, but he suspected the time would fly by all the same.

Between his tasks aboard the rig, shepherding those under his care, preparing for and attending the weekly meetings, keeping up with his personal study, and cramming all of this information into his head, he doubted there'd be any time for boredom. Jehovah had always kept his people busy, and though the work in front of him was like nothing he'd handled as a congregation secretary or coordinator, it was no less demanding or important. But Peter was thankful for it. Busy was good. Busy with spiritual things was great. It left little time for fear or complacency.

Peter turned as a knock on his door caught his attention. He opened it to find Ted standing there, filling up the entire doorway with an odd expression on his face.

"What's on your mind?" Peter asked as the two men took seats around the table. Peter poured Ted a cup of coffee from a small French press.

"A strange thing happened this afternoon."

"Which strange thing are you referring to?" Peter asked, chuckling. "I can think of a few."

"You heard about the guy who arrived from the supply boat? James?"

Peter nodded slowly as he sipped his tepid coffee. "I've heard."

"What do you think? You think he's the real deal?"

"You mean do I think he's really an angel?"

"Well... Yeah."

"I guess it sounds a little odd, but who knows? All sorts of things are happening these days. I guess it's to be expected, given how close we are to the end."

Ted stood from his chair to look out the apartment's window. It faced another block of apartments: hundreds of colorful, stacked containers. "I thought that too. I mean, there's precedent. An angel led the Israelites out of Egypt, another angel rescued Paul and Silas from prison. It could happen, right?"

"I wouldn't rule out the possibility, sure."

"So what would you say is the consensus among the other overseers about whether or not he is who he claims to be?"

"I wouldn't know. I've only heard a couple of brothers mention him in passing. To be perfectly honest, the overseers have bigger things on their plates right now. There's the blackout, which has people scrambling, and of course we need to start rationing everything. Some guy showing up and claiming to be an angel... I mean it's *strange* but... It's also *possible*. Then again, he could just be some emotionally unstable brother who's cracking under the pressure. Or who knows, maybe he was always like this." Peter shrugged.

"So far as I know, he isn't affiliated with a congregation. Word is he showed up out of the blue. That supply boat that dropped him off said he just appeared one morning. Like, out of thin air. And he's only got the one name, *James*."

"Like I said, it's possible," Peter said. "Why are you asking about it, though? Is there a problem?"

"I met him," Ted said.

"Oh?"

"I was on deck when his boat arrived. He requested to be transferred to this rig, you know."

"And? What's he like?"

"He's tall, muscular build, dark hair. No outstanding features, really. Hard to tell his age or his ethnicity. Very mysterious looking."

"Why did he request this rig?"

"He wants to meet Angelica and Evan."

Peter frowned. "*Our* Angelica and Evan?"

"Yeah."

"Did he say why?"

"Didn't give specifics. Just that he had a message for them. He wouldn't say what."

Peter leaned back in his chair and stared up at the ceiling.

"What did you tell him?"

"I said I'd do it."

"I wouldn't let them meet alone."

"Of course. I was going to set up their meeting in the cafeteria and be nearby, just in case."

"Seems wise."

"I just keep thinking, you know... Maybe Chad is behind this."

"Angelica's ex?"

Ted turned from the window and sat back down. Peter noted how his hands trembled slightly. "Am I being paranoid, Pete? Am I? Is it crazy to think that Chad would be capable of something like this?"

"Chad's got friends in high places, Ted, but I'm not sure he has the power to summon an angel."

"I'm serious, man. I just keep thinking about that day, back at Angelica's place. That look he had in his eyes. He had a gun, Pete. He was fully prepared to do something awful. If we hadn't been there to stop him, I don't–" Ted's head dropped a few degrees as he sucked in his lower lip and shut his eyes. He took a few deep breaths until he'd collected himself. "If anything had happened to her or Evan that day, I wouldn't have been able to forgive myself. I know this."

"Ted," Peter said gently, laying a hand on the younger elder's shoulder. "All that is behind us now. You gotta stop dredging up the past. Nothing happened that day. You did the right thing. We got them out of there in time. They're both here, safe with us. Chad can't get them here. Besides just the logistical challenges of him actually tracking us down out here and boarding this rig–which are insurmountable to say the least–you have to remember we've got Jehovah's protection. He wouldn't lead us all the way out here and then deliver us into our enemy's hands."

"You can't know that for certain, Pete. Even the Israelites faced challenges after leaving Egypt."

"Well, sure, but so long as they were obedient, they had Jehovah's protection. And we've been obedient. We've done

185

everything that's been asked of us, from those first letters about simplifying our lives down to the most recent news about rationing supplies here in the convoy. We are doing our best. Jehovah wouldn't remove his protection under these circumstances."

"You're right. I mean, I *know* all this. I just needed to hear it from you."

"Look, Ted, I know how you feel about Angelica."

"You... Wait, what? What do you mean?"

"C'mon, Ted, really? You thought I didn't know you had feelings for her?"

"I... I was being *careful*, Pete. I didn't want anyone to take it the wrong way, you know? Aw man, you don't think it's that obvious, do you? Does Rachel know?"

Peter chuckled with a shake of his head. "Oh, Ted. You've been crushing on her like a kid in middle school."

"Seriously?" Ted asked, incredulous, though a smile had crept onto his face.

"It's ok, Ted. There's nothing wrong with it. She's scripturally and legally free to remarry, and you two seem to hit it off well. Plus, Evan obviously loves you to death."

"I love that kid too. Well, both of them really. I mean, not love, you know, that's a little strong of a word this early on and all but–" Peter cut him of with a gentle pat on his shoulder.

"Just take it slow, all right? She's coming out of a very difficult and abusive relationship. She's a very strong sister, but that doesn't mean she isn't fragile. Take your time, get to know her. And be frank about your intentions when you're ready. I mean, she probably already knows you have feelings for her, but you know, just be honest."

"Thanks, Pete. Great advice, really. I should've come to you sooner, it's just that with everything going on and all..."

"I get it. It's a weird time to date, but we're only humans. We're stuck together now and we're going through the most turbulent time in human history. Romance is bound to happen. I'm sure similar things are unfolding all over, in convoys around the world."

"You think so?"

"I do."

"Ok. Ok. Thanks again, Peter. I… I feel much better. I'm gonna go find her now, tell her about James wanting to meet."

"Sounds good."

Ted got up from the table, a new spring in his step as he crossed the room in two paces and reached for the door.

"Oh and Ted," Peter said as his friend exited.

"Yeah?"

"If you and Angelica do start, you know… *dating…* Rachel and I are here for you. Ok? As chaperones, confidants, whatever. We're here to help."

The smile widened on Ted's face as he wrapped his large arms around Peter Burton in a sudden bear hug. "Thanks, man," he said before disappearing down the corridor.

***

They spent a day on the calm, black waters of Seattle Bay. The air was still and windless, forcing Stacy to rely on the outboard motor to gently propel them through the waters. Joyce sat beside her at the stern, watching as Stacy tugged at the tiller, guiding them beyond the sparsely lit harbor and into near total blackness.

"Man, it's like having your eyes shut. It's just… *black,*" Stacy said through gritted teeth. Joyce looked up at the starless, moonless sky. Were it not for the fresh sea air and low temperature, she could just as well be in a sealed, windowless basement. It almost made her claustrophobic.

"This is bad," Stacy said, her voice dancing on a thin wire.

"What is?"

"These conditions. No wind, total lack of light. You could get stranded out here and never make it back to shore. I don't like this at all."

"Stranded? But the land is just that way, isn't it?" Joyce said, motioning towards what she believed to be East. She felt a tug on her sleeve and looked up to see Stacy's face glowing dimly in the low light of the electric lantern they'd set on the deck. Stacy tapped a fingernail against a small glass dome beside the tiller. It was a small compass. Joyce lifted the lantern to get a closer look.

"That's not possible. We've been heading North this whole time," she said.

"You can't rely on your senses out here, Joyce. They'll play tricks on you. Without the sun, without any visible landmarks to go by, or a working GPS, you could literally get lost less than a mile out. These waters are a deathtrap."

Joyce said nothing.

"And then there's the gas issue. We don't have enough to get us all the way to Vancouver. We'd need a strong southerly wind to get us there. It's like the doldrums out here."

"So what do we do?" Joyce asked without looking at the other woman. Her eyes were glued to the softly rippling lines of foam that bobbed from beneath them. It was the only thing visible beyond the boat.

"Nothing. We wait. We get as close as we can to land and we just sit tight until something changes."

Joyce raised her eyes to gaze into the distance. It was impossible to perceive depth out here. To perceive anything, really. She tried squinting. She tried lifting the lantern high into the air with one arm. But it was hopeless. The darkness enveloped them. Just blackness and blackness as far as the eye could see. Joyce craned her neck, taking in the surroundings, studying them for any irregularities, and that's when she saw it. The tiniest flicker of light.

"Stacy!" Joyce hissed.

"What?"

"Look, there. Do you see it?"

"Just wait for it... There! It's like a speck of light. It's flashing."

"I don't see anything... Oh wait. Yeah, you're right. There's something out there."

"What is it?"

"No idea. Let's find out," Stacy said, adjusting the angle of the rudder slightly to change course.

"Maybe it's another boat out here. Maybe they know how to navigate in the dark?" Joyce said hopefully.

"It's possible," Stacy said, allowing some optimism to ebb into her voice. The speck of light grew larger and larger, flashing in regular intervals four or five seconds apart. As their vessel neared, the light began to take shape. It spread out horizontally and gradually illuminated the outline of a speedboat. It wasn't large, perhaps only sixteen feet long, and it sat much lower on the water, but it didn't appear damaged.

"Abandoned?" Joyce asked as they pulled alongside the craft.

"Yeah, looks like it," Stacy answered. She killed the engine and let their sailboat glide up to the smaller craft. Stacy extended a telescoping gaff hook, snagging one of the speedboat's unicleats. She pulled the boat closer and held the lantern up to glimpse inside the boat.

"Well, good news is there's no dead bodies."

"Ugh, not funny," Joyce scoffed.

"Wasn't trying to be."

"It's spooky, the way it's just sitting out here all by itself like this."

"Maybe a larger vessel came along and the guy abandoned ship. Doesn't really matter much either way. What does matter is if there's any gas in the tank."

"Why?" Joyce asked.

"Well, if there is, we can siphon it. Every little bit helps. Grab me one of the gasoline containers from the cabin, would you? I'm gonna hop over to check it out. Might even be some food and water aboard. Wouldn't *that* be nice?"

"Wait, you're just going to steal it?"

Stacy paused to turn around and look at Joyce in the eyes. "Really, Joyce? We're stuck out here fending for our lives and you're worried about that? Whoever owned this thing just left it, Joyce. He isn't coming back. It's finders keepers. I'm sure my truck will get the same treatment. I didn't even lock it. Why bother?"

189

"Still, Stacy. It seems… wrong."

Stacy took a deep breath and shook her head in frustration as she leaped down into the speedboat. Joyce fought with her feelings for another moment or two before retreating to the cabin to fetch the plastic gas container.

"Joyce!" she heard Stacy call. "Grab a hose, too. There's a rubber one in a cabinet above the lavatory."

Joyce noisily fumbled her way through the cabin until she'd located the items. She exited to find Stacy smiling, her face lit from below by the lantern.

"We caught a break," she said. "Almost a full tank."

Joyce handed her the hose and the container and sat on the bench, watching as Stacy siphoned gas from the speedboat's outboard motor. Stacy had nearly finished when she glanced up at Joyce and froze. Behind her friend stool the tall, dark figure of a man. Stacy screamed.

Joyce's head whipped around, sending her tumbling backwards onto the bench. The figure stood motionless, the glinting blade of a knife held in one hand.

"Who are you?" the man asked in a low, even voice that sent shivers up the women's spines. Joyce was unable to respond. It was as if the air in her lungs had frozen. The man stepped forward, his features coming into focus as the lantern light found him. His blade winked. Except for his face, every inch of his body was covered by a black wetsuit. "I repeat, *who are you?*"

"I–I–I'm sorry," Stacy stammered. "We were just passing through–we saw the boat–we thought it was abandoned."

"It's not abandoned," the man said flatly.

"It's yours?" Stacy asked. The container at her feet was still filling with siphoned gas from the speedboat's outboard.

"Of course it's mine."

"We're sorry. We're so, so sorry," Joyce said, turning to glare at Stacy. "We didn't know. We honestly thought it was abandoned. We're not thieves."

"Then return my gas," the diver said. He raised his knife and pointed the tip at Stacy. She nodded and quickly reversed the flow of fuel back to the speedboat's engine. Standing on one leg, the diver peeled off his flippers and tossed them down into his boat. Joyce looked him over cautiously. He was tall and thin, built like a swimmer, but didn't appear young. A wiry beard of grey bristles poked out from behind the chin line of his wetsuit.

"Why are you out here diving in the dark?" Joyce asked, her curiosity getting the better of her.

"Not your concern," said the man gruffly. He glowered quietly at the two women. When Stacy had finished returning the gas back to the tank, she handed Joyce the container and climbed back aboard her sailboat. The diver reached out and snatched the container from Joyce's hands.

"You must be some kind of crazy," he said, shaking the container and hearing the fuel slosh around inside. "I'm standing here with a knife and you're still trying to steal my gas."

"That gas was in the container already! I was just trying to top it off!" Stacy protested.

"You're lucky I'm a better man than most of the other crazies out here tonight or I'd be taking a lot more than this," snapped the diver, holding up the container. He leapt down from Stacy's sailboat into his speedboat.

"Hey! That's our fuel!" Stacy screamed.

"Now you know the feeling," said the man. He cranked the engine, flipped on a set of deck lights, and sped off into the blackness.

***

Martin wasn't going to last long, of that Chad was certain. They'd only been down here for what—48 hours? And already Chad could see it in the way Martin's eyes shifted from point to point, always looking but not quite seeing, doing without thinking. He saw it in the way Martin fiddled nervously with the radio dials, trying to hone in on a signal but losing it as soon as he'd found it. He was stubbing his toes on the furniture and constantly adjusting the temperature. His mind was coming unglued.

Not that any of this was surprising. Chad had known for a

191

long time that Martin didn't function well under pressure. It had always been this way. Back in their college days, when they'd pitched their first software project to a board of investors in San Francisco, Martin had spent half of the time puking his guts out in the bathroom. Chad had covered for him–he knew Martin's lines and picked up the slack just fine–but Martin's behavior hadn't inspired confidence in the board and had almost cost them a $2 million grant. That basic scenario had repeated itself over the years, so that eventually Chad found himself in the hot seat nearly 100% of the time. Martin was a behind-the-scenes guy. He kept the gears running, and Chad kept him from the high-pressure situations. Chad was Jobs, Martin was Wozniak. It worked.

But what had worked for years as professional symbiosis was now showing signs of trouble. Here they were, stuck three meters below Martin's backyard. The only barrier between them and absolute chaos was a layer of dirt and concrete. Chad could no longer be Martin's protector. And even if he could, would he want to? It was time Martin grew up and faced the world the way it really was, wasn't it? Chad mulled this over as he swigged his warm beer and watched Martin scribble something madly in a notebook as he sat in the metal Faraday box.

A little cuckoo in his cage, Chad thought.

"Martin, give it a rest. The airwaves are empty," Chad said, surprised to feel this buzzed after just a couple of beers. Probably the empty stomach, he thought.

"No way," Martin mumbled from his cage. "No way no one is broadcasting out here. I was just down here last week–there were like forty different guys chatting it up. *No way* they're all gone."

Chad smiled, shook his head, and looked up at the ceiling. "You need some fresh air, dude."

"Yeah, right," Martin scoffed.

"I'm serious." Chad got up from the sofa and wandered over to the radio room. He leaned in. "We should see how things are out there, get a lay of the land. See if we can scrounge up some more supplies."

"But we've got plenty down here–enough to last months. You said yourself–"

"And then what? What if we're down here longer than two months?"

Martin's face went blank, Chad saw only desperation in his eyes. "Look, I'm not saying we will be, but we have to act now, while there are still things to salvage out there. If it gets better, great. But if not, we'll be prepared to last a little longer."

"You're talking about looting," Martin said quietly, gaze lowering.

"I'm talking about going through every room of *your* house and taking what we can use down here. We start there."

"I don't think I can," Martin said.

"Why not?"

"I can still see that man's face. The one you shot. It just keeps replaying in my head like an endless loop. I don't think I can ever go in there again."

Geez, Chad thought. "Martin," he said, grabbing his friend by the shoulders to face him. "You can't spend the rest of your life down here. Sooner or later, we're gonna need to go out there, so you'd better get used to the idea. Now I told you, the body is taken care of. You won't ever see it again. But I need your help now, you got it?"

Martin took a deep breath and slowly nodded. The two men geared up as best they could. They loaded handguns, strapped them to waist holsters, and shouldered a couple of empty backpacks.

"Fifteen minutes, ok?" Chad said to Martin. "We're only out there fifteen minutes. We stick together. First the kitchen, then the pantry, then the bathrooms. We'll hit the bedrooms another time, you got it?"

Martin nodded again, and the two crept up the bunker staircase and opened the door.

It was the smell that they noticed first. A heavy, acrid miasma that stung their nostrils and lungs. It was the smell of fire–burning homes, charred metal, melting tires, oil. The second thing was the darkness. It seemed to consume all but the hazy fields of the orange, flickering light of distant fires.

"What is this?" Martin asked in disbelief as he surveyed the destruction in the valley.

"Fifteen minutes. Keep moving," Chad ordered. The two men quickly shut the bunker door behind them and trudged up the walkway towards the rear entrance of Martin's house. Chad unclipped a flashlight from his backpack and shone it through one of the rear windows. It seemed to have trouble piercing the darkness. The beam just barely illuminated whatever it touched.

"Well, the good news is that there aren't any lights on in there," Chad said.

"That's good news?"

"It means no one's decided to camp out inside your house. That wouldn't be a friendly meeting."

"Sure," Martin said, his voice cracking. He fumbled through his pockets and produced a key to the back door. They let themselves in. The air was much cleaner in the house but still carried a strange scent.

"Kitchen first," Chad reminded. The two men went through drawers and cabinets, taking whatever was edible or drinkable. Chad opened the refrigerator, but the smell made it clear that there was nothing salvageable inside. After five minutes, their packs were already filled to the brim.

"You got any wheeled luggage here?" Chad asked, discovering a cabinet stocked with cereals.

"Yeah, a few. Up in my bedroom."

"Go grab 'em," Chad said. Martin nodded, jogging around the countertop and heading for the stairs. Chad heard his sneakers squeal on the tile floor as he slipped and crashed into a wall.

"You all right?" Chad called out. There was no answer. Chad walked from the kitchen, holding the beam of his flashlight out in front of him. "Martin? You ok?" Chad called out a second time. Silence. Chad swallowed hard, felt his pace quicken. He quietly slipped the gun from the holster at his side as he made his way to the stairwell. He clicked off the flashlight. If someone was waiting for him, the beam would be a dead giveaway. His heart pounded. He stepped silently towards the stairs, one foot at a time. And stopped.

The toe of his shoe had bumped into something on the floor. He wanted to scream. He could feel it clawing up from his throat like a wild animal. *Focus*, he told himself. *Focus*. He knelt slowly on the tile, keeping his gun straight in front of him with one hand while the other explored the object on the floor. It was a leg. A trembling leg.

Chad bit his tongue hard, felt himself bleed from the bite. He heard something. A soft, gasping noise. Chad flicked his light back on. It was Martin. His lips were quivering, eyes wide and wet with fear. He was lying flat on the floor, his hands held in front of his face, covered in blood.

"Martin," Chad said quietly. Martin was unable to respond.

"Martin," Chad repeated. "That's not your blood. You're ok. You just slipped and fell."

Martin's eyes lolled in their sockets, finding Chad's face. They welled with tears.

"You're fine, Martin, do you understand?"

"It's *his* blood," Martin said, his voice a coarse whisper. "The man."

"Get up," Chad said. But Martin wouldn't move. It was as if his limbs had locked. "I said *get up*, Martin."

"*His* blood," Martin repeated.

"Fine. You just keep laying there. I'm leaving," Chad said. He rose and turned back to the kitchen, where he shouldered his bag and headed for the rear entrance of the house.

"Chad! Don't leave me here!" Martin screamed.

"Then get up and *walk!*" Chad screamed back.

"Please! Chad! Please!" Martin said, struggling to scream between sobs. The noises caught in his throat like jagged splinters. Chad heard him scrambling to get up, wet palms pawing the tile and clawing at the walls. *Like a baby learning to walk. I'm a babysitter*, Chad thought.

"I can't see anything! Please! Chad!"

Chad paused, his hand resting on the doorknob. He had never felt such overwhelming contempt, such utter disgust in all the years he'd known Martin. Chad flicked off the flashlight in his hand and turned to face Martin, who struggled in the darkness of his own home. Could he really be so inept, so incapable of handling crisis? Chad took a deep, silent breath, his eyes honed in on Martin's location. He could see nothing, and yet in his mind he could picture it in perfect detail: Martin's skin and clothing smeared in drying blood, the desperate look on his red, tear-streaked face, his eyes wide and dilated from the panic and the dark. He could hear him whimpering. Like a dog.

"Chad? Are you still here? Chad? Hey!" Martin begged, his sneakers squeaking in small, shuffling steps towards the door where Chad stood. He stumbled into a chair, toppled it. Chad heard Martin's knees and palms hit the floor with a smack, heard him crawling on all fours, sweeping the ground with his fingers, trying to find the door.

Chad let his hand crawl across his body like a spider. He felt his hand find the cold steel of the firearm in its holster. He felt the thoughts go through his mind. The wild ones. The ones that had been there just a few weeks back, when he'd sat in his Mercedes outside of Angelica's condo mustering up the nerve. It'd taken so much liquid courage then… But now… Everything was clear. It only made sense. This was no longer Martin's world. Chad ran his fingers along the stock, pressed the edges of his nails into the grooves, felt the screws inset perfectly into the gun. Such an efficient little machine, perfectly designed for its job. *If only everyone were so necessary.*

Chad felt Martin's fingers brush against the top of his shoe and stop, feeling the laces and pulling away.

"Chad! You're still here. Why's the light off?! My god, you scared me, man!" Martin exclaimed, barely able to contain his relief. He stood, brushed himself off, and the two exited the house and trudged back down the path to the bunker.

CHAPTER 15

Angelica Parry strolled down the labyrinthine corridors of Rig 7 as Ted led the way. He'd done his best to explain things: she was meeting a man who claimed to be an angel–no, he wasn't joking–and she was to bring Evan along. No, he had no idea what any of this was about or how long it would take. In the end, Angelica shrugged and agreed on a time to meet the man: James, if she was remembering correctly.

Still, there'd been something odd in the way that Ted had brought it up with her. He hadn't been himself. His carefree smile had been missing; he hadn't joked around with Evan as usual. Even his body was rigid and anxious, as if there were something he wasn't telling her. Angelica thought that Ted looked a bit like he had the day Peter and he and rescued them from her home. That same tense caution. Ted the guardian.

A smile came to Angelica's lips. It was weird, to be smiling with the recollection of that memory, the day she'd almost lost her life, but it was also the day that she knew for sure. About Ted. She'd always suspected something, but that was the day she *knew*. She'd felt it in the way his large, strong hands had gently scooped her up from the floor of her bedroom, the way his dark, warm eyes had looked into hers. The way he'd protected her without a second thought when Chad had shown up with that gun.

She *knew*. But this wasn't the time, she kept telling herself. Under any other circumstances, yes, but not now. Not while their lives were in limbo aboard some floating city on it's way to… to… *Africa*, of all places. She knew Ted cared for her, and she felt the same–more than he knew, more than she'd let on–but it had to wait. More than anything, she needed stability. She'd ached for it for years, since the early years of her marriage to Chad, when she felt him slipping away from her. She'd craved the stability so much that she'd even forgiven Chad for the unthinkable. Not once, not twice, but many times. She'd forgiven until she could forgive no more. But then there'd been the last straw, and she'd left, and the instability had only worsened.

At least now the fear was gone. The fear of Chad showing up from some shadow of her life to suck her back into the vacuum of his control, to play with her mind and feelings the way he played with his games. No more terrors in the night, no more double checking and triple checking the windows and the locks before bed, no more wondering if that creaking floorboard was actually *him*, sneaking back into their lives to wreak more havoc. She could breathe. It might be the *great* tribulation, but as far as she was concerned, *her* tribulation was finally over.

"He's in here," Ted said, glancing back at Angelica as they pushed through the double doors and into the cafeteria. She looked down at her son Evan, by her side, and smiled.

A tall, dark man stood from a cafeteria table at the edge of the room and opened his hands with a broad smile. "Hello," he said warmly. "My name is James."

"Hi, James. I'm Angelica. This is Evan." The three shook hands and sat. Ted joined them. James gave him a look, and then seemed not to notice him again.

"I trust you are both finding it comfortable here, hm?" James said, smile beaming.

"Sure," Angelica said. "It's fine. The apartment's good. Food's good. Our friends are here."

"That's great," James said. He paused to pour them glasses of water. He took a sip and continued smiling.

"So… Ted said that you wanted to talk to us?" Angelica pressed.

"That is correct," James said.

"About what?"

"Actually, I was hoping this conversation would be a private one, between the three of us, as it concerns your family,"

James said, glancing at Ted. Ted eyed James for a minute and then glanced at Angelica. She nodded. Ted stood and walked to the other end of the cafeteria, where he made himself coffee and sat.

"Family?" Angelica asked. "I don't really have any."

"Well, that's not exactly true now, is it?" James said, still smiling.

"Um. I'm not really sure what you're getting at."

"I'm talking about Chad."

Angelica froze. It was as if her blood had turned to ice. She could feel it crystallizing in her veins and arteries. Goosebumps prickled her skin.

"Chad? How do you know about Chad?" she said.

"Oh, Angelica. It's my job to know these things."

Angelica glanced at her side, where Evan was frowning at the floor. This was not good for him. This was not good for any of them.

"I just don't understand. What could you possibly want to talk to me about my ex-husband? And why would you do this here, in front of my son? Do you have any idea what we've been through?" Angelica said. The ice had become fire.

"I *do* know. But I also know that God values *forgiveness*," Thiago said. His hands reached across the table and touched Angelica's hands. She pulled away.

"I still don't get it. What are you trying to tell me?" she demanded.

"Chad still loves you, my daughter."

"Loves me? Do you realize that he tried to kill me and my son? That he literally came into my house with a loaded gun and tried to *murder* us? If it hadn't been for Ted and Peter, I'd be *dead* right now!" she hissed. James merely frowned. He tilted his head and nodded.

"All right," he said finally. "I can't force you. I just want you to know what God wants." James smiled once more, nodded again, and left. Angelica was speechless. Her mouth stayed open as she shook her head in disbelief. Ted was immediately at her side.

"What happened?" he asked.

"I… I… I don't even know. It was weird."

"Well, what did he say?" Ted demanded.

"He… He wanted me to forgive my ex."

"Chad?"

"Yeah."

"He knew about Chad? He actually said your ex's name?"

"Oh, he knew about my ex. He knew *everything*."

Ted turned to look for James, but he was nowhere to be found.

***

It had been a long shot, but still worth a try, Thiago thought as he jogged away from the cafeteria. It would've made things much easier, had Angelica and the boy been willing to simply leave with him of their own accord. Wishful thinking perhaps, but at least he now knew for sure. Now there was only one option left: force.

He would have to sedate them, get them on a boat, and deliver them to the mainland, and then to Chad. Before leaving, of course, he'd need to finish the other job, but one for which he had developed a concrete plan. He now knew for sure who Ted and Peter were. He'd spent the previous day bringing their names up in conversation and gathering all of the intel he needed. He knew their daily schedules and what part of the rig they lived in. He even knew where and when they ate their meals. It wouldn't be a difficult thing. Sure, there'd been hiccups along the way, but the end was in sight and he just needed to persevere a bit longer. It would all come together. It always did.

If your God was real, he would've stopped me long ago, Thiago thought, grinning to himself. He could almost smell the money. This had been a high-paying job, and after its completion, he was sure there would be more. Thiago hadn't failed. Not once. He was too skilled, too smart, too good at what he did. A man with a million faces, even that of an *angel's*, he thought with another smile. It was a story he couldn't wait to tell. *Thiago the*

Angel.

He let himself into the small cabin he'd been temporarily assigned on the rig. He packed the clothes that had been given him–these people were *far* too trusting, *far* too naive–in a duffel bag and quickly left the room. Angelica had been upset when they talked, a reaction he'd somewhat anticipated, and she'd tell others, and they'd come looking for him. And when they did, he'd be gone, hidden away in some other part of the rig, planning his next move.

Thiago left the room and got as far away from it as he could. He'd need to hide out for a little while. He'd need supplies, and he'd need access to certain items that would only be found in a medical ward. And since he'd done his homework, he knew exactly where one was located. It took him only ten minutes to get there.

He entered the infirmary with a feigned limp and a strained look on his face. "Hey doc, a little help here?" he said, leaning against the doorframe as if he might collapse from the pain. A couple of nurses spotted him and instantly ran over, guiding him to a padded bench.

"What happened to your leg?" one of them asked, rolling up his pant leg.

"I think I sprained it again. Old basketball injury. I was going down the stairs and it just popped. It's killing me, doc."

The nurse carefully removed the sock. Thiago gripped the seat with clenched knuckles and grit his teeth.

"Seems like a pretty sharp pain for a sprain. It might be broken."

"Nah, it's not broken, just a bad sprain. Bad ankle. Been like this for years."

"All right, all right. Dorothy, bring him some ibuprofen, would you?" one of the nurses called out. Thiago heard rapid footsteps in the background.

"Thanks, doc. Really appreciate it," Thiago said, wiping sweat from his face.

"Not a problem. I'm not a doctor though, just a nurse."

"Oh, right. Ok. Well, you *should* be a doctor. You're very

201

good," Thiago said, watching carefully as the girl blushed. Another woman appeared with a blister pack of pills. Thiago immediately took them from her hand and pinched one into his mouth. He shoved the remainder into his pocket before the nurses could stop him and moved his foot slightly, bumping against the bench. He pressed his eyes together again and reeled with pain.

"Sorry, sorry," he said. "This stupid ankle does this a lot. It sprains easy when the weather is cold."

"Doesn't look like it's swelling, though," the nurse said, looking at the foot but careful not to touch it.

"No, never swells. Weird, right?"

"That is weird."

"Actually, you know the funny thing is that I was on my way here for someone else, and that's when I twisted my ankle."

"Here for someone else?"

"Yeah. A sister in my congregation asked me to get her some cold medicine. Have anything like that here?"

"Well sure, we've got the usual stuff, like decongestants. Is that what you're talking about?"

"Yeah, maybe something like that, something that'll help her sleep?"

The nurse nodded and left the room for a moment, returning with an off-brand bottle of green cough syrup. The nurse gave Thiago directions on how to take it. He listened intently, nodding where appropriate. He sat for another fifteen minutes, chatting amicably with the nurses, before standing gingerly on his foot. He took a few steps, the limp less pronounced, then managed a courageous smile.

"You sure you're all right to leave?" one of the nurses asked.

"Yeah, like I say, this happens all the time. Just need to rest it a while, pop some Advil, then I'm good to go. I'd love to stay and chat, but I've got a busy day ahead." Thiago took another few moments, pretending to test his weight on the ankle. Then he thanked the nurses and hobbled out the door.

***

The idea was to just keep going down. Down past the residence blocks, down past the maintenance levels, as far down as the stairwells and catwalks could take him before he hit the ocean. The space he finally found was not a luxurious one–no comparison to the cabin aboard the supply boat and the apartment "pod" they'd put him up in the last few days here–but it would suffice. It was out of the way and afforded him enough space to work, and that was all that mattered.

Thiago pushed his way into the supply closet and locked the door behind him. The only source of light was a dim bulb that hung from wire in the center of the ceiling. It drifted from side to side with the movement of the rig, a movement so slight that Thiago's feet barely detected it anymore.

Thiago pulled the tools he'd pilfered from various parts of the rig from his bag and laid them atop one of the shelves: a metal spoon, a bottle of water, a lighter, a glass cup, the medicine from the medical ward, and a bottle of floor cleaner. This was all he needed, he thought with a sense of smugness. For the next two hours, this would become his lab. He had entered with a seemingly random assortment of items, but would emerge with a potent chemical cocktail strong enough to stop a man's heart or cause liver failure, whichever came first.

Thiago hummed softly to himself as he carefully disassembled the ibuprofen capsules, deposited the powdered medicine into the spoon, and placed the emptied capsules on a dry paper napkin. He mixed the powder with a capful of cough syrup and dissolved the concoction over the open flame of the lighter. The floor cleaner was the tricky part–he had to add just enough to create the desired poison, but not so much that the final compound would give off a noticeable odor. It had to be just right.

If the chemicals worked in their desired order, they'd stun the system enough to give the poison sufficient time to reach vital organs, while the cough medicine suppressed the body enough that the subject didn't simply vomit the compound out, instead feeling little to nothing as their organs steadily shut down and eventually failed. The process was painstaking, but Thiago didn't mind the change of pace. It beat the mental fatigue of constantly switching identities and figuring out what he should and shouldn't say to the people he'd run into over the course of the last few weeks. The actual act of killing had always been the easy part; it didn't require much thought. He merely had to turn off that part of the brain where inhibitions come from, something for which he'd become quite proficient.

After all, he was a professional; he'd done this for years. And the only ones in his profession who'd gotten this far were those who were in absolute control of their minds and bodies. The conscience, that sense of morality, was merely a mental mode; it could be switched off. It mattered not that Peter and Ted were likely decent human beings, or that in the end, his client was probably no more than a wealthy, psychotic ex-husband, and the woman and the boy were simply his trophies. What was right and wrong was not Thiago's concern; morality never came between him and the job. When it did was when you started making mistakes, getting sloppy, second-guessing your gut feelings. It had never happened to him before, and it wasn't about to happen now.

Thiago was in control. Breathe in. Breathe out. Finish the job.

Thiago thought about the money. $300,000 would be his biggest payout yet. Not enough to retire, but close. He was almost there. Another five years–seven tops–and this life would be behind him. He would sell the loft in California and take his cash and run. Maybe to Switzerland, maybe to Portugal. Maybe he'd finally find someone, somewhere far away. Somewhere his old life wouldn't find him. And then it'd be ok. He would put it all behind him. It was close enough to taste.

Thiago let the concoction cool as he drizzled it into the empty bottle of water and added the sticky medicinal mix. It would take awhile to congeal, after which he'd have to cut the bottle open and fill the empty capsules with the compound. Two capsules per mark would be enough, he was sure of it. He sniffed the bottle. The heat had removed most of the smell, but there was still a hint of pine. Dissolved in a cup of coffee, though, there'd be little to detect.

An hour later, he filled the capsules with the congealed mixture. He grabbed his tools from the shelf, found a door to the outside, and tossed all of the items into the sea below. It was unlikely they'd ever be found in this dark and forgotten corner of the rig, but he was paid to be a shadow in all aspects of the job. There were to be no traces left. The objects tumbled noiselessly into the waves and disappeared. The roar of diesel engines and churning seas drowned out all else.

It would all be over soon.

***

Joyce awoke to a never ending, maddening darkness that was almost like total blindness. It was supernatural, of course. She hadn't bothered discussing this with Stacy–it would only upset her–but she doubted she thought it was anything else, either. No other explanations remained. It was too absolute, as if the sun and moon and stars had simply vanished from their perches in the heavens.

Joyce climbed out of the confines of the sailboat's cabin and sat in the cockpit, lifejacket still strapped to her chest. The vinyl straps were chafing at her neck but she barely noticed them anymore. She knew it was for her own good that Stacy forced her to keep it on at all times. She could only imagine how easy it'd be to fall into these black waters and never be seen again. Just the thought of it made her uneasy; she tightened the straps.

Stacy joined her on deck an hour later. They'd slept most of the day, waiting for a wind to fill their sails. With no reserve fuel, Stacy had determined that they needed to conserve as much as possible. Frankly, things were beginning to seem hopeless, and they both felt it. They were weary with the stress of the last week, and Burrard Harbor felt farther away than ever. At least on land they had access to roads. Out here there was nothing.

"You never did tell me why," Joyce said softly into the

darkness. She handed Stacy a sleeve of saltine crackers and a jar of peanut butter.

"Why what?"

"Why you left Vancouver in the first place."

"I told you. My house burned down."

"Come on, Stacy. That isn't a reason."

"It's not?"

"Your house burned to the ground so you decided to go back and what, walk through the rubble?"

"Pretty much."

Joyce shook her head and sighed. "Even after all of this, you still manage to be mysterious."

"Maybe that's all I have left," Stacy said. Joyce could hear her scraping a cracker in the peanut butter.

"I never realized how much I'd miss seeing the stars," Joyce said. She leaned against the edge of the deck and looked up at the flat, black, endlessness.

"Did you know I had a brother?" Stacy asked.

"No, I didn't," Joyce said.

"We were only a few years apart. His name was Jerry."

"I don't think you ever mentioned him before."

"I wouldn't have. He died when we were young."

"I'm sorry."

"I wasn't."

"Why?"

"His life was misery. Jerry was born with Down syndrome."

"People can live with Down syndrome and still have productive lives, Stacy."

"Yeah, maybe people with normal families, people surrounded by mothers or fathers who actually care about their well being. That wasn't exactly our situation. And Jerry deserved so much more. He was so sweet and innocent. And *pure*."

"How did he die?"

"Well, the official story was pneumonia. That's what we always told anyone who asked, anyways."

"And unofficially?"

"Neglect. He'd had a cold for months. A bad cough. You

could tell something wasn't right. He was complaining of chest pains, too. I was only thirteen and even I knew my mom needed to take him to the doctor, but she refused. She just kept acting like it wasn't a big deal, until one day he just didn't wake up."

"Oh my god, Stacy."

"My parents held a little service at a chapel, but no one else came. Barely anyone knew about him. I was the only one who was close to him. We were buddies. But after he died, we hardly ever mentioned his name. It was like, I dunno, like my family wanted to just *erase* him. They were some sick people."

Stacy took a deep breath and let it out slowly. "Anyways, Jerry was cremated. It was the cheapest option, so of course that's what my parents chose. I kept his ashes in my room. It felt like... I don't know. It felt like I *owed* him that at least. Like I'd failed him somehow when we were still alive. Like, I should've said something, I should've told *someone*, a teacher or something."

"You can't blame yourself, Stacy. You were just a kid."

"I knew what was going on, Joyce. I wasn't stupid. I simply didn't act. Of course, years later, when I got the truth, and when I knew I'd see Jerry again, that was..." Stacy stopped abruptly. Joyce waited for the words, but they didn't come. Then she heard Stacy's breathing hitch in her chest and moved across the bench to wrap an arm around her friend.

"All these years, you know? And that's been the only thing keeping me going. Jerry."

"I'm so sorry, Stacy. I'm so sorry," Joyce said.

"That's not the worst part, though."

"What do you mean?"

"The worst part is that I forgot about him. With everything going on during the evacuation, I simply forgot about Jerry. After I inherited my grandmother's house, I moved his ashes to a safe. I didn't want to lose him, but I ended up completely forgetting about him when I was packing for the evacuation. It wasn't until after I got to the camp in Vancouver, and then I got that call about my house burning down, that I remembered. Jerry's ashes were still in the safe."

"And that's why you left. To go get your brother," Joyce said, piecing it all together. An enormous weight descended on her shoulders. It was not merely the weight of knowing these awful stories, but the weight of having judged Stacy so harshly. In the end, they'd left for the same reason.

"I know it sounds crazy. I know he's not in those ashes, that it's not like Jehovah needs some physical thing to remember him, but I... I *do*."

CHAPTER 16

Martin exited the shower to find Chad hunched over a backpack on the sofa. He was jotting something down in a small notebook and muttering to himself. Two guns sat on the coffee table beside him.

"Hey, Chad. What're you up to?" Martin asked, drying his hair with a towel. Steam poured from the bathroom behind him. He'd taken a longer time in the shower than he'd intended, but he just hadn't felt clean after the first rinse. It was as if the blood had stained his skin. He'd scrubbed and scrubbed until he was red and raw and wrinkled.

"Going out for another haul," Chad mumbled without turning.

"Now? Why not wait till tomorrow? It's not like we're short on supplies."

"Maybe not, but how long do you expect them to last out there?"

"In the house? I don't see why–"

"No, of course you don't. You haven't thought that far ahead," Chad said, tapping his temple with the back of a pen.

"What are you saying…"

"You think your home is safe? You think any of these homes are safe? You've got fires burning throughout the valley. And you hear that?" Chad said, turning as his eyes gazed up at the ceiling of the bunker. Martin looked up and frowned.

"Hear what?"

"Exactly. Silence. No police sirens. No ambulances. No fire trucks. No one's coming, Martin. Those fires will spread. They'll climb their way right up this hill, right over this bunker, and they'll consume whatever's left of your house and your neighbors' houses. So if I'm going to look for some supplies, I'm going to do it now."

"I'll go with you," Martin said.

"You don't mean that," Chad said with a chuckle.

"Excuse me?"

"You don't mean it. You don't want to be out there and I'm not asking you to do it."

"What? Why?"

"You can't handle it. You could barely handle a little blood in the dark of your own house."

"Look, I thought…"

"You thought what?"

"I thought maybe, you know… Maybe the body was still there. It just freaked me out, is all."

"The body? The body that I told you was buried?"

"Look, I wasn't sure. I know you said you took care of it, but I thought maybe you'd just said that to make me feel better."

"You thought I lied."

"Come on, Chad. I wouldn't have held it against you. I just didn't know for sure. It caught me off guard, all that blood. That's all. I'm fine. I'm over it."

"Great. I still don't want you out there with me."

"We'll be faster if we're together. Safer, too."

"No, we won't. You being out there will not make me safer. You're a liability, Martin. And until you figure out how to wrap your head around this, you stay here, underground, in this bunker." Chad shouldered his pack, holstered his guns, and exited the bunker without another word.

Martin watched him go, watched how easily he moved in this space. As if he owned it. That was always the way it had been with Chad. When he was present he didn't just *occupy* the space, he *possessed* it. It was as if an invisible hand extended from his body and *squeezed* the space around him. It was his charisma, sure, his winning smile. But there was something else, too, something that had always lurked beneath the surface, a subtle but undeniable undercurrent that was always moving.

210

Ebbing. Shifting. Something in his eyes.

Like the way he'd looked at Martin when Martin had found him in the dark, just standing there in front of the door, watching. What had he been doing, anyway? What had he been waiting for? Was this all some kind of game for him? Was he somehow... *relishing* this?

Martin opened the fridge and removed a beer–room temperature, they'd killed power to the fridge to save electricity. He cracked it open and fell into his sofa, trying to think. His mind was a flood, detritus stuck in eddying whirlpools that never settled, nor went anywhere discernible. It was hard to focus down here. Hard breathing recycled air, without natural sunlight, with only the drone of his own subconscious telling him to... to *what*?

Martin threw back the last of the beer and went for another. He carried it up the ramp and up the steps, standing behind the door of the bunker, staring out of the small reinforced-glass window, wondering what Chad was up to. The bunker was too far from the house to see anything, if Chad was even in there at all. Perhaps he was walking the streets by now, casing out the other homes on the block. What would he do if he found someone? Someone injured, say? Someone who needed help?

Well, *that* was a no brainer. Martin had witnessed enough of Chad's coldness to know exactly what he'd do: nothing. Maybe that's what he'd meant when he said he'd be better out there alone. No one to slow him down, no one to question the morality of his actions. Martin wondered how far Chad would go. Killing and death were clearly non-issues with him. What else was left? When it really came down to it, how well did Martin actually know the man?

It had been foolish to give him the door code. That much was now clear. With that bit of information, there was little protecting Martin. He wasn't needed. Heck, Chad had called him a *liability*. Martin frowned out the window and wondered. He turned to a small electrical panel beside the doorframe and flipped it open, revealing a small digital readout and keypad. Martin could always change the code. It was that simple. Martin

211

had at least earned the right to be the keeper of the code. He'd built this place with his own money, hadn't he? He could always let Chad in and out as needed. At least he'd then have a purpose. At least then he wouldn't be so *disposable*.

Martin entered the door code and selected in the reset option. He stopped. Chad would be furious. He could only imagine his face on the other side of that glass when he found out the code had been changed. He'd scream and yell and throw a fit as soon as he entered, and Martin would have to explain himself.

No. It was better to leave the code for now. He could always change it another time. If Chad got dangerous Martin would find a way to get him outside long enough to change the code and lock him out. There was no need to reveal his hand just yet. Now was the time to wait and watch and listen.

***

"Disappeared?" Peter repeated. Ted was nodding. The two men walked side by side down one of the cramped corridors.

"That's what his housing overseer said. They checked the room. Place has been cleaned out. Like he was never there in the first place."

"Weird."

"Angelica's still pretty freaked from talking with him."

"He didn't say anything to you after the two of them talked?"

"Nothing. He stood and walked out, like he'd said what he'd come to say and that was that. I haven't seen him since. That's why I went to talk to his housing overseer. I had no idea what part of the rig he was staying in. I got a call about an hour later. They say it's like he just vanished."

"So you're thinking his angel story was a hoax."

"This guy told Angelica to get back with her ex, Pete. *Chad Harkett*. The guy who tried to kill us. No way is this *James* guy some angel."

"So, where'd he come from?"

"That's the thing. I've been wracking my brains trying to

212

figure it out. But I think we have to consider the possibility that, you know…"

"Chad sent him," Peter said.

"Yeah. I know it sounds crazy, way out here in the middle of the ocean. But it's not out of the question. Chad's loaded, he's connected. He could've hired someone."

"But how'd he just show up on our supply boat in the middle of a storm?"

"I don't know. It doesn't make any sense. Maybe he was airlifted in or something. Maybe he's some ex-Navy seal or mercenary or whatever."

"And he goes through all this trouble just to deliver a message? Five minutes of face time with Angelica and he disappears? That doesn't add up."

"No, it doesn't. But it makes me nervous, Pete. *Real* nervous. The brothers are saying he's disappeared, like that's the proof he was an angel."

"They don't know about Angelica?"

Ted shook his head. "I've only told you so far. We wanted to keep it quiet, not freak too many people out. People are already on edge with the news from the mainland. We don't want to cause a panic."

"Sensible, but I think we should let the overseers know at least, get them to keep an eye out. If he's still aboard, he could be planning something."

Ted's eyes squeezed together as a pained expression wrinkled his face. "I promised they'd be safe, Peter. I told Angelica and Evan they had nothing to fear here."

"I understand, Ted. You did the right thing telling me. We'll all keep an eye on her. Jehovah will keep them safe."

"I hope so, man," Ted said. Peter gave his friend a squeeze on the shoulder as they parted ways. Peter passed through a set of swinging doors into the cafeteria. Bo was waiting for him, as usual, with a Styrofoam cup of coffee laced between his knobby fingers. Peter sat across from him. It was clear from a glance that all was not well. His skin was pale and clammy; a thin veil of perspiration covered his face, plastering the greying hair to his temples. Bo brought two trembling fingers to his lips and pressed.

It was the withdrawals, of course. He'd been ok his first few days aboard, but whatever he was going through now looked like torture.

"You get the doctors to look over you in medical?" asked Peter. Bo's eyes flicked up for a moment and then fell back into his cup of coffee. His head jolted side to side.

"I'm no medical expert, but they might have something to ease the effects a little," Peter said, refilling Bo's cup.

"Not really one for docs and hospitals," Bo muttered. He lifted a sleeve to scratch his arm, revealing tracks of red skin he'd scraped away with his fingernails.

"Been sleeping much?" Peter asked. Bo shook his head.

"I lay there awake for hours, just staring up at the ceiling. My mind is turning over again and again, but without actually thinking about anything. It's like my head's a loop, man."

"I can only imagine, Bo. You just gotta hang in there. It's a sickness, just like any other. You'll get through it. Try to stay active. Get plenty of fresh air, sleep when you can. Eat right."

"No appetite. Not that it matters. I hear everything's been tightly rationed now."

"We'll have enough, just gotta be careful. You eaten anything today?"

Bo shook his head. "Like I say, no appetite. Well, not for *food*, anyways."

"You looked over that chapter on prayer in the *Teach* book? There's some good info in there. Plenty of others have gone through what you're facing right now. Many of them say they couldn't have done it without prayer."

"Yeah, I read it when I couldn't get to sleep the other night. It all sounds nice, like you can just ask for stuff like that and God will just listen and grant wishes or whatever, but it's hard for an old dog like me."

"New habits take time to form. You've got to be patient with yourself."

"What if not everyone's cut out for it? Like, what if some people are just born bad–you ever think about that?"

"Fate, you mean?"

"Yeah, I guess. Fate, destiny, whatever. I spent years on the inside, Pete. I met guys—you'd look in their eyes, right? and there was just nothing there. No humanity, no conscience. It's like they were born without a soul. Just nothing there, man. Like staring into a bottomless pit. You see these guys day in and day out, you start realizing there's just no reforming someone like that. You throw them in prison and they just come out harder than before. There's only one place for 'em."

"What, the electric chair?" Peter asked. Bo's eyes bulged as he wagged his head back and forth, smiling with what was left of his teeth.

"That's just a pit stop, brother. A pit stop on the way down there," Bo said, pointing a finger down.

"Well, you know what the Bible says about hell, Bo. We've been through this. And in any case, what you're describing is a problem with the prison system. That doesn't mean those guys were destined to become that way."

"I dunno. I seen kids like that, too. Barely learned to shave and already serving life sentences for murder."

"There's no denying that humanity is sick, Bo. Add to that the Satanic influence in the world today, and you've got a lot of messed up people."

"Yeah, but… You think people can be *born* evil?" Bo whispered, leaning over his cup of coffee. His bloodshot eyes bored into Peter's.

"That… That's a hard question," Peter said. "But regardless of where someone is born or how he's raised, we all make choices in our life. The choices we make are what define us as good or bad, not our predispositions. I don't believe that fate plays a part, and that's certainly not what the Bible teaches."

"Choices," Bo repeated, as if turning the concept around in his head. A smile flickered in his eyes and he nodded at Peter and nibbled his lower lip. "You're a good man."

***

It was nearly five AM when the sky began to brighten suddenly off of the Northern Washington coast. It was Joyce's watch. She stood gazing at the faint orange light in the distance and scrambled down to the cabin to rouse Stacy. The two women stood staring minutes later on the deck of the sailboat, gazing at the odd light.

It was no sunrise. Instead of a horizontal band of gradually rising light, it was a hazy blob that seemed to rise vertically out of the water. Stacy yanked the outboard motor to life and steered their vessel into the light. As they neared, it became clear that something terrible had happened here.

The water was on fire. Flames spread over the surface of the black sea in a large, undulating patch. Joyce and Stacy felt its heat from a distance, felt the air stirring as wind currents began to form as a result of the temperature difference. Flames licked upward from the water as if attempting to take flight. And at the center of it all stood the mass of a mangled steel structure slowly disappearing into the sea.

"A shipwreck?" Joyce said, struggling to make out an identifiable shape behind the flames.

"Yeah, looks like it. Must've been transporting oil," Stacy said. She nudged the tiller by a few degrees, steering the boat far from the perimeter of the flames.

"You think the crew got off safely?" Joyce asked.

"Doubtful. No one to receive their SOS, if they ever made one. Besides, there'd be no place to escape to. You wouldn't want to be in this water."

Stacy kept the boat moving, skirting around the vast field of burning oil as Joyce kept an eye out for debris.

"Oh my God, Stacy," she said, leaning over the prow.

"What is it?"

"Kill the engine!" Joyce shouted. Stacy did as she was told. As the boat coasted slowly to a stop, Joyce went for the gaffing hook. She fished something out of the water–a long, white cord. She pulled it onto the deck and began gathering the line in her hands.

"What is it?" Stacy asked again. Joyce pointed into the

distance. There, barely lit by the light of the fires reflected on the sea, was the outline of a life preserver. The top half of a human body was visible from its center. Joyce continued reeling in the line. The life preserver approached, creating subtle ripples as it was pulled through the debris-filled waters. Stacy lifted the electric lantern as the preserver neared their sailboat.

The women gasped as the figure came into focus. It was a young girl–perhaps only fourteen or fifteen. Her arms were held stiffly at her sides, a look of shock and agony frozen on her face. Most of her clothing had been burned off, along with much of her skin and hair. Stacy turned and raced to the opposite side of the boat, where her body crumpled over the railing and she retched.

Joyce made no noise. She gathered the remainder of the line in her hands, her eyes locked on the girl, searching for any signs of life. She gently rotated the preserver with the gaffing hook to get a better look. The burns were extensive and severe.

"What is *wrong* with you, Joyce? Just let her go," Stacy said, still hunched over the railing, a sleeve held up to her lips.

"I just wanted to see if she was still alive," Joyce explained. It was doubtful, though. The shock to this girl's system would've been too severe. Joyce took one last look at her before nudging her back away from the boat and tossing the oil-slicked line back into the sea. She watched the girl vanish back into the blackness as Stacy started the motor and they continued northwards in the general direction of Burrard Harbor.

For the next couple of hours, sparse words were exchanged. The women nibbled on peanut butter crackers and sipped sports drinks. As the morning began, the horizon remained dark and invisible. Stacy let them drift; the outboard motor was running dangerously low on fuel. Hope was beginning to fade.

"I gotta hand it to you, Joyce. You handled that like a champ. You've got nerves of steel," Stacy said finally.

"Come again?"

"Back there, with the girl, the fire. Being that close up with something so grisly... I don't have the stomach for it."

"Yeah, well, you work in a hospital for eighteen years, you

217

get over it. I've seen everything. Gunshot wounds, burn victims, broken bones. Worst were always the kids, though. Hated seeing the little ones in pain."

"You worked in the ER?"

"Sometimes, yes. When they were understaffed. Like the last week I was there, when the bomb went off at Seattle-Tacoma. Hard to believe that was only a few weeks ago. Feels like a lifetime."

"That's where you met the girl you were taking care of in the camp, right?"

"Yes. Claire."

"Sounds like a fortunate girl."

"Jehovah's hand was behind all of it, I'm sure. Did you know that we actually got in touch with her family? They were in another camp, way down in New Orleans."

"Huh."

"The more I think about it, the more stupid I feel about this whole thing."

"Why's that?"

"I left because I was scared. Claire was sick, and I was getting news from the hospital about it being some kind of contagious biological disease no one had seen before. They said I needed to do a blood test. When I told Alvin I wanted to leave, he tried to stonewall me, told me it was the wrong thing to do."

"Sounds familiar."

"Yeah. Well. Like you, I didn't listen. At the time, it seemed like the only logical option. Now, when I really think about it, it's clear that things were already worked out as well as they could be. I was in the safest possible place. And so was Claire. And I gave all that up. And here I am."

"Here *we* are."

***

Thiago filled the Styrofoam cup with water and pressed the rim into his palm, using the muscles in his hand to grip the cup. He lifted his hand into the air; the cup went with it. He wriggled his fingers, which were still free. He filled a second Styrofoam cup and set it on the shelf. Then, with a quick movement, he waved his hand over the second cup, coordinating the muscles in his fingers and palm to switch cups as he passed.

It was convincing, but too slow. He tried again. And again. And again. For hours he worked to perfect the maneuver, each time trying to make it as fluid as possible. He tried it as different speeds, from different directions, with varying amount of liquid in the cups. There were many variables–he would need to practice for all of them. He had to be flexible, he had to be perfect. $300,000 was on the line, and he would only have one chance.

Thiago finally stopped at 11:30, massaging out the cramps in his hand and getting ready for the real thing. He took a long look in the mirror hanging from a screw in the wall. He took himself in; the shape of his eyes, the curve of his mouth, the creases in his forehead. And then he went to work.

He started with the toilet paper first, tearing off pieces and rolling them into small wads, which he jammed into the corners of his mouth, between his cheeks and his gums. His jawline gradually began to change, widening his jowls. His lower lip puckered slightly outwards.

Next was the grease. He rubbed two fingers in it and dabbed at the skin beneath his eyes and just under his cheekbones. He rubbed the grease in circles, darkening his skin slightly and giving it an aged, sallow look. The rest of the grease he put in his hair, which he slicked backwards with a comb. He plucked the hairs from the edges of his eyebrows, which, with the slicked back hair, appeared to elongate his forehead.

Thiago stood back, looking at himself in the mirror. He was nearly unrecognizable. He smiled contentedly at his work, switched off the light bulb, and exited the storage cabinet. The pills were in his breast pocket and he was a new man, and a third of a million dollars was just around the corner. He hummed to himself as he climbed up the stairwells towards the upper decks, towards the cafeteria of Rig 7.

Stacy had done her best to conserve gasoline, but she'd been forced to crank the engine to life a few times over the last couple of days to avoid large piles of floating debris–debris that could easily damage the hull of their sailboat or the outboard's propellers. Their fuel was now dangerously low, and land had still eluded them. Stacy suspected they were somewhere near Admiralty Bay, but there was no way of knowing for sure. If land were anywhere nearby, it remained shrouded in darkness and was thus useless to them.

"Well," said Stacy, sighing deeply, "I suppose now is as good a time as any."

"Time for what?" Joyce asked. Stacy didn't reply; she was busy raking through the contents of a cabinet beneath her bed. She removed a small tin of cookies and cradled them in the nook of her elbow.

"I'm going to need your help," she said softly as she flicked on the electric lantern and handed it to Joyce.

"Ok. What are we doing?"

"Just hold the light steady." Stacy opened the hatch to the cabin and climbed out onto the deck. Joyce followed her, keeping the lantern high in the air. The electric bulb illuminated a circle of its surroundings; shadows danced with its movement.

Stacy sat herself on the cockpit's bench, the top half of her body twisted outwards to face the sea. She closed her eyes, took a deep breath, and opened the tin. Joyce gazed upon its contents and sat silently on the bench across from her, holding the light obediently in the air. There was nothing to say; if ever there were an occasion that demanded silence, this was it.

Stacy Owen dipped the tips of her fingers in the ashes, holding them there for a moment as if testing the temperature of bathwater.

"You probably think it's silly, me keeping him in a cookie tin," Stacy said. A single tear streaked down the side of her face and glistened in the lamplight, but her voice remained steady.

"The thing is, these butter cookies were kind of Jerry's

220

thing. The *one thing* that could always put a smile on his face. Even during those final days, when he was basically drowning in the pneumonia, it was the only thing he asked for. So I kept the tin, his last one. It only seemed right. You know?" Stacy turned to look at Joyce. Her eyes held a pleading look that was more vulnerable and honest than anything Joyce had seen her express. Joyce crossed the cockpit, still holding the lantern above them, and reached an arm out, resting it on Stacy's shoulder.

"You did fine, Stacy," she whispered. Stacy gazed into the ashes, eyes hard and unblinking, before reaching a hand out and sprinkling a handful of her brother's ashes onto the sea. Flecks of grey dust sat on the gently rippling water. The women watched as a current carried them beyond the reach of the lantern.

When it was done, Stacy replaced the tin's lid and held it close to her chest. She said nothing. Joyce said nothing. And they continued to drift.

***

It felt like they'd been on the road for weeks. Without the normal cycles of day and night Darren Hughes was having trouble keeping track of time. His sleep had become fitful and irregular. It was as if the world were stuck in some kind of void, where stars and sun and moon and even time itself no longer existed.

They'd stuck with their initial plan, heading eastwards on the interstate towards New Orleans. It had been slow going at first; getting out of the valley had been a nightmarish gauntlet of gridlocked roads and angry motorists. There'd been violence, of course–drivers pulling knives and guns on each other, the highways and thoroughfares gradually becoming spectacles of carnage.

They'd managed to find food and water–a trucker heading in the opposite direction had been willing to trade some of his goods in exchange for some of Rita's medicines–but this was one fortuitous event amid a series of disasters that Darren could hardly imagine emerging from unscathed.

221

They'd talked about turning around, but these discussions became less frequent the farther they got from home. There was nothing to return to—no friends, no hotels, no motels. They were stuck on this road, hoping desperately that they'd find something at its end.

"Tank's nearly empty again. *Man*, this thing guzzles gas," Darren said, glancing at the fuel indicator with a grimace. His wife didn't respond.

For the last two days, their trek had taken them from gas station to gas station, where'd they'd spent a total of nearly five hundred dollars in cash to fuel up. The station owners were gouging, but there was nothing Darren or anyone else could do about it.

"We're gonna need to fill up again. Keep your eyes peeled," Darren instructed. Rita managed a slight nod. Her eyes were glued to the scene beyond her passenger window—overwhelming darkness peppered with the occasional roadside fire. The entire state, it seemed, was slowly disintegrating to ash.

Darren hit the scan button on the radio and turned up the volume.

"What *exactly* are you trying to do?" Rita asked, her face pressed against the glass.

"Just trying to figure out what's going on here. Maybe there'll be something on the airwaves."

"It's gone, Darren. There's no one out there."

"There's gotta be *someone*. There are dozens of radio stations out here; someone has to have found a way to broadcast."

"The power's out, Darren. How's a radio station supposed to broadcast without power?"

"They've gotta have other means, right? Generators? Backup batteries? Someone's got to have figured it out by now. The *government* has to have a way, at the very least."

"Yeah, right. The *government*," Rita sneered.

"Look, Rita. I'm just trying to get information, ok? I'm trying to be proactive here. Is that a problem?"

"You're wasting your time."

"Please. Rita. For once."

"For once what, Darren?"

"Just… Just try to support me here, ok?"

"What, like I've never supported you in the past?" Rita snapped, turning to glare at her husband.

"No, I'm not saying that. I'm just asking for you to back me up here. I'm not asking for anything else."

"Oh, I'm sorry it's just been so hard to live with me–your sick, fat wife with all these diseases. And my God, she doesn't even *support* you."

Darren said nothing. He had no energy to fight.

"It's not like I *choose* to be this way, ok? It's not like I *like* living in this body. What ever happened to marriage for better or for worse, huh? You somehow forget about that?"

"Rita, I *have* been there for worse. I've been by your side *for years*. I've never complained. All I'm asking now–"

"I know you blame me, Darren. I know you, I see it in your eyes. I know that somehow you think us being stuck here now and not on some oil rig with Peter and Rachel is my fault. Right?"

"I never said that."

"You didn't have to. Like I said, I *know* you."

"Please, Rita. Can we not fight about this? It's pointless," Darren begged.

"Pointless?! How can you say that what I'm saying is pointless?!" Rita said, her voice rising and shaking.

"I mean that this fighting is pointless. It's only going to push us further–"

"Stop the car," Rita said.

"What?"

"I said, stop the car."

Darren shut his mouth as he pulled to the shoulder of the road. Rita flung her door open and hefted her large frame outside. She took a puff from her inhaler and marched away from the car. Darren sat and waited.

On the one hand, he loved and pitied her, as he had for all these years. He knew how much her sicknesses had robbed her of life, and living in a vehicle these last few days, constantly on the run, every day full of fear and uncertainty, had only worsened things. But on the other hand, he was tired. Tired of her mood swings, tired of the ailments, tired of struggling to understand Rita's constantly shifting state of health and mind.

Darren watched Rita go. The road ahead swung around a bend and Rita had went with it, leading her out of Darren's headlights. He waited for another few moments before restarting the car. He edged the vehicle back onto the road and proceeded slowly forward. This was always the tricky part: determining how long to let Rita cool off before approaching with his tail between his legs. Too soon and she wouldn't be ready to talk; too long and she'd be mad at him for taking his time. It was an old game with her, one for which Darren had struggled to learn the rules.

He caught up with her around the bend, his high beams sweeping over the asphalt and momentarily revealing an otherwise invisible tree line beyond the highway's guardrail. Darren rolled down the window and pulled up next to his wife. Her face was damp with perspiration and some of the fire had gone out of her expression. Darren opened his mouth to say something when a noise from behind them caught his attention.

He glanced in his rearview mirror, and for a brief moment caught sight of a pair of headlights slicing through the darkness, jolting and thrashing as a vehicle behind them bounded down the highway. Darren heard the screech of tires on asphalt as the driver raced up the road, caught sight of Darren's SUV, and swerved frantically to avoid a collision.

The speeding vehicle fishtailed back and forth on the highway as it passed Darren's SUV. A plume of dirt and dust erupted from the ground as its tires found the shoulder of the road, clouding Darren's view. When the air finally cleared, the vehicle was nowhere to be seen. Darren sat for a few moments in the silence, catching his breath before guiding his SUV to the shoulder of the road and getting out.

"Rita?" Darren called out, looking up and down the road. But there was no one there; it was as if his wife had simply disappeared. It wasn't until he climbed over the guardrail that he saw her.

Darren ran to her, his mind reeling as he collapsed beside her in the dirt. The knees of his pants immediately soaking in the cold dew. Darren placed his palms on her body, gently touching her back. She wasn't moving. Darren trembled as he struggled to speak.

"Rita... Baby? Can you hear me?" he asked, his eyes quickly roving over her. Rita Hughes was lying face down, limbs sprawled out, in the dirt and the tall grass. She wore no visible injuries, though her clothes were torn and muddied in places. His chest filled with the cold tide of dread.

"Please... Rita... Don't leave me, girl..." he said, lips quivering. His hand moved up her back and then her neck, and finally the base of her head. His fingers touched something wet and cold; he drew his hand back with a gasp and pressed his eyes shut.

"No... Please, God. Please not this..." Darren said, his hands clenched before him. He opened his eyes and saw the blood on his fingers and screamed. It was not a sound of fear or horror, but one of utter loss and madness. Darren felt the floor fall away, felt the darkness consume and digest him.

He sat in the damp grass for several long moments, staring at his wife's lifeless body, waiting for a miracle.

CHAPTER 17

"Any news on our rogue guest?" Peter asked, peeling open a packet of mayonnaise. Since the rations had gone into effect, meals had gotten simpler and less appetizing–today, ham sandwiches and juice cartons were the only items available.

"Not yet, no. Still no sign of him–almost two days now."

"How's Angelica?"

"It's been hard, knowing how much to tell her. I didn't mention that I think this guy is connected to Chad, didn't want to scare her. She's smart, though, I'm sure she'll reach the same conclusion if she hasn't already. She seems to have a lot on her mind lately. She's been acting a little… off."

"Well, that might have something to do with just being here aboard this rig, day in and day out. It's wearing on all of us."

"Yeah. Cabin fever," Ted said, raising his eyebrows.

"Is that your lunch?" Peter asked, pointing at the cup of coffee in Ted's hands. Ted shrugged.

"Not really hungry. Plus, with these rations, I figure I'll let those who really need it eat first."

"That's considerate, but you need your energy," Peter said. Ted made a crooked smile and lifted his coffee between two fingers.

"How've you been, otherwise?" Peter asked.

"Like you said, this place is wearing on all of us. Narrow corridors, small cabins, this packed cafeteria. Makes you a little stir crazy after a while. I'm looking forward to Namibia… As weird as it feels saying that."

"Well, you've got another few weeks to get used to the idea. You making use of the rec rooms?"

Ted shook his head. "No time. Between the training and going over manuals and this whole thing with Angelica, I've been pretty exhausted."

"I hope you're not meeting with her alone."

"No, no, of course not. We usually chat right here. Sometimes Marcus tags along. I know you've had your plate full so I haven't bugged you about it."

"Always willing to help. If we're too busy to help the friends, we're too busy."

"Yeah, I thought you'd say something like that. I appreciate it, but there's been plenty of help."

"That's good," Peter said, nodding.

"Still… I just can't get this James character out of my mind. I just keep wondering where he showed up from, and where he disappeared to. The more I think about it, the more uneasy I get. Like, he was here, right? Other people are talking about him, right?"

"Sure, as far as I know. What are you implying?"

"I just want to be sure, you know?"

"Sure about what?"

"Sure that it's not all in my head."

Peter chuckled.

"I'm serious, Pete. Like you say, being out here on this rig… It's not healthy for the mind, man. I just want to make sure I'm not imagining things."

"Why not just ask Angelica? She talked with him, didn't she? And there were others."

"Yeah, no, you're right. There were others. I just wanna be sure, you know? I don't know. Maybe I'm losing it. I've barely been sleeping."

"You look it," Peter said. "My advice would be to take a day off. Head to the upper decks, get some fresh air, walk around outside a little and clear your head. You've been through a lot these last few weeks. And maybe lay off the coffee."

Ted only grinned with the shake of his head. "It's the only thing keeping me going. I'm thinking of having a T-shirt made: 'this machine runs on coffee and holy spirit'"

Peter laughed. "We all need breaks from time to time, Ted. You're not superman."

"Yeah, well…" Ted paused, lifting his head as he sniffed the air. "You smell that? It's like something's burning."

The two men turned to look in the direction of the kitchen.

***

His two marks were there in their usual spots, like clockwork. Thiago knew he could count on them. Better still, both men had their usual Styrofoam cups of coffee beside them. Predictable subjects always made the best targets, he thought, smiling to himself as he strolled along the far end of the cafeteria, keeping Peter and Ted in sight from the corner of his eye.

Thiago skirted around the edge of the cafeteria as the lunch crowd gathered, the usual assortment of the elderly, couples, teens, and small children. The din grew steadily in the small space as Thiago took his place in one of the lunch lines. He grabbed a tray and made his way slowly to the wall separating cafeteria from kitchen, and as the line turned, he slipped casually from his spot and through the door.

He'd cased the place days prior, before meeting with Ted and Angelica, and knew how easily he could slip in undetected. Men and women dressed in sanitary gloves, masks, and hairnets swarmed around him, each preoccupied in a frenzy of tasks: emptying garbage cans, moving trays and silverware, wheeling food carts, washing dishes. No one paid him any mind.

Thiago moved quickly to a rack of supplies, removing a mask and hairnet from a box and slipping them on. He dressed himself in an apron hanging from a peg on the wall and got to work. He needed to create a timed distraction, something small that would cause commotion without posing any lasting danger.

Fully disguised, Thiago casually strolled to a roll of paper towels. He balled a small wad of them tightly in his hands and wet them on a countertop. He casually tossed the damp paper towels into an oven and cranked up the dial. Then, after a final glance around, he grabbed a fresh rack of plates and exited the kitchen back into the cafeteria.

He strolled casually through the crowd, nodding and smiling at several of the people in line, before setting down the plates and pouring two piping hot cups of coffee. He pulled the poisoned capsules from his breast pocket and dropped them in the cups, stirring the mixture with a spoon before palming the two Styrofoam cups. He moved to the far end of the cafeteria and waited.

It took less than five minutes. He smelled the smoke before he ever saw it, and just as the lunch crowd was falling silent and beginning to stand and look for the source of the smoke, he sprung into action. Peter's and Ted's heads were turned to the kitchen, their eyes temporarily away from their meals. Thiago moved up the aisle quickly, switched the cups, and turned immediately to another table to gather several plates in his hands.

Over his shoulder, he could hear commotion in the kitchen as the workers struggled to locate the source of the smoke. It wouldn't take long, and then it'd be all over, and everyone would be back to their meals. Thiago set the dirty dishes and two cups of coffee into a plastic tub near the far wall, and continued to bus tables as he kept an eye on his marks.

***

Peter and Ted stood for a few anxious moments, eyes glued to the narrow, horizontal window separating the cafeteria and the kitchen. They smelled smoke but saw nothing apart from the commotion of the kitchen crew. There was the whoosh of compressed air and foam from a fire extinguisher, then nothing. The tension passed and the lunch crowd settled down and continued working their way through the queue, chatting as all returned to normal.

"Well, that was a little scary," Ted said, taking his seat. A fire aboard a rig like this, can you imagine? Man, that wouldn't end well."

"I'm sure it was nothing," Pete said. "Someone probably just left a burner on or something. No need to worry."

Ted only shook his head and stared into his cup of coffee.

"Got space for a third?" came the gruff and weathered voice of Bo Wharton from over Peter's shoulder.

"Absolutely, Bo," Peter said, scooting over on the bench and pulling his tray with him. Bo sat.

"Long time no see," Ted said. "How've you been? You two still having your lessons?" Ted asked. Bo's eyes darted from one man to the next, as if it took a moment for the question to register.

"Oh, sure. We've been studying almost every day," Bo said, tearing off a large bite of his ham sandwich.

"Sometimes twice a day," Peter added.

"No kidding. So, what do you think about what you're learning?" Ted asked.

"Well, it's, you know… It's all good. Good people here, too. I like the people."

"No people like Jehovah's people, right?"

"Sure, sure. All clean, nice, sweet… You know, good-looking people."

"It's all about living by Bible principles, Bo. The more you learn, the more you'll see yourself changing."

Bo chuckled, but didn't seem confident. "That sounds nice and all, but I'm not sure how much hope there is for an old dog like me," he said between mouthfuls.

"It's never too late," Peter reassured him. Bo shook his head as he bumped his chest with a clenched fist.

"You all right?" Ted asked.

"Fine. Sandwich is just a little dry, is all. I forgot to get myself a cup of joe."

"You're welcome to have mine," Peter said, sliding his cup over. "I haven't touched it. Trying to cut back on the caffeine."

"Much obliged, sir," Bo said with the tip of his head. He snatched the Styrofoam cup and downed the coffee in a single gulp.

"I'm with this guy," Ted said to Peter, pointing his thumb at Bo. "You'd have to pry my coffee from my cold dead hands."

Peter chuckled as Ted put the cup to his lips and took a sip.

"Everyone's allowed a vice," Bo Wharton said, nodding generously. "I'm not sure if that's in the Bible or not, but that's my philosophy, anyway. If yours is simply coffee, you're better off than most."

"I will agree with part of what you just said," said Peter. He made a face and the other two laughed.

"So, you feeling any better, Bo?" Peter asked.

"Sure, now that I've got some food in me."

"I notice your hands are looking pretty stable," Peter commented.

"Yeah, strangely enough. I feel pretty calm. Almost a little…"

"A little what?"

Bo said nothing as he widened his eyes and gave his head a shake, as if trying to keep himself awake. He flexed the muscles in his jaw before his mouth fell slightly open, head tilting forward a few degrees.

"Bo. Hey, buddy. You ok?" Ted asked. The man said nothing. He winced, then grabbed his chest with one hand and fell forwards into the table.

"Ok, we need to get him to the infirmary *right now*," Peter said, shooting to his feet. He grabbed Bo Wharton's bony shoulders in both hands–they felt thin and hollow, as if his body were made of paper. Ted rose to his feet and paused. He was light headed; the room spun slightly

"A little help here!" Peter called out frantically as he watched Bo's frail body begin to convulse, his head thrashing, speckled foam forming at the corners of his mouth. A couple of brothers stepped forward from the growing crowd of spectators.

"What's going on with him?" Ted asked.

"No idea! It's like a seizure or something–any doctors here? Nurses? Anyone?" Peter barked frantically. The crowd shook their heads slowly. Two brothers stepped forward, each taking one of Bo's arms over their shoulders as Peter led the way down the corridors and to the infirmary.

***

231

Thiago had no choice but to leave. The crowd that had gathered around the tables where Peter and Ted had been sitting had forced him to retreat; on the off chance that someone had spotted him switching the cups, he would be putting himself and the rest of his mission at risk. It was better to retreat and gather intel later.

Things had happened quickly and unexpectedly. There'd been no way to know that someone else would've shown up at the men's table. Plans were never failsafe, but at least part of his job had been completed–he'd seen Ted drink from the cup. In any case, now was not the time for analysis and second-guesses; Thiago had work to do.

He fled from the cafeteria and straight to Angelica's quarters. He took the most direct route–one he'd memorized and rehearsed. It was a seven minute walk that took him from one end of the rig to the other, three levels down. As he neared her room, he slipped the mask back on his face, along with a pair of rubber gloves. He paused for a moment outside of her room to pull a small Ziploc bag from his back pocket. He took a deep breath before opening it and removing a damp washcloth. He'd soaked it the night before in a bleach and ethanol concoction he'd prepared from discarded chemicals found around the supply rooms. It wasn't professional grade chloroform, but Angelica had a light frame and Evan was a child; Thiago presumed his creation would be sufficiently potent. He wiped his gloved hands with the rag and entered.

Angelica and her son were sitting together on her bed, pillows propped up behind their backs, a colorful book opened before them. They looked up slowly, a drowsy expression on their faces.

"Sorry, I didn't know it was cleaning day," Angelica said with a puzzled look.

Thiago didn't respond as he closed the door behind him. In two swift strides he was across the room, one knee on the edge of the bed as his hands, smeared in homemade chloroform, reached forward to smother the faces of woman and child. Their eyes filled with panic; Angelica's mouth gaped wide to scream, but Thiago was too fast. The rag was already against her lips; she inhaled only the smell of dizzying chemicals. She clawed at her attacker, trying desperately trying to ward him off while pushing Evan out of the bed. The boy tumbled out from under the blanket; Thiago reached out a hand to grasp him but he had already wriggled out of reach.

"Run!" Angelica yelled with her last breath as her vision began to swim. Her head spun. The colors bled from the room. And then there was nothing at all.

Her body limp, Thiago quickly replaced the rag and gloves back into the plastic bag and threw Angelica's arm over his shoulders. Their significant height difference made it uncomfortable, but there was no other way to transport her without drawing too much attention.

Thiago left the small cabin, Angelica wrapped partially around him, and glanced up and down the corridor. The boy had vanished. It was inconvenient but not altogether unexpected. He would have to make a second trip up to these levels to snatch him away another time. The gears of his plan were already in motion; he had to keep moving.

Down, down, down. Back down to the lower levels, farther down still to the storage closet. He passed a few curious passengers on his way, to whom he'd mutter something about seasickness, or a sudden onset of the flu. He didn't stop. No one asked questions.

Thiago made sure no one was following him before exiting the final door out onto the exposed catwalk and into the underside of the decks, where his storage closet hideout was located. He linked several loops of zip-ties together and chained Angelica's wrists to a thick pipe that ran vertically from the floor to the ceiling. He placed a single strip of duct tape across her mouth and unfolded a chair before her. Then he sat.

And waited.

***

233

Peter sat in the infirmary staring at the floor. It had all happened so quickly; too quickly to process. They'd been talking, and then Bo had collapsed. There had been no other signs that something was wrong, no other symptoms.

"There you are," said a familiar voice from over Peter's shoulder. He stood as Marcus Kelly entered and embraced him with a bear hug. "How is he?" Marcus asked.

"No word yet. They've been in there for like fifteen minutes."

"What happened?"

"No idea. It was so sudden. One moment we were talking and joking like everything was normal, the next he was having a seizure."

"A seizure? Maybe he's epileptic."

"It's possible, I guess. I wish we had some kind of information on his medical history. I'm worried, Marcus. By the time we got here, he wasn't breathing. His face was purple."

Marcus's brow was furled as he slowly shook his head. "I'm sure everything will be ok. We're *here*, after all."

"Yeah, well I'm not sure if that guarantees anything."

Marcus took a seat next to Peter on the bench. "What's on your mind?"

"I just want to be sure we're telling the friends the right thing, Marcus."

"About?"

"About how safe they are here."

"What do you mean?"

"Look, we know that Jehovah will protect us as a group, but we also know that doesn't guarantee the individual safety of every single person. We've said that before, right?"

Marcus nodded slowly. "Sure."

"So maybe we shouldn't be telling the friends that nothing bad will happen to them as long as they're with us. We've said that—*I've* said that—but now I'm really questioning it."

"Peter," Marcus said, reaching out to place a large hand on the younger elder's shoulder. "You don't know what's going on behind those doors. Bo had a complicated past. Who knows what kind of medical conditions he had. Maybe it just caught up with him. Maybe he'll be fine."

"It's not just him, Marcus," Peter said. "You've heard about Angelica's situation?"

"Bits and pieces."

"Ted's terrified. He thinks Angelica's ex is after her."

Marcus raised his eyebrows. "Peter, that seems a little farfetched."

"I know, I know. And I said the same thing. But it doesn't change the fact that there was some stranger on this rig who showed up mysteriously and disappeared just as suddenly. All I'm saying is that maybe we're not as safe as we've been saying we are. I feel like the friends need to know the truth, and the risks. You should've seen the faces in that cafeteria, Marcus."

"Brother Burton?" said a voice from the doorway across the room. Peter stood, giving the doctor an intent look, trying to decipher his expression. The man removed a cloth mask from his mouth and stepped slowly forward.

"How bad is it, doctor?" Peter asked quietly. The man's eyes lowered to the floor for a moment. His face shone with a sheen of sweat.

"I'm sorry. We did everything we could, but Mr. Wharton didn't make it."

"You can't be serious," Peter said, shaking his head.

"I'm sorry. Whatever this was, it was very sudden. His heart stopped shortly after we got him up on the table. There was nothing we could do."

"But I was just talking to him, I mean just *minutes* ago. He was—"

Peter was cut off as the swinging doors at the entrance of the infirmary burst open. A large figure entered, legs wobbling beneath him as if he might collapse at any moment. It was Ted Watkins.

"Ted?" Marcus said.

"I... Need... A doctor," Ted said, before crumpling onto the floor.

CHAPTER 18

The floor of Martin's bunker was littered with items from the previous two excursions: tins of foods, rolls of toilet paper and paper towels, a few bottles of water and energy drinks, and of course plenty of beer and liquor. Chad had hit something of a jackpot on his last trip out; he'd returned with a bag near to overflowing with booze–booze eagerly consumed by the two men sprawled out on the couches. The bunker reeked.

Things had been tense when Chad had first returned. Martin knew the goods weren't from his house, but when he'd asked where everything had come from, Chad had been tight-lipped. Martin had pressed him for details and it became a yelling match until someone had the idea to crack open the beers. Chad was eager to get drunk and Martin didn't pose any objections. They drank until their faces were red and their pores sweated alcohol. It took the edge off; the two calmed down and abandoned their argument.

Chad was slumped in the couch, his bare feet draped over the coffee table as if he'd landed in that position after being tossed across the room. Martin's head was leaning against the headrest of the other sofa as he tried to whistle a familiar tune that he couldn't quite seem to get right.

Chad stood and stretched. He gazed for a long moment at the pile of items on the floor before trudging through it with his bare feet. Tins of chili and green beans clanked and clinked on the polished concrete floor as he walked.

"So… I've put together a list," Chad announced, making his way to the dining table.

"List?" Martin asked.

237

"A list of items. For you."

"For *me?*"

"You said you wanted to get out there and help out. Here's your chance." Chad returned with a page torn from a notebook. He slapped it against Martin's chest and collapsed back on the couch. Martin gazed over it disinterestedly.

"We're already stocked, here, Chad. What's the point?"

"This isn't about supplies. It's about you."

"I don't understand."

"You will when you get out there. It's a changed world, man. You've got to change with it." Chad peeled the tab from another can of beer and drained half of its contents as his eyes bore down on Martin. "We've known each other for how long now–fifteen years?"

"Something like that."

"In that time, I've been watching. I know how those gears work," Chad said with a wily grin as he jabbed a finger into his temples.

"Okay…"

"In some ways, you're a *prodigy*. I've never known anyone to code like you. Your mind is a machine. Fast, efficient, precise. I couldn't have built Alphi without you."

"Well… Thanks."

"Yeah well, unfortunately, none of that stuff matters now. You know what your problem is, Martin?"

"No, but I'll bet you're gonna tell me."

"You reject reality."

"Right," Martin said, rolling his eyes. He reached for another beer but Chad beat him to it, sweeping the cans to the far end of the table.

"I'm serious. It's what made you a good programmer. You were never satisfied with the status quo–you always had to push the technology further, always had to explore the possibility space. You defined the cutting edge. And I think that's why you built this place, too.

"Maybe, in some way, work had become too mundane for you. Reality wasn't interesting enough, so you invested in a fantasy scenario where some zero day bug took over the planet's digital infrastructure. It kept your mind occupied with the possibilities. The irony, of course, is that your wish has been granted. You got exactly what you wanted, and now you're pretending it isn't happening. Rejection of reality, man," Chad concluded with a self-satisfied grin.

"Wow, nice psychoanalysis. You should've been a shrink."

"So you deny it? You think you're mentally capable of handling reality?"

"Chad, I freaked out once. Come on, man. Given the circumstances, I think that's–"

"You have to *change* with the circumstances, Martin. That's my whole point. All the old rules don't apply out there anymore."

"You make it sound like there's no possibility of things turning around. Things can still happen. The power can still come back on, maybe we'll get news that this was just some freaky weather pattern, like tied to global warming or whatever."

"Global warming. Right."

"All I'm saying is, is it really wrong to hold onto some sort of hope that things will change? Instead of, you know, acting like this is the end of days and resorting to violence, looting, whatever. It's only been a few days, man."

Chad just smiled his Cheshire smile and leaned his head back on the sofa. "You have no idea, Martin. Which is why you need to go outside and take a look for yourself. You'll see. I promise."

***

Joyce opened the final sleeve of crackers, careful not to spill a single crumb. Her stomach rumbled from hunger pangs and it took incredible willpower to keep from devouring her half of the sleeve. She ate three of the crackers and washed them down with a sip of Gatorade. She was dizzy from the dehydration and the endless rhythm of the sea beneath their feet.

"Well, you can't say we didn't try," Stacy said, grabbing

239

her share of the crackers. She smirked in the dark for no one to see.

"No, I suppose you can't," Joyce agreed.

"You think he'll bring us back?" Stacy asked.

"You mean in the resurrection?"

"Yeah."

"I… I don't know, Stacy. To be honest, I'm trying not to think about it."

"Well, he reads the heart. He'll know why we did what we did."

"I don't think it's wise to presume on his mercy."

"I'm not presuming anything. I just don't see him punishing us with eternal destruction for this. I needed to save Jerry. You needed to save Claire. It's not like we were Lot's wife or something, going back for some jewelry or whatever."

"We still disobeyed, Stacy. That's the bottom line."

"Well, I'm sure glad you're not in charge of the judging, then," Stacy snickered.

"As am I," Joyce said.

Stacy disappeared down into the cabin for a few minutes. Joyce heard her fumbling through drawers and cubbyholes before returning with a plastic gasoline container.

"You had more gas in there?" Joyce asked, surprised.

"I just remembered it. It's been in here for a while, the fuel is probably bad by now. But, seeing as we've got nothing else…" Stacy uncapped the tank of the outboard motor and began filling it with the contents of the container. Joyce caught a whiff of the aged gasoline fumes and waved a hand in front of her

"Smells like paint thinner," she said.

"It practically is. Must've been in there at least three years, I think. Won't have much of a kick to it, and it'll probably ruin the engine, but we're kind of out of options here," Stacy said, holding the canister at a steep angle to get the last of the liquid into the tank. The nozzle of the canister was leaking; gasoline dripped down the outside of the tank and created a small pool in the cockpit's foot well.

Stacy rinsed the empty gasoline container in the water

240

beside the boat and tossed it back below deck.

"Well, I'm going to call it. We're just about out of fuel, nearly out of food and water, and we're stranded on an ocean that refuses to give us even the slightest breeze to sail on. I know you hate me for always raining on your parade, but I'm afraid we're at the end of the road."

"I never hated you, Stacy. We're just different people. And what does it really matter, in the end?"

"Not a whole lot, I guess."

The two women shared a laugh, but it was a dry, humorless sound, like a winter breeze through dead grass.

"I'm just glad I'm not out here alone," Joyce said softly. "I would've cracked long ago by myself out here. I'd probably be–"

Joyce's words evaporated from her lips as a distant but powerful sound filled the air. The two women stood suddenly at attention, shifting their gaze from one point to another, desperate to find the source of the noise.

"That sure sounded like some kind of boat," Joyce muttered. Stacy raised a finger in the air, shushing her. The women kept deathly silent for the next few minutes, hoping to hear another sound. When they did, it was much closer, and had clearly come from the north.

"I knew it," Stacy said, cranking the engine to life and pointing the sailboat in the direction of the noise. "That's the channel."

"The channel?"

"Yeah, where the waters off Washington's coast merge with those of Canada."

"Are you saying we're close to Burrard Harbor?" Joyce asked, allowing herself a bit of hope.

"No, there's no way. It's still dozens of miles to the north of us, but at least we're nearing open waters. That means a better chance of running into other vessels, and possibly getting help."

"Great. Let's do it," Joyce said, feeling her pulse quicken.

***

Martin Landretti stood in the middle of the street, gazing down at the valley. It was like some scene from hell. Rampant fires now covered the entire landscape. Thick smoke billowed into the air, radiating heat. Martin pulled a rag from his pack and tied it over his face as glowing red embers and dark ash swirled around him like swarms of agitated insects.

And the screams were everywhere. Screams of the injured, the dying, the crazed.

Martin darted for the edge of the road as a large truck roared up the street, horn blazing, speakers blaring rap music. The driver chucked a half-emptied glass bottle at him as it sped past. It missed Martin narrowly, shattering to a million pieces against a rock wall just behind him. Martin turned to watch the truck disappear down the road. Chad had been right about one thing; this was a changed world. He pulled a flask from his pocket and took a deep swig of whiskey before staring at the torn sheet of paper in his hand.

He didn't think it really mattered what was on this list; it wasn't as if the bunker's supplies were lacking. Chad had merely sent him on this errand to test his mettle. He had to simply survive his errand, fetch a few useful items, and that would be that. Chad would be satisfied that he could handle himself. And perhaps, after that, he could shake the nagging feeling that told him Chad thought he was becoming a dead weight. That cold, unsettling look in his eyes, perhaps, would then be gone for good.

Martin made his way down the street, passing several homes before finally finding one that appeared unoccupied. The gate to the property was wide open, as was the front door to the house; several of the windows had been smashed in. Perhaps there would be nothing remaining worth taking, but perhaps not?

Martin approached the door warily, eyes flicking from window to window, checking for movement. He paused at the driveway to draw his weapon–a small handgun he'd jammed under his belt, just like a tough guy in the movies. His heart was racing. The blood thrummed in his ears. He collected himself for a long moment, crouched at the entrance of this stranger's home, then entered. Glass cracked beneath his boots.

Martin pulled a flashlight from his pocket and cast the beam of light over the foyer. An overturned bookshelf. Clothes strewn everywhere. More broken glass. A pile of vinyl records. He spun slowly around as the light peeled away the layers of shadows. He walked slowly to the kitchen, sweat dripping from his face, slicking down his back and legs. The pantry was empty. A shattered jar of pickles lay on the ground; the scent of vinegar filled his nostrils.

He glanced at his watch and could hardly believe he'd only been gone fifteen minutes. Chad wouldn't let him back in empty handed, he knew. He had to keep going; he had to find *something*. Martin wiped the sweat from his face with a trembling arm and made his way to the staircase. His head throbbed with anxiety and nerves, but his feet carried his body up the steps, one by one.

On the second floor, he searched the bathroom first. The place had been stripped like the kitchen, but a single bottle of shampoo stood on a shelf in the shower stall. He stuffed it quickly into his bag and exited. He found an office next. A computer, printer, and expensive stereo system remained untouched, along with a bookshelf, which had been vandalized with spray paint. None of it interested him. At the far end of the hall, Martin found a master bedroom. The sheets had been torn away from the mattress and the end tables had been ransacked. A few miscellaneous items of clothing hung from a bar in a walk-in closet, but Martin could tell from a glance that they were a few sizes too big for either him or Chad.

Martin turned to head down the stairs when he noticed another room at the other end of the hall. The door was closed. He held his ear against the door for a minute, but heard nothing. He opened it, an odd odor washing over him. He pressed the rag tighter against his mouth and nose and swung the beam of light across the room.

Martin's heart sank when he saw the posters: Taylor Swift, Katy Perry, a few bands he didn't recognize. His light crossed to the corner of the room, where a small music box sat perched on the edge of a child's desk. He knew he should leave, that there would be nothing for him here, no item that he could possibly bring himself to take. He wished that he could somehow stop himself from continuing to look around, that somehow he could force his feet to turn and leave this little girl's room forever. And yet the beam of light continued, slicing through the darkness like a surgeon's knife.

She was still in bed. The look on her face was almost peaceful, as if she'd died in her sleep. Several layers of blankets were wrapped over her body, her blanched fingers still clenched to their edges. Stringy, matted hair was plastered to the sides of her pale, lifeless face. Martin moved the light to the foot of her bed, where the girl's feet were exposed. Both wore several layers of socks and had been wrapped in torn strips of cloth at the ankles. The feet sat elevated on a pillow; the ankles swollen to an abnormal size.

Martin gasped as the pieces fit together.

The man who'd come looking for help. The man who'd left his ten-year-old daughter at home with broken ankles. The whole story had been true. And this girl had been laid up in bed for days, waiting for her father to return home.

Martin drew a jagged breath and felt himself collapse onto the floor. His arm fell away from his mouth as the odor of death and decay filled his lungs. The death that he was, in at least some way, responsible for. Tears welled in his eyes as he sobbed on the ground, hating himself.

***

In spite of the total lack of visibility, it was instantly evident to the two women that their sailboat had passed into open waters. The temperature dropped by several degrees as cold arctic waters joined the warmer Pacific waters from the south. The current here was stronger, too, and a light breeze stirred the sea, making its surface choppy.

"I don't know about these waves, Stacy," Joyce said uneasily as she steadied herself and sat on one of the benches. It was like experiencing a mild earthquake while blindfolded.

"It's a good sign. It means we're on the right track. We just have to keep traveling north from here and, you know, try not to crash into any rocks or islands."

Joyce groaned. Between the rollicking of the boat, the lack of light, and the lingering smell of gasoline, Joyce found her seasickness quickly intensifying. She flipped on the electric lantern and surveyed what little they could see of the white-capped ocean around them. The sight did nothing to calm either of their nerves.

But then they heard the sound, the same one they'd heard before they'd hit the open waters.

"That's definitely a foghorn," Stacy said.

"From a ship?"

"Yes, it has to be. There must still be boat traffic out there. Probably shipping liners or supertankers or something. If we can just track one of them down..."

And then, in the distance, they spotted it; a faint smudge of horizontal light swaying back and forth over the water.

"There! That's the ship!" Joyce exclaimed, momentarily forgetting her nausea as she stood and pointed.

"All right. That's where we're headed," Stacy said. She yanked the line on the engine. It sputtered on the first few attempts but finally kicked over and came to life. Stacy nudged the tiller gently to one side, pointing the prow of the boat in the direction the distant vessel was headed. It was a slow crawl, but at least the clarity of the light in the distance reassured them that there was nothing to crash into on the way.

"I need you to hold her steady," Stacy said. "I'm going to look for the flare gun."

Joyce complied, taking the tiller in her hands as Stacy went below deck. There were noises from the cabin as she fumbled through drawers and cabinets and finally returned with a small pouch. She zipped it open, examined the plastic gun and flares before loading one into the barrel.

"We're falling behind," Joyce said nervously, glancing back at Stacy, who was still fiddling with the flare gun. Then, without warning, Stacy lifted her hand in the air high above her head, and pulled the trigger. The flare ignited at first, flying brightly for a few short feet before fizzling and dying, disappearing completely in the darkness as it arced through the air.

Stacy cursed under her breath.

"What was that?" Joyce asked. Stacy was shaking her head.

"A dud. These flares are old. Hopefully it's just the one." Stacy yanked a second flare from the bag, taking a few moments to brush off the sides and the back of the percussion cap on her sleeve before loading it and raising the pistol. This time, the flare didn't even ignite. It launched into the air a few feet from the force of the gun's hammer before falling uneventfully into the water not far from the boat.

"Not good. Really, really not good," Stacy was saying. Her hands were trembling now as she removed the final flare from the bag.

"Wait, Stacy. Just hold on a second," Joyce said. She reached one hand out to grab Stacy's arm and pull her close.

"What are you doing?"

"Let's say a prayer first."

Stacy stared at Joyce with a strange look for a moment before her expression softened. She nodded. "Ok. Good idea. Go ahead."

The two women closed their eyes and bowed their heads.

"Jehovah… We know we sinned. We know we did the wrong thing. But we are begging for your mercy. Please don't forget us now. Please remember all the things we've done for you and your name in the past. Please give us this one last chance. We are out of options. *Please…*"

Joyce could feel her pulse drumming a rhythm from her chest to her jugular to the pit of her stomach. Her senses felt sharpened and attuned. Suddenly the sea no longer existed, nor the sailboat beneath her feet nor the strong stench of aged gasoline. There was only their singular hope—a retreating smear of light in the distance and the flare gun in Stacy's shaking hands. She loaded the final flare, raised her hand, and fired.

Nothing happened. Joyce was silent as the two exchanged a horrified look. Stacy checked the pistol—the flare was still in the barrel. She lowered it, and finally realized that it had been a simple, silly mistake: she'd forgotten to cock the hammer. She chuckled to herself at her forgetfulness and pulled the hammer back slowly, when they suddenly heard it: the powerful, throaty bellow of a nearby foghorn. This one was from a different direction, and much closer and louder than the first.

Startled, Stacy felt her thumb slip from the hammer. It snapped forward into the loaded barrel. It hit the percussion cap with a loud crack, sending the flare whooshing out of the barrel like a lit rocket. The flare became a blinding red light, jettisoning wildly into the cockpit, charging around like a wild animal. It slid along the cockpit floor.

And then it found the gasoline.

Everything that followed unfolded in an instant. Fire erupted. It covered the transom, the floors, and the benches. It covered the women's clothes and shoes. Stacy Owens screamed as she dropped the gun, staring at her hands in horror as the flames engulfed them, incinerating her hair and charring her flesh. But she could not feel the pain; all she felt was pure, bright panic.

Joyce was better off, but not by much. The fire covered her sneakers and the legs of her pants. She patted out the fire on her legs quickly and removed her sneakers by kicking them off into the sea. She cupped her hands in the icy waters and splashed some at Stacy, who was still standing in place, screaming as her body turned into a human torch. Joyce managed to block it out. Years of training in the ER had prepared her for moments just like these. Her thoughts were singular: she had to put the fire out. Handful after handful, she splashed water at Stacy, slowly dousing the fire on her clothes, her hands, and the cockpit. The air was an acrid miasma of burnt hair, polyester, and plastic.

When the fire on Stacy's jacket was finally extinguished, Joyce pulled her by the arm towards the edge of the boat, forcing her hands into the chilly waters. They sizzled as they dipped into the icy sea. Stacy howled in agony.

Stacy collapsed on the cockpit bench, eyes wide, her body trembling all over. She was drenched in cold seawater. The jacket she wore was now covered in holes and chunks of hardened, melted polyester. Much of her hair had been singed off.

"It's ok, Stacy. It's all over. You're ok. We're all right," Joyce said, placing a hand behind Stacy's head. "Let's get you down to the cabin, all right?" She gently pulled at Stacy's shoulders, but she wouldn't budge. It was as if she'd turned to stone.

CHAPTER 19

It was clear to Martin what needed to be done. Clearer, in fact, than anything else had been in the last week. He collected himself off of the ground of the dead girl's bedroom floor and walked over to her bed.

"Don't worry," he said softly, his voice still shaking. "It'll all be set right."

He pried the blanket from her fingers and draped it over her head and left. The terror had finally gone. It was as if he'd spent all the fear that he had bottled inside, and now there was nothing else. Nothing mattered now except the one thing.

Martin closed the door to the house as he exited. With the fires devouring their way up the valley, he expected it wouldn't be long before this entire area succumbed to the blaze. Then it truly would be hell.

Martin marched back down the street, down to his house, down the walkway to the bunker, and keyed in his code.

The door didn't budge. He tried again, but the readout on the small screen told him it was *INVALID*. He frowned, his pulse quickening, as he banged his fist on the bunker door.

"Chad?! You in there?! Is this some kind of sick joke?"

"No joke," Chad replied casually. Martin whipped around to see him standing on one of the retaining walls behind him, just beside the walkway. He stood erect, hands in the pockets of his down jacket.

"Did you do this?" Martin snapped through his teeth.

"Sure. Not an especially hard thing to do."

"Why?"

"Did you find her?" Chad asked.

"Find who?"

"The girl. With the broken ankles."

Martin swallowed away the lump in his throat and nodded. Fury bubbled up from his throat; it felt like he was about to explode.

"Good. I figured you'd enter the first house with an open door and busted windows."

"My neighbor wasn't lying. He was just trying to get help for his little girl and you shot him!" Martin screamed.

"Yeah, well, that's life. You don't show up on a stranger's porch with a loaded gun without considering the consequences."

"He was just trying to save his daughter!"

"And I was just trying to save you. I succeeded, he didn't."

"How can you be so cold-hearted?"

Chad shrugged. "I'm tired of this conversation. We've been here before."

"So you knew about the girl."

"Sure. Found her yesterday. And I figured it was your turn."

"Why? Why would you possibly want me to see her?"

"So you can stop freaking out about it. It's over. Her dad's dead, so is she. And so are another thousand people right here in this valley. Death is everywhere, Martin. Just look around you. You can smell it in the air. This is reality, and it's time you came to accept it."

"No. I refuse," Martin said.

Chad threw his head back and laughed. "You refuse! So what happens now?"

"I want you out of here, Chad. Out of my bunker, out of my life. You're going to give me the code, and then you're going to pack your things and get out."

"Or else?"

Martin drew the gun from his waistband. He held it at shoulder's height, pointed straight at Chad's chest. Chad only smiled.

"So what? You kill me and your conscience is soothed? Between the two of us, I'm the only one holding it together."

"I don't want to shoot you, Chad. Just give me the code."

Chad grinned crookedly as he cocked his head to one side. "Nah," he said.

The gunshot rang out into the night air, shattering the silence. Chad pulled his hands from his pocket, where he'd hidden the gun. The hole from his down jacket was still smoking. Martin felt the force of the bullet push him back, but there was no pain. The gun dropped from his hand as he pressed his fingers against the hole in his chest. He staggered backwards a few steps before falling into the grass.

"You... You... Shot me..." Martin struggled, lips quivering.

"Sorry buddy," Chad said, hopping down from the retaining wall and picking up the dropped firearm. "But you're too much of a liability out here."

"I wasn't... going to... shoot. You're... my *friend*..."

"Well, you should've known I don't respond well when guns are pointed at me. This is not the kind of world where those chances can be taken."

"How... how *could* you..." Martin whispered. The pain was flooding his body now; the wound was white hot with it. It took all his strength to keep from shaking uncontrollably. He began to cough; bits of spittle flecked with blood spattered onto his sleeve. Chad crouched at his side, reaching out and pressing the collar of Martin's jacket against his lips to wipe away the blood.

"I kept telling you, man, you gotta change with the times. The old world is dead. You didn't have to die with it."

Martin's face contorted into an expression of hateful fury, but there was no strength left for words or retaliation. His body shivered as a wave of cold swept over him, but his eyes remained open, boring into Chad's, as he exhaled for the last time.

***

In the end, Joyce had practically carried Stacy down into the cabin, where she peeled off what remained of her tattered jacket. Stacy screamed as her arms were pulled from the sleeves.

251

Joyce realized too late that in places the fabric had partially fused with the skin of her arms. But her hands, by far, were the worst. The blackened, charred skin was cracked and bleeding. Stacy's entire body trembled with the shock of pain. She whimpered, eyes still wide open and fixed on some indiscernible point on the ceiling.

Joyce raked through the contents of the drawers and the cabinets, but there was nothing except for a small first aid kit with Band-Aids for minor cuts and a tiny bottle of hydrogen peroxide. She dumped the items out onto the bed beside Stacy.

"I need to clean the wounds, Stacy. Do you understand?" Joyce was saying, doing her best to keep the panic from her throat. She uncapped the bottle and paused with a long look in Stacy's eyes. "I'm sorry, Stacy. But this is all we have. It's going to hurt." Stacy cast a brief, wild glance into Joyce's eyes as she began hyperventilating.

Joyce squeezed the contents of the bottle onto Stacy's hands. Stacy's back arched, her entire body writhing in pain as she screamed at the top of her lungs. The cuts on her hands foamed and frothed with the chemical reaction. Joyce sopped up the drips with Stacy's discarded jacket. Stacy's head flopped from side to side. Finally, she was too exhausted to scream anymore. She breathed heavily as tears ran from her wide, glassy eyes.

Joyce sat heavily on the opposite bed, wincing at the sight before her. Stacy whimpered, her hands held out in front of her like dead trees shaking in a cold wind. Her hands would never be the same, Joyce knew. Joyce buried her face in her arms and allowed the weight of everything to settle on her shoulders. Their last hope of rescue was gone, as was their food, water, and captain. This was the end.

They would die here, on this sailboat, in the middle of a strange ocean, without a single soul knowing of their fate. Joyce took a deep breath, sat upright, and forced the thoughts away. She climbed back out into the cockpit, sealing the hatch behind her to keep the cabin warm. She stared up at a starless, black expanse, and wondered for the last time about her husband,

Alvin, and Claire Aberdeen, and the friends from their congregation. She closed her eyes and remembered the last time her husband had held her, the last time they'd shared a laugh.

And she remembered Jasmin. Her smile. Her laugh. Her smell. Joyce Tucker smiled one last time as a tear rolled down her cheek.

***

Peter Burton felt a hand on his shoulder gently stirring him from his sleep. He sat up slowly on the infirmary bench, squinting as the light flooded into his eyes, silhouetting a familiar face hovering over him. It was his wife, Rachel.

"Hey, there," she whispered.

"Hey," Peter replied. Rachel sat beside him, patting her husband's hair down and brushing it from his eyes. "What time is it?" Peter asked.

"Almost five in the afternoon."

"I don't even remember dozing off."

"It's all right, babe. You've been pushing yourself the last few weeks. Your body needed the rest."

"I guess you've heard the news."

"I heard about Bo. And I heard Ted's in here, too," Rachel said. Peter nodded. He hunched forward on the bench, elbows resting on his knees as he rubbed his face.

"I just don't get it, Rachel. I don't know what's going on. This shouldn't be happening."

Rachel said nothing as she rubbed the back of Peter's arm.

"Does Angelica know about Ted?" he asked.

"I'm not sure. I went to her room twice looking for her, but she wasn't there. I asked around, no one's seen her yet. She may have taken Evan to one of the rec rooms. I can go look if you'd like."

"No, no. It's fine. She'll find out soon enough."

"Do the doctors know what happened to Ted?" Rachel asked.

"No word yet. They're not equipped for this kind of thing

253

here. They've only said that they're running tests. He's unconscious. They say he's critical."

Rachel pressed her head into Peter's shoulder and hugged him.

"You hungry?" she asked after a minute of silence.

"No."

"You sure? I can bring you a plate from the cafeteria."

"I don't feel like eating."

"Some coffee?"

"Thanks, but no."

"Ok."

"It's ok, you can go eat," Peter said, catching his wife's expression.

"I can sit here with you, babe."

"No, no. It's all right. I want to just... be here a little longer. In case he needs me."

"I understand." Rachel leaned in to kiss Peter's cheek and headed for the doors.

"Could you do me a favor, Rachel?" Peter asked. His wife paused to look at him.

"Sure. Anything."

"At dinner, ask around the cafeteria. See if anyone else had any symptoms after lunch. I want to know if this was some type of food poisoning."

"Sure. I'll ask," Rachel said. She managed a smile at her husband and disappeared.

Peter sat alone on the bench, his mind turning over the events of the day again and again. He stood and stretched and waited for another hour before deciding to take a walk. He roamed the corridors aimlessly. It felt good, on some level, to be moving, to be not sitting and contemplating and feeling like a prisoner of his thoughts.

It wasn't long before he found himself at Angelica's room. He knocked, but there was no response. Perhaps she and Evan were at the cafeteria, standing in the lunch line. Perhaps she was getting the news at this exact moment. She'd already been through so much, yet somehow her problems had found a way to

254

follow her here. This was supposed to be a safe place. Peter was miserable. He kept moving.

Another ten minutes passed before he arrived at Bo Wharton's room. Peter stared at the closed door for a few moments, and then entered.

Bo had brought few things with him when he'd boarded the rig. There were the clothes on his back–the ones Peter had first seen him in, before he'd been given others–and of course his Polaroid camera. It hung from a small hook on the wall, just over Bo's bunk.

Peter stood in the middle of the room with his hands in his pockets and inhaled deeply. The scent of Bo's aftershave filled his lungs–that cheap, tangy smell that flooded his mind with memories, and all at once it hit him. He'd only known the man for a week, but in that time they'd become close. As the details of Bo's background had filled themselves in, Peter couldn't help but feel pity for the man. He'd simply been dealt a bad hand. He'd made the wrong friends and the wrong choices and now he was gone.

Just like that. Gone.

Peter shook his head as tears welled in his eyes. He attempted to pray, but found himself too distraught to get the words out. None of this made sense. It was all wrong. Peter felt the strength leak from his body, felt his knees weaken. He sat on the edge of Bo's bunk–a thin foam mattress, and laid back across it. As his weight spread over the mattress, he heard the creak of the metal frame beneath him. But there was something else. Something like the crinkle of paper, coming from below the mattress.

Peter stood, frowning at the bed as he pressed his fingers into the mattress, searching for the source of the sound. He reached his fingers below the mattress and lifted it.

And gasped.

***

Joyce Tucker awoke to a blinding white light. It bore

through her eyelids, rousing her from her spot on the cockpit bench as she sat up and shielded her eyes with the back of her arm.

"Hello?" she called out. She could see nothing. "Is someone there?"

"Are you injured?" responded a voice. It was speaking through some sort of megaphone. Joyce's heart leapt in her chest.

"Oh my! Someone's there! I–I–I'm fine! But my friend, she's–"

"We can't hear you from there, ma'am, just wave your arms if you need assistance."

Joyce complied immediately, frantically crisscrossing her arms. The light pulled away, but its intensity left spots in her vision. It had been days since her eyes had been exposed to such bright light and it had put an immediate headache between her temples.

She struggled to see where the light had come from, but it was hopeless. Her surroundings had once again been submerged into darkness. But there was a sound now where once there had been only silence: the low grumble of an engine below the surface of the water, the churning and splashing of waves in its wake.

Gradually, the shape of a ship took form. It flanked the sailboat and dwarfed it–it was at least four times its length. It slowed to a near stop and someone called out from behind the railing.

"We spotted a fire aboard your vessel, ma'am. You need assistance?"

"Yes!" Joyce nearly screamed. "We're out of everything– water, food, fuel, and my friend–she's badly injured from the fire."

But the man on deck held out his hand and shook his head. "We can give you some food and medical supplies, but I'm afraid we can't offer much else."

"Anything you can give is fine. Please, we're desperate. We need to get off of this sailboat! We were trying to head north, but it's been impossible without the wind to sail on."

256

"We're coming from the north. Trust me, you do not want to be there."

"We're going to be with family and friends. It's a place in Vancouver called Burrard Harbor. Do you know anything about the place?"

The man fell silent as a funny look settled on his face. He stuffed his hands in his pockets. "Burrard Harbor, huh?"

"Yes. You've heard of it? Do you know what it's like there now?"

"I sure do. We just evacuated from there."

TO BE CONTINUED...

AFTERWORD

So here we are, at the end of another novel, and two-thirds of the way through this trilogy. I know the ending here was a cliffhanger, and it honestly couldn't be helped–getting into the scenes following these events puts us firmly on track for the final arc of these stories and into the events culminating in Armageddon. There's still so much to tell, and so many angles to explore, and all of it belongs in another book, so you'll have to wait. (Sorry.)

It was interesting, during the process of writing this installment, to witness the unfolding of actual world events. There was, of course, the increased persecution of our brothers and sisters in Russia. Meanwhile, just south of that country, China's parliament was making international headlines as it did away with a two-term presidential limit that had been in place for nearly four decades. In Europe, backlash in response to mass immigration was leading to the rise of openly discriminatory political agendas. And in America, the tension between races and political parties continued to intensify. And all this was to say nothing of the spreading conflicts in the Middle East and frayed relations between North Korea and the rest of the world.

No matter where you looked, it was conflict after conflict, threat after threat, scandal after scandal, and it only continues to worsen.

It's no wonder, then, that I received more than a few emails from readers wondering if I'd even be able to finish this series before the outbreak of the *real* great tribulation. (Who knows? I certainly hope not!)

Whatever happens, this is certainly the time to keep on the watch and be ready to take whatever action will be required of us. While so much of what the near future holds is still a mystery, we can be sure that faithfulness, obedience, and humility will play a large part in our escaping the great day.

As always, this book couldn't have happened without the support of my wife, who patiently allowed me to bounce plot ideas and characters off of her, and who allowed me the space and time to bring this completed novel to realization.

In addition, I want to thank my dear editors and proofreaders for all of their hard work. So thank you, Lisa, Veronica, and Orville. I hope you were able to enjoy the story even when it was still riddled with typos and inconsistencies. This simply wouldn't be the book it is without your input and corrections.

Finally, I want to thank all of my readers out there who have been so supportive over the years. I appreciate greatly your emails, comments, and reviews on Amazon. It brings me immeasurable joy and satisfaction to be able to write wholesome fiction for you dear friends while stimulating your imagination about future events. I also commend you for having a balanced outlook regarding these stories and seeing them for what they are–fiction, not predictions.

-EK Jonathan

If you enjoyed reading STAY, please consider taking a moment to leave a review on Amazon!

For more information on this series and my other books, as well occasional ponderings on the craft of writing and story telling, please visit:

www.ekjonathan.blogspot.com

For any and all feedback, email me at: allthingsnewnovel@gmail.com

46884794R00145

Printed in Poland
by Amazon Fulfillment
Poland Sp. z o.o., Wrocław